BITS AND PIECES

This Large Print Book carries the
Seal of Approval of N.A.V.H.

A ST. ROSE QUILTING BEE MYSTERY

BITS AND PIECES

ANNETTE MAHON

WHEELER PUBLISHING
A part of Gale, Cengage Learning

GALE
CENGAGE Learning

Detroit • New York • San Francisco • New Haven, Conn • Waterville, Maine • London

GALE
CENGAGE Learning

LIBRARY OF CONGRESS CATALOGING-IN-PUBLICATION DATA

Mahon, Annette.
  Bits and pieces : a St. Rose Quilting Bee mystery / by Annette Mahon.
    p. cm. — (Wheeler Publishing large print cozy mystery)
    ISBN-13: 978-1-4104-2507-2 (pbk. : alk. paper)
    ISBN-10: 1-4104-2507-X (pbk. : alk. paper)
    1. Quiltmakers—Fiction. 2. Cold cases (Criminal investigation)—Fiction. 3. Large type books. I. Title.
  PS3563.A3595B57 2010b
  813'.54—dc22   2009052167

Published in 2010 by arrangement with Tekno Books and Ed Gorman.

Printed in the United States of America
1 2 3 4 5 6 7 14 13 12 11 10

For all the women who quilt with
church groups.
You may not solve murders as you
stitch,
but many other problems are probably
resolved
over the quilt frame.
Happy stitching.

ACKNOWLEDGMENTS

Many thanks to those who answered my numerous questions during the writing of this book — with special thanks to Deni Dietz for the Jesse Jackson quote, to Rae Monet, Lee Lofland, and the knowledgeable people at the crimescenewriter listserv — especially founder Wally Lind and firefighter Joe Collins. Any mistakes are mine and not theirs.

AUTHOR'S NOTE

Scottsdale residents may recognize similarities between the Upland case and a real incident in recent Scottsdale history. While the latter provided inspiration for the story, all the circumstances and characters in this work of fiction came from the author's very active imagination.

"Our lives are like quilts — bits and pieces, joy and sorrow, stitched with love."
— Author unknown

"Methinks it is a token of healthy and gentle characteristics,
when women of high thoughts and accomplishments
love to sew;
especially as they are never more at home with their own hearts than while so occupied."
— Nathaniel Hawthorne,
The Marble Faun, 1859

1

It began with a whispering voice on the telephone. Maggie Browne found it disconcerting. Villains in suspense novels often whispered to disguise their voices, but Maggie hadn't realized how effective the technique could be. She had no idea whose voice had just whispered her name.

"Who is this?"

She hadn't meant to sound so harsh, but then why not? Was it a teenager playing a joke? Or one of her friends with laryngitis? If it was the latter, she would apologize immediately.

"Maggie, it's Clare."

As she continued to whisper, Maggie asked if she was feeling all right.

"Yes, fine." Dismissively. "Maggie, I'm in Big-mart," she continued. A sense of urgency infused her words. "And Kenny Upland is here!"

"Kenny Upland?" Maggie could hear the

excitement in her friend's voice. She shouldn't have said what she did then, but the words popped out of her mouth before she could stop them. And she hated herself as soon as they were spoken. "You must be mistaken."

Maggie winced when she heard Clare's sharp intake of breath. Poor Clare was so easily hurt. She had a very active imagination and probably heard similar words all too often. Though not usually from Maggie.

"Clare, I didn't mean it that way. It's just that he's been gone for all this time, and everyone is looking for him. The police, the FBI. He's been featured on *Wanted Criminals.* He can't be here in the area, in his old neighborhood. It would be beyond foolish, and a foolish man couldn't have eluded capture for so long."

"Nevertheless, I saw him." Clare's resolute voice came clearly across the phone line. She was using a normal tone now, though she still sounded furtive. "In fact, I can still see him. I'm in that Big-mart on Pima, right here in the housewares department. And I can see him, over in the aisle with the camping and hunting stuff."

"Then you should be calling the police."

Maggie wondered if the fact that she'd called her instead indicated that Clare was not certain of her identification. It was true that the Quilting Bee members all knew the Uplands. They had belonged to the St. Rose Catholic Community for many years, and both Kenny and Kate had been active in various church activities. They always brought the children to the Fall Bazaar, too, which was the main fund-raising venture for the Senior Guild, of which the Quilting Bee was an integral part. The Fall Bazaar had been held the previous weekend, and they had all grieved over the absence of Kate and her family.

Could Clare possibly be correct? Was Kenny back in the area, flaunting himself, challenging the authorities? It didn't seem like the Kenny they knew, but then neither did the man who stood accused of murdering his entire family. Almost everyone in the Senior Guild had trouble believing Kenny capable of harming his family, especially the twin daughters he doted on. But in the six months since the deaths of Kate Upland and her children, no other explanation had come to the forefront, and Kenny had remained missing. What else could they believe?

So . . . was Kenny no longer among the missing?

The thought frightened Maggie. Kenny

knew Clare. Would he see her and realize that she recognized him? What would a man wanted for three murders do if confronted? The obvious possibilities were not pleasant. He wouldn't attack an old woman in a crowded store, would he?

"I wasn't sure what to do." Clare's voice had lost some of its bravado. "That's why I called you. I knew you'd know how to handle it."

Maggie sighed. How had she established this reputation for knowing about such things?

"They did his story on *Wanted Criminals,* Clare. They called him a dangerous man. You'd better call 9-1-1 right away."

But Clare did not disconnect so that she could place the emergency call.

"Do you really think he did it, Maggie? Killed his whole family?" Clare's voice sounded small and distant. She had never wanted to believe the worst of Kenny.

"I don't *want* to believe that he did it," Maggie replied. "But the police are certain he did. They must have reason. Evidence. They don't tell us everything, you know. They often keep things from the public to help make their case later."

Quietly, Clare agreed that Maggie was probably right.

Then she finally disconnected. And called 9-1-1, Maggie sincerely hoped.

Maggie stared silently at the phone. Should she call the police? No. She still found it difficult to believe that a man who'd successfully eluded law enforcement for the past six months could be shopping in a store in his old neighborhood, where chances were good someone would recognize him. Though a niggle of a thought tickled her brain — that old adage about hiding in plain sight.

No. Maggie shook her head, then forced herself to return to the sewing project she'd abandoned to answer the phone. She was stitching the binding on the latest of the Quilting Bee's finished quilts, a lovely Dresden Plate in thirties' reproduction fabrics. An old but still popular pattern, they tried to do one every year for their increasingly well-attended annual auction. This one was the second they had completed during the past year, too late for last weekend's auction. Because they had to send in descriptions for an auction catalogue well ahead of the auction date, they usually had at least one quilt finished and in their closet at the time of the bazaar. When Maggie finished the handwork on it, this Dresden Plate would be the second quilt stored in their closet for next year's auction.

Maggie pressed the button to pick up her audio book where she'd left off. Audio books were wonderful accessories for quilters. There was nothing like listening to a good murder mystery while relaxing with her stitching. She'd much rather fill her mind with the adventures of Amelia Peabody than think about Kenny Upland. As far as she was concerned, murder mysteries were only exciting when they were fictional works. Too close to home, there was too much heartache involved. And the Uplands had lived a mere two blocks from Maggie.

But before she could fully immerse herself in early twentieth-century Egypt, Maggie was once more interrupted by the ringing phone.

"Maggie."

This time Maggie had no trouble identifying the whispering voice on the other end.

"What is it, Clare?"

"He's leaving. And the police haven't arrived. I'm going to follow him so I can tell them where he goes."

"No, Clare, don't!"

But it was too late. The line was already dead.

Frustrated, and afraid for Clare, Maggie

immediately dialed the emergency number herself.

"I hope this isn't a complete waste of your time, but I just received a call from a friend of mine. She's in the Big-mart on Pima, and she claims to have seen Kenny Upland. She says she called 9-1-1, but no one has come yet and he's leaving. She told me she was going to follow him so she could direct authorities. It has me worried, whether or not it is Kenny Upland."

The operator was very professional and didn't tell Maggie she and her friend were both crazy. Instead, he said someone would be sent out to investigate.

Maggie hung up the phone, still unaccountably worried about Clare. Clare was so enamored of detective novels, especially the "cozy" type that featured amateur sleuths. She probably thought she was living one of the stories, that *she* could be an amateur sleuth and solve this biggest of all Scottsdale mysteries. It wouldn't occur to her that she might be in danger.

Maggie didn't believe for a minute that the man Clare saw was Kenny, but she was still worried. How would a man react if he saw an elderly woman watching him, a cell phone to her ear? Then following him in her car! He'd think she was a stalker.

Who could she have seen? What if this person had some other reason to fear such action? Kenny Upland was certainly not the only fugitive in the Phoenix metropolitan area.

Maggie reached for the phone.

2

The Upland story began six months earlier, with the explosion of an ordinary house in a nice family neighborhood.

As South Scottsdale awakened on that quiet morning, one house remained silent. At number 8345 Butternut Lane no alarm clock trilled, no lights blinked on, no doors slammed, no television chatter disturbed the silence. Afterward, a neighbor reported finding the Upland dog wandering in the street that morning. When she tried to take him home, there was no answer at the Upland house, which she thought extremely odd for a school day.

Later that morning, Kate did not walk out to meet her kindergarteners at the bus stop as she usually did. Indeed, the Upland girls were not on the bus, not in school that morning. Neighbors who were at home were having lunch, perhaps watching a soap or the local news. Gladys Jablonski, who lived directly across the street from the Uplands, had returned from Senior Guild at St. Rose just after noon and was having a bowl of soup while watching *Geraldo* as she waited for *As the World Turns* to come on.

The blast came at approximately 12:42 P.M. It startled an area far beyond the immediate neighborhood. Gladys told her friends at church that she almost had a heart attack from fright at the loud noise. She thought a small plane had crashed on top of her house, she said — there was that much noise and vibration. Down the block, a young boy, just home from morning kindergarten and playing outside, looked at his mother then up into the sky, asking where the fireworks were. Two blocks over, a National Guard member recently returned from the Middle East dived for cover on the floor beneath the kitchen table, pulling her toddler with her and causing him to giggle at this fun new game.

By 12:44 P.M., 9-1-1 operators were taking calls from all over the Scottsdale area — calls about explosions, sonic booms, even gun fire and plane crashes.

Gladys Jablonski, once her heart settled back into a somewhat regular beat, realized that her house remained intact and looked out her front window. And almost fainted.

Flames leaped up into the sky from what had been the roof of the house across the street, flames so high that Gladys not only feared for the houses on either side, but for her own as well. Debris littered the street and all the yards within sight. People were running down the street, yelling. At least, their mouths were wide open, so Gladys assumed they were yelling.

That was when Gladys realized that she couldn't hear a thing, just a dull roar, a faint echo of the recent larger one. Crying out, she collapsed on the sofa where firefighters evacuating homes found her fifteen minutes later, sobbing hysterically and claiming she'd gone deaf.

The Upland house explosion caused a spate of gossip at St. Rose Catholic Community, especially at the Senior Guild sessions. The Senior Guild met at the church every morning where members worked on all manner of crafts for the grand annual St. Rose Fall Bazaar, held on the weekend prior to Halloween. The Guild served as a place where retired parishioners could meet and socialize. They shared their craft expertise and felt they were helping their church at the same time because the bazaar was a tremendously successful fundraiser. Father Bob had been able to paint the church and outbuildings recently because of the efforts of the Senior Guild and the results of last year's bazaar. Two years ago, the bazaar funds had paid for a new roof for the church.

Not least among the fundraisers was the St. Rose Quilting Bee. Members of the Bee gathered every morning to quilt the tops made by their members or donated to the church. At the end of the year, they had some dozen or more quilts that were auctioned as part of the bazaar. The quilt auction had achieved a wide reputation for the quality of the quilting, and more bidders arrived each year, causing the prices to soar.

Gladys didn't quilt, but she did like to sew and she often pieced tops for the women to quilt. So it was natural for her to join the Quilting Bee the day after the disaster. Although devastated by what happened to her neighbors, she seemed to glow from all the attention.

"It was just terrible," she told them, sitting in an unoccupied chair at the quilt frame. The Quilting Bee members listened with attention, their fingers busy with their stitching, while Gladys sat with her pocketbook in her lap and her hands clasped tightly over the straps.

The other women had all seen the pictures on the news. "Terrible" seemed a mild description, inadequate for the devastation shown. It was horrible and fascinating at the same time. Along with everyone else in the parish — and probably all of Scottsdale — they had been glued to their television sets the previous day.

"The house was on fire, flames leaping up so high I thought the whole neighborhood would burn," Gladys told them, her lips drawing downward in concern. "I thought the explosion had burst my eardrums," she added. "When I looked out the window, I could see people running with their mouths open, but I couldn't hear a thing."

"You poor dear." Anna commiserated with Gladys. Her health was not the best, and she always had compassion for others with health problems. "You must have been terribly frightened."

"I was." Gladys had spent the previous afternoon at the hospital, having her hearing evaluated. It had come back slowly, just as the firefighters on the scene had assured her it would, though she still heard a slight ringing when all around her was quiet.

"I was so afraid that more houses would burn," she repeated. It was obvious to all the women that the fear of the previous day was not entirely gone. Her knuckles showed white where she grasped her purse straps. "The flames were so high, they might even have carried across the street to my house."

"Was it a gas explosion?" Louise asked.

"That's what they think," Edie said, "according to the morning news report. The theory is that someone left the gas on in the house."

"Is that enough to make the house explode?" Anna asked.

"There was probably a candle lit somewhere, or something along that line," Edie replied. "They don't tell us everything, you know."

Gladys lowered her voice, as though she was afraid to say the next words aloud. "Did you hear they found bodies in there?"

All around the quilting frame, the women nodded solemnly.

"Does anyone know whose bodies were found?" Maggie asked. "Was it the whole family?"

Murmurs of murder-suicide were making the rounds at St. Rose. Kenny was in the National Guard, had seen action in Iraq, and everyone had heard stories of returning soldiers and post traumatic stress disorder. In fact, rumors about Kenny and PTSD had been rife ever since his return.

Gladys shook her head. "I don't think they've released the information yet, but the word in the neighborhood is that the family was inside." She paused, unable to resist the drama of providing such tantalizing news. "All of them except Kenny. He's missing."

There were gasps of sorrow as well as surprise. They all knew the Uplands, who were active members of St. Rose. Kate Upland was a lovely young woman, devoted to her twin daughters. She'd been a stay-at-home mom until forced to take a job while Kenny was in Iraq. Kenny loved to camp and always helped with the church youth group trips. He worked hard to support his family, holding two jobs last they'd heard — as a security guard at the shopping center during the day and as a nursing assistant at a care home nights and weekends. When church members told him they didn't know how he managed, he claimed not to need much sleep.

"No one saw any of them yesterday morning," Gladys went on. "I talked to some of the neighbors last night. No one saw any activity around the house. And the dog was outside! Roberta Blackwood, who lives on the corner, took him in, said she found him wandering around on the next block when she had her morning walk. She knocked at the Upland's kitchen door, figuring they would be in there having breakfast, but no one answered."

"Is that unusual?" Clare asked. "For the dog to be out?" She had a miniature Schnauzer that she spoiled, and who spent all of his time inside the house, except for walks and potty breaks. But she knew that not everyone kept their dogs inside twenty-four/seven. And some dogs were excellent escape artists.

"Yes, it is. That dog was always with the girls. In the morning, he'd be inside while they had their breakfast and got ready for school. He'd walk with them to the school bus in the morning and meet the bus in the afternoon. With Kate, of course." Tears filled her eyes at her mention of her three well-liked neighbors.

Maggie nodded. Like the others, she'd talked to Kate often and liked her a great deal. They always came to the bazaar. The Upland girls, five-year-old identical twins named Kelsie and Kerrie, were beautiful children who garnered a lot of attention wherever they went. Not only were they lovely to look at, the girls were polite and well behaved. Everyone loved them.

It made Maggie's heart ache to think of

those beautiful little girls, gone. A tear stole down her cheek at the thought of such young lives taken in a senseless accident. At least, she hoped it was an accident. Horrible as that would be, it was better than the alternative, that someone had deliberately ended the lives of an entire family.

But if Kenny truly was missing, could he have something to do with it?

"So, Kenny is missing, is he?" Edie asked. "You know what that probably means."

"Oh, no." Anna's exclamation was almost a wail.

"There's been a lot of talk about post traumatic stress disorder," Louise said.

But Edie merely nodded in a firm, decisive manner. "It *could* be a monster of a mid-life crisis. That happens with some men, you know."

Maggie supposed it did. Still, she could barely comprehend such an action. If a man wanted his freedom, why not get a divorce? Or just disappear? Why would it be necessary to kill his family? It didn't make any sense, especially in association with the nice young family man Kenny seemed to be.

"It's just awful," Gladys went on. "There are police and fire people all over the neighborhood this morning. They're sifting through the rubble and questioning everyone who lives in the area. The street is still blocked off, too, and you have to show your ID to get through. I don't know when it will end."

Maggie wondered, too.

3

Six months later, Maggie still wondered when it would all end, as she and Victoria entered the Big-mart on Pima. Every now and again, the subject of Kenny Upland and his disappearance would come up at the Senior Guild sessions. It was still hard for most of them to believe that Kenny had destroyed his family. He'd been such a devoted husband and father, how could he have killed them all? He helped at the church; he worked with the youth groups. Still, he'd been missing all this time; what else could have happened, they asked. Wouldn't an innocent man have come forward and tried to help the police? Wouldn't a loving family man have been there for the funerals?

"Did she say where she was?" Victoria asked as they entered the store. She kept her voice low, as though someone might be trying to eavesdrop.

Maggie had no such compunctions. She spoke in her normal, no-nonsense tones. "Yes, she did. She said she saw the person in the hunting and camping area."

Maggie hurried toward that part of the store, not bothering to take a cart. No use trying to pretend that this was an ordinary shopping trip. All she wanted to do was find Clare and make sure she was all right.

They quickly found the camping department. However, it was deserted except for a young man with long, unwashed hair, his arms covered with tattoos, who was examining canteens. He didn't look anything like Kenny Upland and was too young to be an expertly disguised Kenny. There were no women in the area.

"Clare said she was in the housewares section," Maggie suddenly recalled.

They looked across the wide aisle toward shelves filled with pots and pans and small appliances.

"Clare needed a new toaster oven, remember?" Victoria said. "She was talking about it the other day."

Together, they walked toward the aisle of small appliances. But already they could see that there was no one shopping there.

"I'll go up this way," Victoria suggested, pointing toward the back of the store. "Why don't you check that way?" She gestured in the opposite direction, toward the paper products and pharmaceuticals.

Maggie quickly agreed, and the two women separated. Five minutes later, they came back together in the aisle between the fishing poles and the small kitchen appliances.

"Nothing," Victoria said.

"Same with me," Maggie said.

"Shall I try her cell again?"

Victoria was already reaching for her phone when she spoke, and she quickly found Clare's number and pressed the button to send. But they could both hear her voice mail pick up as soon as the call connected. Victoria flipped her phone closed and tightened her lips.

"Her battery might have died," she suggested. "Or she's in an area without a signal." There were still dead spots, even right in the heavily populated valley.

Maggie nodded, continuing to look around. "She said she was going to follow him. I really hoped she would change her mind, but if she did where is she?" She looked around the store, agitated because there was nothing they could do. "I wish there was someone working here. It would be nice to know if they saw anyone."

33

She'd barely finished her sentence when a middle-aged man wearing a Big-mart vest appeared. Maggie approached him immediately.

"Excuse me."

He looked at her, a smile of greeting on his lips, ready to be of aid.

"My friend called from the store about an hour ago, and I expected to meet her here." Maggie improvised as she spoke, happy with this particular scenario. "Have you noticed an older woman, about five foot three, not too thin, thick gray hair? She wears glasses," she added.

The man took a moment to consider this before replying. "I recall seeing a woman somewhat like that. She left suddenly. Left a cart with some cleaning supplies in the aisle right over there." He pointed to the small appliance aisle. "In fact, I just got back from returning the items to the shelves. I didn't think she'd be back for them."

Maggie thought he seemed more irritated than regretful.

"Oh, dear. That's not like her — to be so inconsiderate," Victoria said.

"We think she saw someone she recognized and got upset," Maggie said.

The man looked at her for a moment. "There was a police officer who stopped by, just a few minutes ago. He asked about that man, Kenny Upland. He had a picture he showed all the employees. He said a woman had seen him here."

"And did anyone recognize the man in the picture? Could he have been in the store this morning?"

"There was a man here looking at sleeping bags who looked a little like him. Not much." He shrugged. "Could have been him, I suppose."

Maggie waited for the man to say more, but he did not. "Was he still here when the police officer came?"

"Oh, no. He'd been gone some time. But I don't think it was that man, Kenny Upland."

"Too bad," Maggie said. "There's a big reward for his capture."

If Maggie thought this would elicit a further response, she was disappointed. He merely shrugged. "I remember that man, Kenny Upland. Terrible thing he did."

"Yes," Maggie agreed. "I knew his family, and his children were the most beautiful little girls you've ever seen. It *was* a terrible thing." She swallowed the lump that caught in her throat whenever she remembered Kate and her beautiful little girls. Such young people, especially children with so much to look forward to, should not be dead.

"Well, thank you for your help." She offered the man a friendly smile that quickly morphed into a frown. "We are a little concerned about our friend though. I thought sure she would wait for us."

"I think she is gone. It would be odd for her to select her supplies and then just abandon them unless she was going to leave the store."

"Yes, I believe you're right." Maggie thanked him again, then turned to go.

"She's probably fine," Victoria said. She could see that Maggie was upset by the furrows that wrinkled her forehead. So Victoria took control. "We'll go back to my place and call everyone else." It wasn't a suggestion. And she didn't have to specify who it was they would call. Maggie knew she meant the other Bee members.

"Maybe she's already called Anna or Louise," Victoria suggested, as they left the store.

They were in the car and adjusting their seat belts when Maggie's phone rang. It almost landed on the floor as she grabbed quickly for her purse.

"Yes?"

"Maggie?"

Her voice sounded thin and trembly, but

Maggie immediately recognized Clare.

"Clare, where are you? The connection is bad."

"Maggie, I feel guilty saying this, but I'm having so much fun. It's like being a real Jessica Fletcher."

Startled, Maggie realized that the quiver in Clare's voice was not from fear but from excitement.

"Clare, where are you?" Maggie's voice was sharp with frustration and concern.

"I'm following Kenny. We took the 101 to the Beeline highway, heading toward Payson. I think he might be going up to the Rim. That's where he always went camping, isn't it?"

Maggie barely made out her final words. The connection was breaking up, some of her words lost; it failed completely before Maggie was able to ask for more details.

Victoria watched, her forehead creased with worry for her friend. "Did she tell you where she is?"

Maggie nodded, anger making her voice irritable. "She's following Kenny, heading toward the Mogollon Rim, she thinks."

The Mogollon Rim was a popular camping spot for those who lived in the Valley of the Sun, the temperatures there being cooler than in the desert. Basically a 200-mile-long cliff, the Mogollon Rim was formed in the Mesozoic Age — the same period that saw dinosaurs roam parts of Arizona — when pressure within the earth pushed the land upward as much as 2,000 feet. Not only cooler, the Rim area was picturesque, with rocky cliffs, Ponderosa pine forests, and hidden green valleys. It was Zane Grey country, literally. Grey wrote some of his books in a cabin below the Rim. Unfortunately, the original cabin was destroyed by the 1990 Dude fire.

Maggie closed the phone, pushing it into her purse and starting up her car. "We'll just have to follow, Victoria, and see if we can find her before something terrible happens. She said they went out the 101 to the Beeline Highway."

Without listening to Victoria's mounting apprehension, Maggie put the car in gear and turned the car toward the Route 101 entrance ramp.

4

As Maggie and Victoria drove toward Payson, Clare's excitement began to wane. She'd driven much farther than she'd ever expected to, watching the sky darken as a storm moved in. It looked like a monsoon storm to Clare, even though the monsoon season was over. The sky was heavily gray and forbidding, and streaks of lightning shot from it, connecting earth and sky. Thunder loud enough to shake the car rattled Clare and her nerves.

Clare peered through the worsening rain. Hard drops pinged against the windshield and she wondered if some of it was hail. The pavement was slick, the road unfamiliar as it curved through the pine forest. Gerald came up this way all the time to fish, but she hadn't accompanied him in years. She had the Quilting Bee to keep her busy on weekday mornings, and she did hate to miss attending, so any memories she might have of the area were hazy and outdated. And anyway, Gerald always drove when they traveled somewhere together.

Clare almost giggled, thinking that Gerald might be somewhere nearby, taking shelter from the rain. He was off on a fishing trip this week, with Dan from church, who had a fishing spot so secret no one seemed to know exactly where it was. Gerald had told Clare that it was on the Rim, but the rain was so heavy, Clare wasn't even sure she had attained the Rim itself. The road was still heading upward, but she didn't know if that was a definitive clue.

Unbelievably, the rain seemed to intensify. She could barely see through the fierceness of the pellets hitting the window so hard and heavy. Thank goodness the road ran uphill; at least she didn't have to fear a flash flood. At least, she hoped she didn't. She thought they were a problem in the desert anyway, not this area. She prayed to the Blessed Mother to help her out, wondering briefly who might be the saint for weather related issues. She needed to talk to him — or her — and in a hurry. Desert storms usually didn't last long, and she would pull over and wait it out — if only there was a place to do so.

Then she remembered that she was no

longer in the desert, but in the transition area between the desert and the high country — where they had cold weather and even snow. This area got more rain than Phoenix or Scottsdale, as evidenced by the Ponderosa pine forests on either side of the road. So perhaps the storm would not pass as quickly as she hoped. With a sigh, she continued to pray. If the rain hitting the roof of the car hadn't been so loud, Clare was sure she would have been able to hear her heartbeat in the close atmosphere of the car. She could feel its heavy pulsing in her chest. If she took her eyes off the road for a moment to look down at her chest, would she be able to see the cloth of her shirt moving up and down with the accelerated beats? It certainly felt that way, but she didn't dare take her eyes from the road. So she couldn't worry about that. She had to pay attention to the road, to the weather, to the car ahead. At least, she hoped it was still ahead of her. With the rain so thick and heavy, she wasn't even sure of that.

Visually, it seemed to be early evening, even though she knew it couldn't be. She'd left for Big-mart right after lunch. And what an adventure had begun with that seemingly ordinary trip. Clare chanced a quick glance down at the dashboard clock. Only four-thirty, but the storm had brought an early gloom to the afternoon.

Clare swallowed. She had followed Kenny's car in a burst of adrenalin-laced excitement. She was so sure it was Kenny, the person every lawman in the country was looking for — without success. Yet she, Clare Patterson, had found him. Why, it was just like the amateur sleuths in the mystery novels she read, just like Jessica Fletcher from television.

Despite the rain and the unfamiliar road, Clare smiled. She'd always wanted to be an Annie Darling or a Faith Fairchild. New strength surged through her, and her vision seemed to improve. Taillights gleamed ahead of her, glistening through the lessening rain. She felt sure it must be Kenny's car.

But Clare quickly moved beyond smiles, beyond the smugness of her successful sighting of Scottsdale's most wanted fugitive. Beyond debating Kenny's guilt or innocence. She tried again to tell herself that storms like this passed quickly, squashing down any doubts she had about weather patterns in this unfamiliar region. But although the rain was no longer pounding like a hammer on her car's roof, the storm system seemed to be stalled over the area.

Fat raindrops continued to fall and visibility did not improve. She could think of nothing beyond keeping the car on the road and keeping the windshield clear enough to see through.

She tried calling Maggie again but was unable to get a signal. She didn't have a lot of experience in using the phone while driving, and it made her nervous. There was nowhere to pull over.

And she thought she'd lost Kenny, too. It had been almost ten minutes since she'd last seen those taillights on the road ahead. Still, she would keep at it until there was an obvious place for her to turn her car around. She had to.

Who knows, she thought. *I might just spot him on the road back to Payson. He couldn't go much faster than I have in this weather, so if he's not up ahead of me, he could have turned off.*

Rounding yet another bend, Clare was startled to see a large cat run out of the forest to her right, streaking across the road in front of her. Not a wild cat, but a big, beautiful calico. Automatically, her foot slammed down on the brake pedal.

But she was no longer in Scottsdale, on that city's wide, dry roads. Her tires couldn't handle the sudden cessation of movement on the slick, wet pavement. Clare's heart rose to lodge in her throat as the car went into a skid, sliding across the road and continuing over the grassy verge and into the trees. When it stopped, the car tipped at a forty-five-degree angle and the view out the windshield was partially blocked by green shrubbery. Clare slumped against the seat belt, her eyes closed, while smoke-like dust settled. Her cheeks were pink with contact burn from the airbag. Her heartbeat finally slowed its frantic beat.

5

Maggie and Victoria spoke barely a word on the long drive from Scottsdale. They were both worried, and best left to their own internal musings. They were almost to Payson when the storm clouds moved in, and the afternoon began to look more like night.

Victoria was the one to break the silence, with a needless comment. "There's a storm coming," she said. "Odd time of year for it."

"I know." Maggie tried to remain focused on the mechanical act of driving. If she allowed her mind to stray, she would be wracked with worry over Clare and what she was doing. Sometimes Clare could be as naïve as a child. While being a creative person was a good thing for a quilter, having an active imagination was not always the best of attributes. "But these off-season storms can be bad."

Victoria shifted uneasily in her seat. "Do

you think she imagined seeing Kenny?"

There was no need to say who she referred to. Maggie knew, and thought it interesting that their thoughts were so similar.

"I'm sure she saw someone," Maggie said. "I just have trouble believing it was Kenny."

The rain began as they reached the outskirts of the town. Fat, heavy drops that made it impossible to see and drove them into a shopping plaza to park. Luckily, there was a small café there, and they braved the weather to go inside.

"It's no use continuing," Victoria told Maggie when she expressed her unhappiness at having to stop. "We can't see anything through this rain."

"And you didn't think we'd have any luck catching up with her anyway, did you?" Maggie asked, brushing at her damp clothes.

Victoria didn't reply, merely glanced at Maggie with raised brows. Her facial expression was answer enough.

"I hate going back to Scottsdale without her," Maggie said.

The waitress, filling their coffee cups, heard her comment. "If you're heading up Route 260 you might as well go back to Scottsdale. The road's closed. There's been an accident — a motorcycle and a car.

46

Pretty bad from what I hear. The road's closed in both directions, probably for a couple more hours. That's why it's so busy in here. Usually the place is empty this time of day."

Victoria's eyes widened at this bit of news. "Do you have any idea who was involved in the accident? We were following a friend, an older woman driving a Cadillac Seville."

But the woman shook her head. "Sorry. I just know what I'm hearing from the people who are in here." She shrugged as she moved off to the next table.

Maggie sighed. "I guess I didn't really believe we would find her this way, but I had to do something. Admit it, driving out here was better than sitting at home worrying, wondering if she'd really found Kenny and what on earth would happen if she did."

"You said yourself it's highly unlikely that he would be shopping in Scottsdale when he's a fugitive, and in a store so close to his old neighborhood. It wouldn't be smart, and Kenny is an intelligent man."

Maggie nodded, comforted by her friend's effort to ease her worry.

"Let's call the others," Victoria suggested, "and see if anyone else has heard from Clare. Perhaps she tried calling someone else."

So they divided the Bee members between them and placed their calls while they ate their greasy meals.

"At least the coffee is good," Victoria said.

"At least it's hot," Maggie corrected. "And not bad at all," she conceded.

By the time the rain let up, all the other members of the Quilting Bee had been called. No one had heard from Clare since they left the church at noon.

6

Clare opened her eyes, disoriented. The ceiling was dark, gray and smutty-looking, not the cool cream shade she usually awakened to in her Scottsdale bedroom. She shifted slightly and realized her body ached — everywhere. She felt as if she'd been beaten up — not that she knew what that was like, but she imagined it would make one feel just the way she did right now. Even filling her lungs with air was uncomfortable.

With a soft moan, Clare rolled onto her right side and looked into the room. She lay in what appeared to be a small cabin. And, unless she was still asleep and dreaming, half of the room seemed to have burned away. Dark, stained wood showed uneven, jagged edges at the top, and most of the ceiling and roof were gone, replaced by plastic sheeting. She lay on a fat sleeping bag, and, at the foot, sitting on a campstool, was Kenny Upland himself.

Clare swallowed. She was alone in a wreck of a cabin, heaven knew where, with Kenny Upland. The same Kenny Upland whom police claimed had killed his wife and his two daughters, then arranged to blow up and burn his house to cover up his crime. Sure, she'd seen him earlier, and followed him. But she never meant to confront him; she'd thought the police would do that.

He looked different. Tamping down a giggle that verged on hysteria, Clare told herself that of course he looked different. . He had been on the run for six months, with not even a sighting. Of course his appearance would have changed.

His hair was long, much longer than she'd ever seen it, and he'd grown a beard. Always a lean, athletic type, he was now much thinner, more wiry. But it was Kenny, she was sure of that. He was wearing the clothes she'd seen him in earlier, looking like any other outdoor enthusiast who was camping out. Quite a difference from the Kenny she'd known who always dressed in preppy style polo shirts and neatly pressed khakis, his hair in a short, military-esque style.

With a start and a gasp, Clare sat up, instantly seeing the room spin crazily. *Bad idea, Clare,* she scolded herself, *to rise so abruptly.* In addition, her arms, legs and

50

back all protested the sudden movement, causing her to emit another moan.

"Mrs. Patterson?" Kenny asked. "How are you feeling?"

Clare stared. Here she was, sitting on a sleeping bag in a strange, burned-out cabin, and a fugitive who had been featured on that *Wanted Criminals* TV show was sitting beside her asking how she felt. And he sounded absolutely sincere.

"I'm fine, I guess," she replied.

After all, what else could she say? He didn't want to hear about how dizzy she got when she sat up, about the way her chest muscles felt sore and bruised and her knees seemed too weak to support her body. Or that her face stung as if she had a sunburn and her lungs burned when she inhaled.

Unconsciously, Clare rubbed her collarbone. She did feel very sore there, and down across her chest.

"The car ran off the road," she said, suddenly remembering the rainstorm and the cat streaking across the road — a beautiful calico. It should have been black for all the trouble it caused.

Like a movie preview, she could see it all, flashing before her just as it happened. With an intake of breath that created another involuntary gasp, Clare realized that her sore chest was probably the result of the seat belt restraint holding her back and away from the windshield. And that her face and lungs must hurt from the airbag deployment. Still rubbing at her collarbone, she told herself that a sore chest was better than a smashed skull.

Kenny was up now, and crouching beside her, reaching for her arm. Clare realized he was offering her help to get up.

Was it today, or yesterday? It was dark, but she had no idea if it was just past dusk or deep into the night. *The storm must be over,* she thought. There was no sound of raindrops, though she could hear trees rustling beyond the room and a whine, almost a whistle, as the wind moved through the remaining walls of the broken cabin.

"I'll help you get up, if you want to, Mrs. Patterson, but mostly you need to rest. Your car skidded in the rain, and you lost control. I found you tipped into a ditch in the woods and brought you back here. If you feel up to it, I'll get you something to eat. You've been out for hours." He looked into her eyes, as though trying to judge her condition. "You don't seem to have hit your head. I examined it for bumps or cuts and there aren't any. And you seemed asleep rather than unconscious, so I let you sleep since there doesn't seem any chance of a concussion. I'm sure you needed the rest. Maybe it was just exhaustion after the adrenalin rush of the accident."

Clare's hands went up to her head, feeling carefully through her hair, but she didn't feel anything there. No bumps, no bruises, just as he said. "I seem to ache everywhere *except* my head," she said.

"Are you hungry?"

Clare thought it over. All she felt was a deep exhaustion. "No, I don't think so. I think I need more sleep before I can go back. Will I be able to drive my car?" she asked.

"Don't know yet. I'll get someone to help me get it out of the ditch in the morning, and then we'll see. It doesn't look bad," he added, making her feel a little better. "There'll probably be some dents in the front end. Do you need to call your husband? I have a cell phone, though the reception is spotty."

"Thank you, but Gerald is off fishing this week. Oh, dear. But my dog is there alone."

He took a cell phone from his pocket, handed it to her, then heaved himself to his feet.

"See if you can get a signal, and I'll get you something for the aches."

He moved toward a counter that must have been part of the kitchen. Clare couldn't really tell much from her position on the floor, but trying to get up was more than she could cope with at the moment. He was reaching for a bottle of water when she opened the phone. She saw immediately that there were no bars at all, and snapped it closed with a sigh. She hoped her neighbor who sometimes watched Samson would notice that she was gone and take care of him.

"No signal," she told Kenny as he came back with the water and another, smaller bottle. She put the phone down beside her, near the spot where Kenny had been sitting.

"I have some ibuprofen. That should help the aches. You can take up to three or four," he said, making it almost a question as he shook a few tablets out into his hand.

"Okay," Clare said, leaving the number up to him. "Thank you." She took the pills he handed her, popped them into her mouth and swallowed most of the water in the bottle.

"Go ahead and lie down again," Kenny urged. "Close your eyes. I'm sure you'll feel better soon."

Clare screwed the cap back onto the water

bottle and lay down. The sleeping bag was very comfortable, with a nice pillow. She could feel her heart pounding, and hoped it was just worry over Samson, her spoiled little miniature Schnauzer.

Then her eyes popped open. "How did you ever find my car?"

She thought Kenny looked sheepish. He seemed nervous; she'd caught him looking behind himself more than once. But then he *was* a fugitive.

"I knew someone was following me. I guess it was foolish heading back down to Scottsdale, but I wanted to see someone who might have some information for me. And then I thought I might as well get a few things at Big-mart. Not a good idea, I guess."

"Maggie — you know Maggie Browne — told me it couldn't be you, because you would never have come back to the neighborhood."

"It was taking a chance, but then too no one expected to see me there." He shrugged. "I noticed the car behind me, and it didn't look like a police car, but I wanted to be sure. I thought I'd lost it there after the storm hit, but I backtracked to check before I took the turnoff leading here. Didn't want to lead someone right to my place. And just as I saw your car, that cat flew across the road and you skidded right off it."

"Thank you for saving me." Clare was finding it an effort to speak, and her eyes refused to stay open. For one brief moment, she wondered if those pills Kenny had given her — and she'd taken so trustfully — really were ibuprofen. Had he just killed her, too?

Why was she still alive? That car accident could easily have caused serious injury, even death. She sent a quick prayer to the Virgin Mary, her special devotion, thanking her for saving her life. There must be a reason she'd been saved. The Virgin meant her to do something, and it must be something important.

This realization brought comfort and a feeling of well-being missing until then. She felt sure the pills really were an innocent pain killer, and she was profoundly grateful to Kenny for taking care of her. She *had* always liked him, and had trouble believing he was a cold-hearted killer. Especially now, after what he'd done to help her. She had to get his side of the story. Perhaps it was going to be her role to speak up for Kenny, to let everyone know that he had been wrongfully accused.

With that last and quite pleasant thought, Clare dropped off to sleep.

7

Maggie lay in bed, staring up at the shadowy ceiling. She wondered if Victoria was also having trouble falling asleep. At least Victoria had nothing to feel guilty about. She wasn't the one who'd taken Clare's calls. Perhaps if she'd called 9-1-1 immediately upon hearing from Clare . . . Would the officers have arrived before Kenny left the store? Would such action have prevented Clare taking off on her own?

With a sigh, Maggie rolled onto her side, hoping a change in position would help her rest, and eventually, sleep. Her rosary beads slid through her fingers and she grabbed onto them before they were lost in the sheets. Saying the rosary often helped bring sleep, but so far not tonight.

Where was Clare, and was she okay? At least Michael had gotten back to her about the accident on Route 260. Clare had not been involved. She'd called Victoria immediately to let her know, then between them they'd called the rest of the Bee members.

Maggie made another call before getting into bed, checking in with Joan Cummins, Clare's neighbor whom she'd spoken to earlier. "I'm sorry to call so late," Maggie began.

But Joan knew the reason for the call and was not put out. "I've been keeping an eye out," she told her, without being asked. "No one's come back."

Her chest tight with concern, Maggie hung up.

Now, still unable to find a comfortable position in her usually comfy bed, Maggie threw back the quilt and got up. Sleep experts recommended getting up out of bed if you could not sleep, so Maggie decided to take their advice. She settled down in her "sewing chair," turned on her CD player and worked on a quilt block for an hour.

When she returned to her bed, she started another rosary. She prayed for Clare, and for Kenny Upland as well. She prayed that Kenny was the upstanding young man he'd always appeared to be. Just in case Clare had caught up to him and was with him now.

8

The next time Clare woke up, it was bright daylight. She could see the condition of the cabin now, and it was not a pretty sight. Soot blackened the walls and ceiling, and a large section of wall and roof were replaced with black plastic. But she no longer felt exhausted, no longer felt as though she could not keep her eyes open. And her lungs didn't burn when she took a deep breath.

Then she shifted her legs and winced at the aches in her old bones. Perhaps she wasn't much better after all.

Kenny was quickly beside her, helping to support her as she tried to sit up.

"I can't believe I slept for so long."

Kenny gave her a sheepish look. "I slipped another tablet in with the ibuprofen last night," he admitted. "An anti-anxiety medication." He looked down at the ground, apparently embarrassed by what he was about to share. "I've needed something like it since . . . well, you know. It helps you to sleep, too, so I thought it would be a good thing for you. You seemed to sleep very well. Do you feel better?"

Clare was sitting up on the sleeping bag now, having maneuvered herself up without feeling ready to faint. And her head seemed to be okay. She did feel better, although she wasn't sure she liked the idea of someone giving her medication without her consent. Still, she was all right and feeling more comfortable this morning. As soon as she could get to a restroom, that is.

She was even able to stand, although she was grateful for the support of Kenny's strong arm. Otherwise, she would have flopped right back onto the sleeping bag when she first tried to rise and her knees almost collapsed beneath her. Now, though, with his steady hand on her waist, she was able to not only stand but take a step toward the door.

"I wouldn't mind some more of that ibuprofen," she said. "And a trip to the little girls' room." She blushed as she said it, unable to deviate from her use of the silly euphemism she'd learned from her mother so many years ago.

But Kenny didn't laugh. He merely stayed at her side, directing her outside and to the door of the tiny, old-fashioned facility. It even had the obligatory half moon cutout on the door.

"The one inside isn't properly connected up, but this old outhouse is still usable. Can you manage on your own?"

Clare recalled that Kenny worked at a nursing home. He was probably used to taking elderly people to the restroom, but she was definitely not ready for *that* kind of help.

"I'll be fine."

"Okay." He watched her take a few steps on her own. "I'll have some ibuprofen ready for you when you're done."

"Thank you, Kenny."

Clare felt tears dampen her eyes at his kindness. And everyone thought this nice man had killed his family. What on earth could have happened that everyone would believe such a thing?

When she came out of the little hut, Kenny was waiting for her. He walked her back to his campsite in the cabin and handed her two tablets and a bottle of water.

"No surprises this time, just some ibuprofen," he promised.

He watched her take the pills, gulping down more water afterward. He kept looking back and forth — not like a viewer at a tennis match, but like one of those actors playing a secret service man on presidential protection detail in a movie. Did he expect someone to find him here, in the middle of nowhere?

"Are you hungry?"

Clare realized that she was indeed hungry. The water had felt so good going down her dry throat and seemed to stimulate her taste glands. Now they were ready for something more filling.

"Thank you, I'd love something to eat."

9

Maggie looked haggard on Thursday morning. Victoria was her usual put-together self — mostly because she was skillful with her application of makeup. It made Maggie wonder if she should try to wear make-up herself, but she quickly dismissed such a thought. She'd never worn more than lipstick, with a bit of mascara and blush for dressing up, and she was too old to try anything new.

By the time they entered the Bee room, everyone else was there and eagerly awaiting them. Their first words changed the air of expectancy to one of chagrin.

"Has anyone heard anything?" There was no need to explain that they were asking about Clare, that they had no word themselves.

"No." Both Edie and Louise looked concerned.

Anna was near tears. "Do you think he's

killed her, too?"

"It's hard to believe he killed anyone." Louise shook her head. "I talked to him often enough about the youth programs, and he was a dedicated family man. I just can't believe he killed those beautiful girls."

"Anyone can become a killer," Edie said. Her voice oozed authority, though no one asked how she felt qualified to know this. It was just a typical Edie comment.

"But two little girls? His own children?" Louise said.

Maggie had to agree. Kenny Upland had been an upstanding member of the parish, active in many different areas, but especially with the youth groups. It was unimaginable that he could have killed his wife, much less his young children. Still, in six months' time, no one else had emerged as a suspect, and most of the parish had accepted the word of police and prosecutor that Kenny was the guilty party.

"He always went on the youth camping trips," Louise said. "The kids loved him, said that he knew all about surviving in the wilderness." Louise's voice, too, was authoritative, but she at least had credentials. Her granddaughter, Amanda, participated in many of the parish youth activities. "Amanda had quite a crush on him. She was horrified after the explosion. Still is." Louise stabbed her needle into the quilt top, pushing it back up when it hit her finger on the underside of the fabric sandwich. "She doesn't want to believe someone she knew and admired could be capable of such horror. But she also feels that those in authority must have good reason to suspect him. So mostly, she won't talk about it."

"And Clare claimed to have seen him in the camping supply aisle." Maggie's voice was resigned. Without much enthusiasm, she sat at the quilt frame, picking up a needle and putting her thimble on her finger. Perhaps the familiar movements would help her relax.

"Did you call Michael?" Louise asked.

Maggie nodded as her fingers began the familiar up and down movements. "I did. He was able to tell me that her car wasn't involved in any accidents yesterday. But there isn't anything else he can do, officially. Clare is an adult, and there's no evidence of foul play. He told me that the Upland sighting would have been reported to the FBI, since we called 9-1-1 about it. And the man at Big-mart did say that someone showed him Kenny's photo and asked if he'd seen him. Michael said he expects that was the tribal police." Her fingers worked automatically at her stitching. With burning, red-rimmed eyes, she watched the line of tiny stitches appear and felt better. The uniformity pleased her.

"This was a terrible time for Gerald to go on a fishing trip. Can anyone reach him by cell phone?" Anna asked.

"Clare told me once that he turns his cell phone off when he goes fishing because he goes to get away from everything. Plus the reception is bad out there, or non-existent. He usually calls her on their way back, once they get to a populated area." Maggie set another row of stitches and began to feel the tension ease from her. "Michael said to let him know if she doesn't turn up after twenty-four hours and he'll file an official report. He's started an unofficial inquiry, though, since she was last reported being around a known fugitive."

"What about Samson?" Anna asked.

"I called Joan Cummins — that's Clare's neighbor who watched Samson when they went back to Missouri in the summer. She said it was no problem for her to take care of Samson for now. She's very concerned about Clare, too, especially when she heard about her following Kenny. She said she would call if she heard anything."

66

They all had to be content with that for the time being.

10

Clare didn't know what to say to Kenny. He'd saved her from a cold night alone in her crashed car. Or from wandering around alone in the wet, dark forest trying to get help. From what he told her as they ate, her car was off the road, out of sight in the trees. It might have been days before someone noticed it. But he'd managed to find her and bring her to this snug retreat. He'd put her on a sleeping bag to rest, kept an eye on her, to make sure she was all right. Then he'd made her a bowl of soup, the most delicious meal she'd ever had. How could this gentle man be a killer? Worst of all, the killer of his own children?

She kept her counsel while they ate, her mind working frantically the entire time. She reviewed recent reading material; there must be a book she'd read that covered something like this. She read dozens of mystery novels each year, and she could usually pull some appropriate episode from one of them when faced with an iffy situation. But by the time the delicious soup was gone, she still hadn't come up with anything even remotely like her present position.

Kenny was silent, too, but watchfully alert. When they finished eating, he collected the empty bowls.

"That was the best soup I've ever had, Kenny. Thank you."

He laughed, and Clare couldn't help thinking that he looked startled at the sound, as though he thought he'd forgotten how.

"It was just canned soup, Mrs. Patterson. But I appreciate your enthusiasm. Just as I want to thank you for not running screaming from the house when you woke up and saw me sitting beside you. I guess I have to thank you for not turning me in back in Scottsdale, too."

Clare was glad he kept his back to her, busying his hands with the cleanup. She was sure her face was red with guilt, since she had indeed called about seeing him.

"Kenny, you're like a guardian angel, helping me this way. Who knows what would have happened . . . I might have died if you'd left me in the car. Please, call me

Clare. We're old friends from church after all."

"Clare."

He turned then and Clare realized there were tears in his eyes. She couldn't look directly at him, not without confessing that she had indeed turned him in. "I, ah . . . I'm afraid I did call 9-1-1 at the store."

His outburst startled her.

"You turned me in? Did you call from out here, too?" The tears were gone. His voice was deep and scary in its intensity. His eyes darted around the room, covering every inch and then going back again. Clare was suddenly glad he didn't have a gun. At least, she hadn't seen any evidence of one.

His hands grasped her shoulders. He wasn't really rough, but she was still sore from the accident and winced.

Instantly, he released her. He turned, hanging his head, running his hand over his face as if to wash away what had just happened.

"I'm sorry, Clare. I don't know what gets over me sometimes. I know you didn't call from here, or someone would have showed up already."

"No one came when I called," Clare said. "That's why I started following you. I should have turned around when I realized

70

you were heading out of town. I don't know what I was thinking."

"That makes two of us," he said. "Am I forgiven?"

He offered his hand; she took it. They shook as friends. Then Clare threw her arms around him and squeezed. She couldn't help it. He was just the age of her youngest son, and he looked so pitiable.

His arms went around her plump body, and he held her tight. They stood that way for over a minute, both seeking to gain control over roller coaster emotions.

"You need to rest," Kenny said, when he felt her come close to collapsing as her knees weakened. He held her firmly as she grabbed on to him for support. "Come on over here. There's a couch that's not too bad."

He led her back toward the wall where the sleeping bag was laid out, in the part of the cabin with the least damage. There was an old couch covered by an older afghan with a battered coffee table before it. Newspapers and magazines covered the top of the table.

"Thank you," Clare said, as soon as she was sitting, half reclining, on the sofa. "Tell me what happened." There was no need to explain what she meant. Kenny knew immediately.

"I didn't kill them," he said instantly. He gestured toward the stacks of paper on the coffee table. "I've read all the accounts, and I know what everyone thinks. But I didn't do it." He took a deep breath. "Like the police have said, I was having some issues with post traumatic stress. But I would never have taken it out on my little girls. Or on Kate. I loved them."

Tears streamed down his face, but he continued to speak as though unaware of them.

"I used to go camping when the PTSD was really bad and I was having trouble coping. It was my way of taking myself away from people until I was someone they could be around again. Without fear. Kate was afraid when I had the nightmares. I think she was scared that I'd forget where I was — think I was back in Iraq and do something to harm her. I was afraid of that myself. So I'd go off for a few days, practice the meditation techniques I learned to help me cope."

He paused, and Clare remained silent. She could see that he needed to talk about this. Had he kept it all bottled up inside for the past six months? How on earth had he remained sane?

"I was up near Heber, camping, when it happened. I've been back here hoping to find someone who could verify that I was here during the time the murders occurred. But so far, nothing." He ran his fingers through his long hair, then patted it back into place. Clare got the impression that he still wasn't used to the longer style.

He took a deep breath, then continued. "I didn't hear about it until I headed back to town four days later. I stopped at a fast food place in Payson. It was one of those places that has a TV set in the eating area that's always playing the news. And I saw photos of my family on the television. I couldn't believe it. And while I sat there, stunned, unable to eat any of the food I had in front of me, I saw my driver's license photo flash on the screen and heard the anchor asking for anyone who'd seen this man to contact the police. The banter between the two anchors made it plain that they felt I was guilty of killing my family and blowing up my house. My home!"

Once again the tears streamed down his face. He wiped at them with his hands, as if disgusted at this show of weakness.

"Didn't the people in the restaurant recognize you?"

A wry smile twisted his lips.

"I'd been camping, alone, for ten days. I was dirty and had a beard. Hadn't showered in days. No one wanted to get too close to me. I should have just used the drive-up, but by then I was ready for some people contact." He shook his head as if sickened by his brief desire to be social. "Also, my hair was much longer than it is in the photo they keep showing. As you can see, I've kept it long. Not that it seems to have helped as a disguise. You knew me right away." He frowned at her.

"I wasn't positive it was you," Clare said. Sometimes she was a little afraid of him. He seemed so up and down emotionally. It made her wonder if he was bi-polar. But then his fugitive status, and the reason for it, was surely enough to cause such extremes of behavior.

"I called Maggie Browne and told her I saw you." Clare's face fell. "Oh, dear, she's probably looking for me, especially when I didn't get back to her. She would have called her son, too, and he's a police officer in Scottsdale."

"Michael," Kenny said, looking resigned. "Yes, I know him. Sometimes I think it would be better to turn myself in and just get this running over with." He ran his hand over his beard. "You know, I used to love that movie *The Fugitive.* Thought it was great the way Dr. Kimble was on the run, trying to prove his innocence. Looking for the one-armed man. Isn't it ironic? Now I'm Dr. Kimble."

Clare almost smiled at his mention of the movie. He was so young. She remembered the original television series, the one with David Janssen that the movie was based on.

"But do you have a one-armed man?" she asked him.

Kenny gave her a confused look before he worked out what she meant. Then he offered a grim smile.

"You want to know if I'm chasing a suspect."

11

"I'm glad you were able to come to dinner, Michael. I'm so worried about Clare."

Although Michael regularly came to dinner on Monday evenings, Maggie had called and invited him for a second night that week. She was terribly worried about Clare and hoped he could offer some good news. Or at least lessen her concern.

Michael hugged his mother. "I know. I'm not sure there's anything I can do to help, but you know I love having dinner here." He leaned down to place a kiss on her cheek then grinned as he released her. "You did make dessert, right?"

Maggie couldn't resist grinning back. "Pineapple upside down cake."

Although she was anxious to consult her police officer son about Clare, Maggie managed to wait until they finished eating. Or at least, until she finished eating. Michael's appetite far surpassed hers. While they ate, they talked about their newest family member, the child of Maggie's son Bobby and his wife Merrie. Born with a heart defect requiring immediate corrective surgery, the baby was doing very well.

"Merrie took her for her twelve-week checkup yesterday and said she's doing as well as any other three-month-old." Maggie smiled. "It was just what I needed to hear after all that concern over Clare's phone call."

"Yeah, Bobby called me. Bragged like crazy about what a great kid she is."

He tried to sound bored about the whole uncle thing, but Maggie knew he was nuts about the baby. And all his other nieces and nephews. He'd make a great father, if only he would find the right woman and settle down.

When Maggie brought in the pineapple upside down cake, she finally couldn't put it off any longer. As soon as she put the cake plate on the table, she gave her son a pleading look.

"Where could she be, Michael? We've called everyone we can think of."

Michael stood, laying his arm across his mother's shoulders. "There's a call out for her and for her car. Someone will have seen her, or will see the car. We'll find her, Ma."

His quiet, confident voice flowed over Maggie, soothing her nerves. How often she'd heard those reports of missing senior citizens that ran on the local news programs. She never expected to be seeing such an announcement for one of her dear friends. Not all of those other news stories ended with good news. She just hoped there would be a happy ending to this particular tale.

12

"Oh, my."

Despite a beautiful, sunny morning, Friday at the Quilting Bee started out as glumly as Thursday, until Anna's gasp drew everyone's attention to her startled face. Anna's eyes were fixed on the door, her eyes wide, her mouth slack. Everyone else immediately turned in the same direction.

"Clare!"

Maggie rose with her one-word cry, and rushed around the quilt frame, getting to the door before any of the others, who had all risen and started forward too.

After exchanging hugs and having everyone exclaim over her sudden appearance, they moved back into the quilt room and sat down.

"Goodness," Clare said. "You all act like I've risen from the dead!" She gave a nervous laugh, that also managed to convey how touched she was about their concern.

"It's almost like you did," Anna informed her. She threw her arms around her for another intense hug. "We couldn't imagine what had happened to you, and it was easy to imagine the worst. With all that's being said about Kenny . . ."

"Where have you been?" Maggie asked. Her voice came out stern, almost accusatory, and she tried to compose herself before Clare took offense. She took a deep breath. When she spoke again, her voice was calm. "We've been very worried, Clare. Victoria and I tried to follow you on Wednesday. But we'd only made it to Payson when that storm hit."

Victoria nodded. "We couldn't go any farther. The road was closed because of a bad accident."

There was no need to explain their fear about who might have been involved in that disaster. Clare immediately understood, and her eyes grew wide.

"I didn't know about an accident."

"We stopped at a little place in Payson to see if the storm would blow over, and a waitress there told us about it," Maggie said. "She said that Route 260 was completely closed because of an accident between a car and a motorcycle."

"Maggie called Michael and asked him if

80

he could find out what kind of car was involved," Victoria added.

"So we knew it wasn't you," Anna said.

Clare was visibly upset by this. "I'm so sorry. I didn't mean to make everyone worry. I thought I would just drive a little way after him, then call the police when he stopped, and go home." She sighed. "Things often don't work out the way I think they will."

Maggie didn't say it, but she would have liked to tell Clare that that was because she wasn't a character in a book. In the real world, impulsive acts were often ill advised. In the real world, impulsive acts did not end up providing the vital clue that allowed a book's heroine to solve the mystery and call the police in triumph. Didn't Clare notice that the amateur sleuths in novels were often put in dangerous situations? Life or death situations?

They moved back to the quilt frame as they spoke, and soon everyone was seated. The women picked up their needles again, all except Clare who sat with her hands in her lap.

"You look like death warmed over," Edie said, causing the others to object.

"Now, Edie." Anna's voice held a gentle reproach.

Maggie did think Clare looked tired, as though she'd missed getting a good night's sleep. And she probably had — as had she herself, and most of the other Bee members.

Still, Maggie was sure that Clare was excited about something. Did she think she knew where Kenny was hiding out? Was she anticipating calling the FBI and collecting the reward?

But Clare dismissed Edie's comment with a wave of her hand, though her hand continued on to fluff at her hair. "I'm sure I do look dreadful. And you would too if you'd been caught out in the middle of nowhere for two days."

It was a day and a half, Maggie thought with an inner smile. But then, who was counting?

But Clare surprised her with her further words.

"Well, I guess it was really only a day and a half," she said. "But it seems like longer."

"What happened?" Louise asked.

"I told you. I saw Kenny Upland in Bigmart, and I followed him out toward Payson."

"You shouldn't have!" Anna was still shocked at such daredevil behavior.

"That was a very dangerous thing to do," Louise said. "He's wanted for killing his entire family."

"I know that!"

Maggie could tell Clare was getting irritated. She'd practically snapped Louise's head off. But this was an unusual and possibly dangerous situation they were discussing.

"So you still think it was Kenny you saw?" Maggie asked.

Clare looked offended. "I told you when I called from the store that first day, Maggie. I'm sure it was him. I've known him for years, and the man I saw was Kenny."

"Why didn't you approach him in the store and say something?" Edie asked.

Anna gasped. "Oh, that wouldn't have been good." She shook her head as she spoke.

Good question, Edie, Maggie thought. As Anna's gasp indicated, it would have been a foolish thing to do, but no more foolish than following him all the way up to the Rim in a thunder storm.

"I was going to, but then I caught myself. I remembered all the articles about him, and how I saw that episode of *Wanted Criminals* that he was on. Everyone was so sure he did it." Clare hung her head. "I was too nervous to go up and say hello, in case he really did kill Kate."

"That was probably a wise move, Clare," Maggie said. "The police and the FBI are pretty certain he did it, so it's best to be cautious."

"I couldn't help thinking that a character in a book would have gone right up and said something. And done something, too," Clare said. "I'd like to be that brave," she added in a small voice.

"But you're not a character in a book," Victoria told her, her voice soft and soothing. "You're a real person, and following him as you did was very brave."

Clare looked mollified.

"You should have called 9-1-1," Edie said. "You might have collected the reward."

"I did. Call 9-1-1, I mean. But no one came, and then I saw him leaving. I was afraid they'd miss him. So I thought I could just keep him in sight until they arrived and caught up with us."

Maggie wondered at such faulty logic but didn't interrupt.

"But then my phone battery died. And the rain got so bad. I was doing all right until a cat ran across the road, and without even thinking I slammed on my brakes."

Edie shook her head. "You should be very careful braking when the road is wet, Clare."

"I know that," Clare snapped.

Then she took a deep breath. Maggie imagined she was counting to ten.

"I know what I should do when driving in the rain, Edie. But it's a different thing when you're in the middle of a situation and there's no time to think."

As Clare paused in her story, Maggie noticed that other members of the Senior Guild were arriving at the Quilting Bee door, stepping inside or peering in at Clare, anxious to find out what had happened to her. Everyone knew she'd been missing; everyone knew she claimed to have seen Kenny Upland at Big-mart. Someone must have seen her enter the Bee room and passed the word.

"Let's all go and get some tea." Maggie rose, looking pointedly toward the door.

"Excellent idea," Victoria said, rising as well. "You could probably use a cup, Clare. And you can tell us *all* what happened. There's room enough in the kitchen for everyone to sit and hear your story."

13

When the Senior Guild met, urns of coffee and hot water for tea as well as pitchers of iced water and iced tea were always kept ready in the kitchen. The kitchen in turn opened up into the community room, filled with tables and chairs. This worked well for break times but was also excellent for meeting with large groups of Guild members.

Which is why the Quilting Bee women headed there now, the other Senior Guild attendees trailing in their wake. Since it was the week after the bazaar, attendance was not heavy, but there were still a fair number of people. While work went on as usual for the Quilting Bee, in other craft rooms they were cleaning up, sorting out unfinished projects and planning for next year. They would be discussing the turnout, what sold best, whether or not things had been priced well. For most of the craft groups, real work would not begin in earnest until after the new year.

There was already a large group visiting in the break room. Once all the newcomers had their desired refreshment and settled down, Clare began her story.

"Did you all hear that I saw Kenny Upland — right here in Big-mart?"

She told them about calling 9-1-1, and how no one came. When she got to the part about following him after he left the store, there were many who appeared to be of a mind with Anna as regarded Clare's impulsive action. As earlier, there were gasps and warnings.

Clare tried not to feel offended that so many of them did not agree with her hurried plan and proceeded with her tale. "Well, I certainly didn't think I was going to catch him myself," Clare said, her voice turning defensive. "I just meant to keep an eye on his car so I could direct the police to him when they came."

"How could you do that if you were in your car, following him?" someone asked.

Maggie had to smile. Here was another person who recognized fuzzy logic.

But Clare continued with her story as if the woman hadn't spoken at all. *Probably because she doesn't have an answer for her,* Maggie thought with an inner smile.

"In the beginning, it was fun. I felt like the heroine in a cozy mystery, you know? Until a big storm hit. Did you get it here in the valley, too?" she asked, and there were nods around the table.

"Odd time of year for it . . ." one of the men began. He was ready to go into more detail, but Clare jumped back into her tale, effectively shutting him off.

"It was really a bad storm out there on the road going up to the Mogollon Rim," Clare said. An involuntary shiver shook her at the memory of the rain pounding the car, the flashes of lightning, the shrinking visibility. "Big, heavy raindrops were blowing against the windshield, making it hard to see anything. I don't like driving in storms, but I was doing really well until a cat ran across the road." She sighed heavily. "It was instinct — I just stomped on the brake, without even thinking about the water on the road. Big mistake."

"What happened?" Anna asked. She turned toward the others in the room. "That's where she was in her story when we moved over here."

Clare waited for complete quiet before she answered the question. This was her big moment, and she wanted everyone to hear.

"My car skidded off the road and into a

ditch. I was really lucky that there was no major damage and that it started again the next day. But the airbags released, and I passed out." Clare's hand reached up to her face where there were burn marks and bruises caused by the airbag.

There were gasps from more than one of the women in the room. Many of them lived in fear of having some type of accident and losing their drivers' licenses. The men probably had similar fears, Maggie thought, but managed to hide any anxiety behind a façade of confident arrogance in their superior driving ability.

Maggie also thought that Clare was milking the moment, but she couldn't really blame her for enjoying her fifteen minutes of fame.

Clare waited until all the comments died away, until there was complete silence. Then she dropped her bomb.

"I was rescued by Kenny Upland," she said. "Kenny saved my life."

Once again, there were gasps and comments. This time, the murmurs turned into a roar. Even though Clare had started out by saying that she'd seen Kenny and then followed him, no one expected this.

"He saved you?"

"How did he do it?"

89

"You passed out?"

"Did you hit your head?"

When all the comments had died down, Clare picked up her story by answering the final question.

"I didn't hit my head. I was wearing my seat belt. But I definitely passed out. I don't know how long I was unconscious, but when I woke up it was dark. I was in a cabin — more of a hut, actually — and Kenny was sitting right there, looking after me. He said I was out for hours. Kenny saved my life." She nodded firmly, as if to tell them all that it had truly happened and Kenny was a good guy after all. "He had taken me from my car and put me in this abandoned cabin, out of the rain. He gave me some ibuprofen and looked after me. I ached all over," she confided.

"But Kenny Upland!" a woman exclaimed. "How could you take those pills? He might have poisoned you."

Clare shook her head, though Maggie saw a quick look of consternation pass over her face. Perhaps, after all, she *had* had a momentary concern about taking pills from the notorious Kenny Upland.

"I guess you had to be there. I wasn't worried. He was just as nice as he always was when he was here at St. Rose. He reassured

90

me that I would be okay and suggested I take some ibuprofen and go back to sleep. He said then I would feel better, and I did. I knew he worked in a nursing home, so I figured he knew what he was talking about."

Clare didn't mention the anti-anxiety pill he'd sneaked in with the pain reliever. She had yet to resolve her own feelings about *that*. But she had never felt that her life was endangered. Not really.

"When I woke up again, I did feel better. A lot better. And he had some soup he'd made for me on a little camp stove."

"Did he tell you what happened to Kate and the girls?"

"He told me how he heard about it — afterward. And where he was when it happened," Clare said. "He has post traumatic stress disorder, you know. From his time in Iraq with the National Guard." Clare continued to speak over the murmur of voices as those present commented to neighbors on this revelation — which was hardly a surprise. "He had really bad dreams, and they scared Kate and the twins. He said he would go off into the mountains to camp and be alone when it got real bad. He was worried that he might hurt someone inadvertently."

Maggie noticed several people exchanging

looks and nods. It was obvious — to her at least — that they considered this a confession of sorts. Unlike Clare, who seemed to think it absolved him, to others it sounded like a good reason to *blame* Kenny for what had happened.

"He wasn't even here in Scottsdale at the time," Clare explained. "He was camping, out near Heber. He's still devastated by the whole thing."

All around her, questions flew. Where was he? What did he say? If he hadn't done it, who had?

Clare waved her hands for quiet. "All I can tell you is what Kenny told me. And that I really believed what he had to say. He was very sincere. I don't think he did it."

Maggie could see that the room was divided. She knew there were many people who had never wanted to think Kenny was capable of murder. But plenty of others were ready to believe all the media hoopla and speculation; there were still people who firmly believed that whatever was printed in the newspaper was the truth.

"Oh, but he has to be guilty. They had him on that TV show, you know the one. They said to call the FBI if you knew where he was."

Maggie amended her previous thought to

include people who firmly believed everything they saw on the television news was
the absolute truth.

"You'll never convince me Kenny killed
his family. He was a good father. Why, the
way he worked with the youth group . . ."

"My grandson thought he walked on water . . ."

"My granddaughter had quite a crush on
him. She's only twelve . . ."

When the buzz of comments finally died
off, Clare resumed her story.

"Kenny was camping out near Heber
when his house exploded." Clare nodded, a
quick affirmation of her belief in Kenny's
statement. "He said he was returning to
Scottsdale four days after the explosion,
when he stopped at a fast-food restaurant
and heard about his family. It was one of
those places that has TV screens, you know,
and plays the news all the time." Clare's
voice edged upward as she ended the sentence, making into a question of sorts. "He
heard then that his house and his family
were gone and that he was wanted for
questioning. He said he knew from what
the anchors said that he was the major
suspect, and he figured if he turned himself
in he would be arrested right away. He'd
been camping alone, and he hadn't seen

anyone."

Clare brought her hands up in a gesture that begged for their understanding.

"But, the thing was, he didn't *want* to see anyone. That was his whole reason for going up there. So he had no proof of what he'd been doing. And he figured if he didn't turn himself in, he could try to figure out what happened. He thinks the police aren't really looking for an answer because they assume he did it. You remember that movie *The Fugitive?* He said he's Richard Kimble, trying to find the real killer."

Maggie could see that Clare, who liked to compare herself to characters in novels, appreciated Kenny's comparison.

Steve, a retired doctor who had taken up knitting and made socks to sell at the bazaar, had a comment about PTSD. "I don't know," he said, shaking his head slowly. "Post traumatic stress is an odd thing. Some people can get quite violent. Killing his family wouldn't be completely out of the picture. And he'd be just as devastated as you describe afterward — even if he did do it himself. The thing is, he might not even remember doing it."

There was a momentary silence as the others in the room digested this information. It was Edie who broke it.

"How did he look?" she asked.

Maggie was surprised at Edie's question and at the sincere interest in her voice. She'd expected Edie to be the first to denounce Clare for following a known fugitive.

"He looked just the same, except that he's lost a lot of weight. And he seems more rugged, somehow. His hair's grown out, and he has a beard. He looks a lot like one of those wild mountain men who ride in the Parada del Sol parade every year, the ones who bring the Pony Express mail."

"That sounds pretty different to me," Edie said.

Me, too, Maggie thought, recalling the preppy Kenny they'd known. But since Clare had recognized him so easily, she probably felt he looked just as he had.

"Ohh," one of the women said. "Maybe the FBI will send an artist out to sketch a picture of him from your description, and they can add it to their wanted poster. Wouldn't that be something?"

"Just like on *CSI*."

"Or *Bones*," someone added.

Clare's eyes sparkled with interest. "Oh, wouldn't that be exciting?"

"I always liked Kenny," Gladys said. "He seemed so genuinely interested in helping the young people. I still can't believe what he did."

"But that's the thing!" Clare protested. "Haven't you heard anything I've said?" In her frustration, her voice rose up to a steep pitch. "Kenny *didn't do it.* He wasn't even in town when it happened. He's been wrongfully accused!" Clare was close to tears. "What happened to innocent until proven guilty?"

There were murmurs of agreement, but also mutterings of Kenny's probable guilt.

Contradicting Edie's earlier observation about Clare's condition, a member of the Guild's sewing League complimented Clare's appearance. "You look good for someone who's been in an accident and then out in the wild for two days."

"I got back late last night, so I had a chance to clean up and to rest. Gerald came home right after me, and that helped, too. And you can't see that I ache all over." Clare winced. "Having your car go into a ditch is hard on an old body."

Around them, the other Guild members continued talking among themselves, the voices blurring into a heavy murmur. They seemed evenly divided among those who believed Kenny guilty and those who sided with Clare, wanting to believe in his innocence.

As the debate over his guilt reached an impasse, the groups of Senior Guild members began to drift back to the workrooms.

14

As the Quilting Bee started back to the room, Maggie broached a question that she felt all the Bee members wanted answered.

"Why didn't you call someone once you were back in town?" She meant, of course, *why didn't you call one of* us *once you returned?*

"It was so late when I got back, Maggie. And then Gerald came in a few minutes later. He was so upset with me!"

"Can't blame him," Edie said.

Clare did look apologetic for worrying them longer than necessary. She chewed on her bottom lip as she continued. "It was really late by the time I finished telling him the whole story. And I just hate to call anyone after ten o'clock. After nine, really, but definitely after ten. A lot of people are in bed by then. And it was midnight by the time Gerald and I finished talking."

They'd reached the quilt room by then,

and each woman found her previously abandoned spot at the frame. There was some shifting of chairs as they maneuvered to get the best position to pick up their quilting again.

"I guess John was able to find Gerald then." Louise picked up her needle and fitted her thimble on her finger. "He said he knew where Dan's secret fishing hole was."

Clare nodded as she sat down and picked up a needle in a reflective movement. "I wasn't really concerned about him — worried that he would worry about me, I mean. Because I knew he was out of touch." Clare rolled the needle between her thumb and forefinger, still not ready to stitch. "It's an awful thing to say, but I was more concerned about Samson being alone." She turned to Maggie. "Thank you for calling Joan, by the way."

Maggie nodded, wondering why Joan hadn't called to let her know Clare was back. Perhaps she thought Clare had done it?

They were all settled around the quilting frame now, thimbles on their fingers, needles in their hands. The familiarity of the scene wrung a quiet sigh from Clare. Maggie heard it, but knew it wasn't an unhappy sound. She too could feel the serenity of their quilting room, of the familiar smells of new fabric and a hint of herbs from their favorite blends of tea.

"What was Gerald's reaction to it all?" Anna asked.

"What you'd expect," Clare said with a heavy sigh. "He yelled at me, actually. Then he got real apologetic and all, but I knew he was angry. He couldn't believe I didn't just call the police from the store and go home. He said it was awfully foolish for me to follow him like that. That I could have been killed, just like Kate and the girls."

There was nothing the others could say about that. Most of them agreed. And while they, like Clare, enjoyed reading mystery novels, none of them were quite so anxious to project themselves into the stories on a real life basis.

Then Clare smiled. She almost giggled. "But in the end, Gerald and I made up. He apologized for yelling. But he just did it because he loves me and I scared him." She smiled again and a rosy flush crept into her cheeks — a coloration completely unrelated to the airbag burns.

In that moment, Maggie missed Harry terribly.

"So how did you get away?" Edie asked.

"Well, I didn't escape, if that's what you

mean," Clare replied indignantly. "I wasn't a captive, after all."

"I never said you were," Edie said. "I just wondered when you left Kenny and how you did it."

"You said you were able to drive your car?" Victoria asked.

"Yes. I could hardly believe it. It looks pretty good for going into a ditch, mostly just scratches in the paint and a dent in the front fender. But Gerald says I have to take it in to be checked anyway. Something about possible problems underneath." There was a twinkle in Clare's eyes as she remembered returning to her damaged car. "Anyway, when it was time to go, Kenny drove me back to my car on a motorcycle!"

Surprise widened Anna's eyes. "You rode on a motorcycle?"

"Yes." Clare's eyes were bright with excitement. "Kenny didn't want to use the car in case they knew about it from his trip to Scottsdale. I'd never ridden a motorcycle before — not in my entire life. It was certainly exciting."

Edie snorted. "I guess you'll be out shopping for one then."

Maggie and Louise chuckled, but Clare looked startled.

"Oh, no. It was fun for a one-time experi-

101

ence, but I wouldn't want to do it on a daily basis." She shook her head. "It was very noisy for one thing. And very cold."

"Honestly, Clare." Edie harrumphed, like she couldn't believe Clare had answered her so seriously. "I was *joking.*"

They all laughed then, at Clare's startled expression. But then Edie rarely joked. She usually just pontificated, most often about the dangers of modern life and the rising crime rate.

"So then you just got into your car and drove back here?" Maggie said.

"Well, I did snoop around a little while Kenny left to get the person with the tow truck." There was a mischievous look in her eyes when she admitted this, though Anna was horrified.

"Clare, you didn't!" Anna said.

"There wasn't a whole lot to see." Clare shrugged. "The cabin must have been in one of the forest fires some time ago. One wall was completely gone, and part of the roof, and someone had pulled black plastic over to try to cover it. But it was okay for me to sleep in, out of the rain. And there was a nice sleeping bag. Kenny must have put me in his because I didn't see another one. But I don't think Kenny's been in that cabin for the past six months. There wasn't nearly enough in the way of supplies. Except for a small bag with a change of clothes and some camping-style food, all I found were newspaper accounts of the case."

"Lucky he didn't catch you snooping through his things," Edie said.

"I keep telling you, he's okay." Clare sighed loudly, with a particularly cutting look at Edie.

Maggie jumped in to ease the strain between the two. Heaven knew Edie could be a trial, but she was a wonderful stitcher. And a good person at heart.

"So after that you drove back to the valley?" Maggie said.

Clare nodded. "Like you, I stopped in Payson to eat. I would have called you then, but the battery on my cell phone was completely dead. And have you tried to find a pay phone recently? No one has them. They assume everyone has their own cell phone and just don't bother getting pay phones or keeping up the ones they have. There was a pay phone at the station where I stopped for gas, but it didn't work. I really have to get one of those car chargers for my cell phone," she added. "I never realized how important it could be to have one."

Edie began to expound on the importance of a working cell phone for a woman alone, but the others quickly cut that short.

"So you didn't call the police either?" Anna asked.

"No." Clare shook her head as she said it. "Anyway, I didn't think Kenny would hang around once I got going. I don't think he trusts anyone, so I'm sure he'll move on." She shrugged. "As I said, the cabin didn't look used enough to account for six months of hiding. I'm sure he's moved on by now."

"Did you at least call the police when you got home?" Louise asked. "To tell them you saw Kenny?"

Clare turned bright red.

"You didn't, did you?" Edie sounded both accusatory and reproachful.

"I called them when I saw him at Big-mart. It was late when I got back yesterday — after dark. And I told you Gerald came in right behind me. He told me about everyone looking for me and how they had tracked him down. He insisted on talking immediately, and I had to feed poor Samson and change out of those awful clothes. I'd been wearing the same clothes for two days, and slept in them . . . I was desperate for a hot shower. I told Gerald I couldn't talk until I had my shower. I didn't want anyone to see me looking like that either," she added in a small voice. "It was bad

104

enough that Gerald did."

Clare smiled, love radiating across her wide face. "He was so wonderful. While I was in the shower, he fixed some soup for us. Then, afterward, he insisted that I have a long soak in a hot tub — to help the achiness. After that, all I wanted to do was get into bed and sleep for a long, long time."

Maggie didn't know whether to hug her or shake her. "I still wish you'd called one of us, so that we could stop worrying about you. We were talking about trying to drive out that way, hoping that we might see some sign of your car."

"The car was fairly well into the shrubbery, and lower than the roadway. Even if you'd gone on Thursday morning, I doubt you would have seen it. Kenny found someone he knew with one of those old-fashioned tow trucks, the kind with the chain that attaches to the bumper. I haven't seen one in years."

"They don't attach to the bumper," Edie interrupted. "The bumper would just get pulled right off. It attaches to the undercarriage."

"Oh, what does it matter?" Clare snapped. Then she took a deep breath and pushed her needle into the quilt. Maggie thought her pause was just about long enough to count to ten.

"Once my car was back on the road, it started up right away. I sure was grateful for that. I'd been praying to the Blessed Mother," she said. "I don't know what I would have done if the car hadn't started."

There were several comments from her friends on how lucky she was that her car wasn't totaled. And that she had come out of it with nothing more than aches and a few airbag burns and bruises.

"But here's the best part," she went on. "I couldn't say anything with all those others around." She abandoned her needle, looking quickly from right to left as if checking that only the Bee members were in the quilting room. Then she leaned over the quilt frame, dropping her voice to a dramatic whisper. "Anyway, Kenny told me he's been trying to work out what really happened. I guess that's why he had all those articles about the case. And," she paused for dramatic effect, "he told me his theory of what really happened." She smiled happily at the others.

This time Maggie couldn't let it pass. After everything Clare had just been through — and it sounded like they hadn't heard all of it yet — Clare was acting like someone in the middle of a movie script.

Maggie had not wanted to believe that Kenny had killed his family, but over time had come to accept it as the truth. Sure, Kenny was a nice man who did a lot for the parish. But hadn't the neighbors of Ted Bundy expressed surprise at his arrest, claiming that he was a very nice, quiet man? Only Kate and Kenny knew what went on inside their home. And even Kate may not have realized the extent of Kenny's post traumatic stress.

"Honestly, Clare, be realistic. This isn't a book or a TV show. You're not an amateur sleuth."

Louise nodded. "I liked Kenny, too, but the police and the fire investigators seem so sure that he was involved. All you have is Kenny's word. And as Steve said earlier, someone suffering from PTSD could do something as horrible as what he's accused of and possibly not remember it afterward."

"The police have all kinds of evidence, so they say," Edie said. "Haven't you seen those *Wanted Criminals* episodes about him? They're sure he did it. And the people who knew killers always say that on the evening news — 'I can't believe it. He was so nice.' It's become a cliché," she added.

"That may be true," Clare said slowly. But Maggie could see her grit her molars and set her head at a stubborn angle. "But you weren't there. I could see how sincere he was. Truly devastated by all that happened."

Victoria's soft voice intruded, before any more could be said about Kenny's likely guilt. "Why don't you tell us his theory, Clare."

Clare sent her a grateful smile. Her posture relaxed noticeably.

"It was just the most exciting thing," she began, looking around at the faces of her dearest friends. Her fingers stilled on the quilt top. Where she had been preparing to fill her needle with stitches, it now stood upright, unmoving, as she concentrated on her story. "There I was, sitting in this horrible, burned-out cabin, with an actual fugitive right there in front of me. But he wasn't violent, or scary. He was just nice Kenny Upland. And he explained how he was innocent. Can you believe it? He told me — *me!* — his alibi and why he didn't turn himself in."

Maggie's and Louise's eyes met in a silent exchange of information, Louise's eyebrows rising upward. They didn't have to say it out loud; they knew they were thinking the same thing. *Don't all criminals claim to be innocent?*

Victoria was more understanding of Clare

and her present emotional state. "What did he tell you?"

"Well, I already explained *where* he was when his house exploded. And he talked to me about the post traumatic stress."

"That's a terrible thing to have to live with," Louise said. "It can really change a person. Did he get treatment? The VA is doing a lot more these days for the veterans who suffer from it."

Clare shook her head. "He said he went to the VA, but there's all kinds of paperwork and it can take months to get treatment. He said he would go there and have to wait for hours — sometimes he spent the whole day there. So he started working out his own treatment. He talked about going off on his own, said that he had some kind of meditation he could do that helped. He didn't explain it, but I got the impression it was some kind of communing with nature thing. We all know how comfortable he was in the wilderness. Certainly much more so than I."

Clare pushed her needle into the quilt sandwich, taking several stitches and pulling it through. She barely noticed that she did so. She appeared to be deep in thought as she placed a few more stitches in the top. When she spoke again, her voice was thoughtful. "He did seem more on edge than he used to be. Kind of jittery, almost. Any sound at all, and he would be instantly alert, turn and look all around. Once I even thought he was reaching for a rifle that was there in the cabin. A hunting rifle, you know, not an army type gun," she clarified.

As though that made it all right, Maggie thought. Maggie's family had always had hunting rifles of one kind or another. She knew how to use a gun, and she was comfortable around them. But she would *not* be comfortable around a man who was jittery with PTSD and who had a gun — any kind of gun — near at hand.

Louise was nodding. "Sounds like typical post traumatic behavior. I've done some reading on it. That aspect of the syndrome is called 'hyperarousal'."

Edie snickered, and Maggie almost rolled her eyes. She caught herself just in time, not wanting to react to an immature response with an even more childish one.

"What it means is that the person never lets his guard down. They might be jumpy, and they're always on the alert in case of attack. I would think Kenny especially might be prone to that, as he's a fugitive whose photo has been widely circulated. He not only has to watch out for non-existent warlike dangers, he has to be constantly on the alert for law enforcement. Or citizens who think they recognize him," Louise added, throwing a particular look toward Clare.

Clare herself nodded vigorously. "That's just what was happening. Even though he was very nice, and thoughtful and everything, he was always watchful. I thought he was just nervous, but what you're saying makes a lot of sense."

There was silence as they all thought this over. But as Clare was eager to share the rest of her story, the moment quickly passed.

"This war in the Middle East is just awful. Kenny's story brought that home to me more than anything I've read in the newspaper or heard on the news. Because the thing was, it made everything so difficult for his family here at home."

"War is often hardest on those left behind," Victoria said. She'd been a history teacher before retirement and could have related many stories to support this position. But she didn't.

"Vince works with the St. Vincent de Paul group here at St. Rose, and they have been helping many families whose main wage earner is in Iraq," Louise said.

"Really?" Clare said. "I didn't know that.

I wonder why Kate didn't go to them to help her out?"

"Pride, probably," Edie said. "Lots of people are too proud to ask for help."

The others chose to ignore Edie's comment. Kate had been so shy, she was probably just too embarrassed to ask for help.

"Should she have?" Louise said. "Gone to St. Vincent's for help?"

"Oh, yes. You see, that's what started it all, according to Kenny."

"Started what?" Edie asked, impatience obvious in her tone. "What happened to Kate while Kenny was overseas?"

"She was a stay at home mother, wasn't she?" Victoria said. "Without his income, it must have been very difficult for her. The media has done some coverage of the effect of the war on family left behind, and even working mothers are having trouble making ends meet without their spouses here working their regular jobs. It's a fact of life that men earn more than women."

Clare nodded her eager agreement. "That's just what Kenny said. He was downright angry about it. He said Kate decided she had to get a job, but she didn't want something full time. And she was shy, and Kenny says she was embarrassed that she didn't have a college degree. But she

112

was really good with math and knew how to do bookkeeping work. He said she was a whiz with numbers and with budgets. That's why they could afford to let her be a full-time mom."

"Actually, I think I heard that she worked in the office at the Lutheran preschool," Maggie said, referring to the large and active Lutheran church just a block away from St. Rose. Victoria was an official member there, even though she spent so much of her time with her quilting friends at St. Rose.

Clare jumped on that. "That's right. Kenny mentioned that, and I remembered hearing it, too. He thought that was very clever of her because when she took a second job, she could trade her work there for the girls' tuition."

"Very intelligent," Victoria agreed.

"Kenny was over there for more than a year, so she had to take other jobs, too."

Maggie thought that over. Jobs would mean contact with others, and some interesting possibilities arose. Still, it was hard to believe that shy little Kate might be the cause of what had finally happened.

Clare looked at Maggie. "I can see your mind working," she said with a smile. "I bet you're thinking what I am. If she was getting out of the house to work, she was meeting and interacting with other people. My first thought was that she might have met a man. Love triangles make great plot devices for mysteries involving murder. Love, revenge, the woman scorned — all that."

Louise shook her head. "We keep reminding you, Clare. This isn't a book. Or a movie."

"And Kate of all people . . . she wouldn't have been acting that way." Anna shook her head for emphasis.

But Clare remained undeterred. "I know. But Kate is dead, and her girls, too. And Kenny says he didn't do it. And I believe him."

"So, did he say who did kill them?" Maggie asked.

"Sort of."

"Sort of?" Edie made a noise that sounded much like a snort. "What kind of an answer is that? Either he did or he didn't."

"Well, he doesn't know yet," Clare admitted. "But he's working on it. And he told me his theory." Her excitement was back.

"His theory?" Anna repeated. She seemed confused.

"All he has is a theory?" Maggie stared at Clare. On the quilt top, her fingers continued to move automatically, creating the outline of a maple leaf sketched onto the top with pencil.

"It's a good theory," Clare insisted. "Wait till you hear it."

The Bee members exchanged looks before turning back to Clare. They were more than ready to hear the rest of the story.

"Kate ended up with three part-time jobs," Clare said. "There was the one at the preschool. The girls attended the morning preschool there before they started kindergarten, so that was an important job for her. Then she took a job with a car dealership and one with a grocery store. They were all bookkeeping-type jobs."

"And?" Maggie prompted.

"Kenny thinks she had an affair while he was gone."

"What?"

The exclamation came simultaneously from every member of the Bee. No one could believe that shy little Kate Upland, devoted mother and wife, would have an affair.

"Kate?" Louise said. "Shy little Kate?"

Edie snorted. "Kate? Why she was the poster girl for prim and proper." She shook her head. "Men think sex explains everything."

"I couldn't believe it either," Clare said.

"But Kenny said he began to suspect it while he was in Iraq, because the tone of her emails changed. You know, they mostly communicate with their loved ones by computer these days."

There were a few nods indicating that the others knew about the prominence of email for corresponding with the military.

"But that's not unusual," Louise said. "Things were difficult, and she was probably worrying about him, too. She could have been hedging, trying not to make it harder for him."

Maggie nodded her agreement. "Things were bound to change in the course of a year."

"It's hard for the women when their husbands are gone, especially those with children," Louise said.

"Kenny thought Kate seemed very nervous, like she was afraid of something." Clare pursed her lips. "He thought she was worried he would find out about the affair. But he said he didn't care, really. He just wanted things to be like they were before."

"They all say that," Edie said. "I'll bet it would be a different story if he had proof that she was unfaithful."

Louise shook her head, ignoring Edie's comment and replying to Clare's statement.

"That was an unrealistic expectation. Whatever the problem was, nothing was ever going to be the same after such a long separation. And after his war experience. He would be a different person after that, even if he didn't suffer from post traumatic stress."

Clare stubbornly stuck to her story. "He said some odd things happened after he got back that only reinforced the idea. Not that the affair continued once he returned, but he thinks the man was getting after her about it. Maybe even stalking her. He says their marriage just wasn't the same."

This time Edie did snort. "Lots of marriages aren't the same after that kind of a separation. And if he was suffering from the post traumatic stress, and not even being treated for it . . ." Edie let her voice trail off.

Victoria quickly jumped in. "I have to agree with Edie on this, Clare. With him being gone for so long, and then having serious problems on his return, I'd be surprised if it *didn't* affect their marriage."

"He needed to admit he had a problem and get some real treatment," Louise added, "not some type of meditation he developed on his own."

Clare seemed frustrated by their lack of

support. "No, no. I must not be telling it right. If only you could have heard Kenny. He said there were things the girls mentioned, about a man who would come over. It must have been something serious if he would visit the girls, take them out and all."

"Or, he could have been a friend of Kate's who wanted to help her out while her husband was gone," Maggie said. Her firm tone might have discouraged another person, but not Clare.

"He thought someone might have been stalking her. He said he would see this man sometimes, following them. But he could never get a good enough look to see who it was."

"PTSD patients can be quite paranoid," Louise said. "It's possible he just imagined someone following them."

At Clare's frustrated sigh, Louise elaborated. "He might have actually seen someone behind them at times, but that person may have been going about his own business. It's the idea that the person was actually stalking them that I question, not the fact that he might have seen an actual person."

"You weren't there." Clare's voice sounded strained, as though she was close to tears. She blinked rapidly a few times.

"You couldn't see how sincere and honest Kenny was. He was just torn up about his family. When he talked about missing their funeral, he actually had tears in his eyes."

Clare looked very guilty all of a sudden and turned her attention toward the quilt top and her abandoned needle. She kept her head down, speaking in a soft voice they had to strain to hear. "I told Kenny how we'd helped find two killers already. I told him we could help him prove his innocence."

For a brief moment all hands stilled. Needles remained in place in the fabric, quivering gently as though missing the warmth of the guiding fingers. Then there was a collective intake of breath and stitching resumed.

Except for Edie, who continued to stare at Clare, her expression formidable.

"You said we would aid and abet a wanted fugitive?"

15

Clare's face crumpled. Once again she was close to tears. "Oh, dear. It sounds awful when you put it like that. I just wanted to help." She hung her head, appearing to study the quilt top with an intensity bordering on obsession. "I don't want Kenny to be the guilty one. I used to talk to him all the time at church events and he was such a nice man. And he just seemed to dote on those darling girls. How could he . . . ?"

She stopped there, unable to continue. What had been done to the family was unspeakable, especially to the children. Two beautiful children who should have had long and fruitful lives. All three, dead in their sleep. Supposedly, they were found in their beds, as though dreaming peacefully. Then the gas was turned on in the kitchen and rigged so that the house eventually exploded into flames. The police and fire department had not given out details on how that was done — perhaps not to encourage copycats, or perhaps to have something to question Kenny about when he was captured.

The true horror was that the Uplands lived in their neighborhood. Just a few minutes from the church. Just a few minutes from any of their homes. For such an awful thing to happen, right there on their familiar streets — that was the hardest part to take in. It was a miracle none of the other houses on the street had burned. Debris had flown many hundreds of feet. Other parishioners who lived in the area said they would never forget it, that it sounded as though a plane had crashed in the middle of their neighborhood. Gladys was deaf for hours afterward.

Maggie and Louise exchanged an understanding look.

Victoria, sitting beside Clare, reached over and patted her hand in an affectionate gesture.

It took a moment, but Clare finally glanced around the frame at all her friends. She swallowed, looking embarrassed, as though she knew she shouldn't have plunged ahead without consulting them all. In a small voice, she apologized. "I guess I should have asked you all first. But it's not as if we're going to help hide Kenny, or even support him in hiding. I just want to help him prove someone else did it. Couldn't we just ask around a bit? See if we can uncover anything that might prove Kenny's theory? That's more or less what we did before."

Maggie did not appear happy about this suggestion. She didn't mind playing the busy body when she had a real goal. Speculating about Candy and her life had been one thing. She'd *known* Louise was incapable of suffocating their friend. She didn't *know* anything about Kenny. Much as she'd liked the young man, she thought him fully capable of doing the terrible things he was accused of. And nothing Clare told them had changed her opinion.

"I don't know what it is you expect us to find, Clare."

Victoria's quiet voice dropped into the tense moment. "What car dealer did she work for? And what grocery store?"

Her calm tone provided an instant soothing effect. Clare's eyes brightened immediately, and she sat up straighter, her shoulders losing their discouraged slump.

"K. C. Gilligan."

Everyone nodded. K.C. was not only an active member of the St. Rose Parish, he was constantly seen on television commercials for his various car dealerships.

"What about the grocery store?" Victoria

prompted.

"It was that small store near here, the one that specializes in health foods."

"Nature's Best," Maggie said.

"That's it," Clare said. "I've been in there a few times, but I don't shop there much. I've often wondered how it can survive because it never seems to be very crowded. And it's expensive."

"It's been there forever," Anna said. "The name has changed a few times as it's changed ownership. I used to shop there all the time before they remodeled a couple of years ago, when they changed ownership. That's when they started calling it Nature's Best. It's supposed to be organic foods. The prices went up a lot then, and the more upscale young people started shopping there. I still see them go in there all the time, athletic-looking young people. They're still wearing their exercise clothes, most of them."

"They have some nice ethnic food," Edie said. "Special spices for Mexican and Thai foods, among others."

"Ah, but what they also have there," Louise said, "is a compounding pharmacy."

The others took a moment to digest this pronouncement.

"What's a compounding pharmacy?"

Anna asked, obviously puzzled.

"If your doctor gives you a prescription for something he wants mixed up special, most of the chain stores won't do it. In fact, I don't think any of them will. They mostly just count out pills and dispense meds that are already made up by a larger company. But the pharmacist at Nature's Best will mix a medication to the physician's specifications."

Louise gave them a moment to absorb this information.

"I had to go there last year for a special cream the dermatologist prescribed for Vince. He had a persistent rash," she added, without elaborating further. "Inez Torres — you know her, she always goes to nine o'clock mass on Sunday — her dog has Valley Fever and she told me she goes there for his medicine. The pharmacist mixes it up special for people who need it for their dogs, and it's cheaper than buying the name brand or even the generic."

Valley Fever, a fungal infection rife in the desert, could afflict both people and dogs. Most valley residents caught it at some time or another and didn't even know it, getting by with mild, cold-like symptoms. But some people became very ill with respiratory problems, and a few even died. Many dogs also contracted the illness, from spores thrown into the air during the valley's incessant construction. The canines became very ill. It could be controlled by medicine — in both humans and dogs — but many dogs required medication for life, and it became an expensive proposition.

"That's very nice of him," Anna said. "My friend Trudy lost her dog to Valley Fever a few years ago. He was only three years old."

"I talked to the pharmacist when I picked up the cream for Vince, and he was very nice. Friendly, polite. He belongs to St. Rose, too, said he'd seen me here a few times. He goes to the nine o'clock mass, too."

Sunday mass times at St. Rose were seven, nine and eleven, with one mass on Saturday evening at five. Because the congregation was so large, parishioners mostly knew the people who attended the same mass they did.

"What's his name?" Maggie asked.

"Antonio Sandoval. Tony . . . very personable — looks like an athlete. I noticed some other athletic young men in there, buying vitamins and supplements and talking to him. He has more vitamins and supplements than I've seen in any other store, so I guess that's why they shop there."

125

"Well, any of us can go into the store and shop," Clare stated. "And I'll bet there are Senior Guild members who shop there, too. We could just see if anyone ever saw Kate with a man while Kenny was gone." She ticked off one finger. "Lots of people here know K.C. Even I know him," she said, ticking off a second finger." She turned eagerly to Victoria. "Do you know anyone over at the Lutheran Preschool?"

Victoria nodded. "I happen to know the director, Eleanor Wells. She's been after me to join her bunco group, but I've been reluctant to commit myself for every week. I have gone a few times and enjoyed it. Perhaps this is the time to finally join." She pulled her needle through the fabric before looking up at Clare. "They meet on Monday evenings."

"Oh, Victoria, that would be wonderful. Now what else can we do?"

"I think Kenny was from the Midwest originally, but Kate was Arizona born and bred," Maggie said. "So what about her family? Why didn't she go to her family when she needed help?"

"Wasn't she from Lake Havasu or Bullhead City?" Edie said. "One of those places on the Colorado River?"

Clare was already nodding. "She was from

Bullhead City. Her parents have a bed and breakfast there."

"Goodness," Anna said. "How on earth do you know that?"

"I think it was in the paper after the tragedy," Victoria said.

Maggie nodded, but Clare was already answering.

"I asked Kate about her family once. She told me about her parents and their bed and breakfast. They took it over from her grandparents, her mother's family, and she grew up there. It was a rooming house back in her grandparents' day. She had to help her mother in the kitchen and help clean the rooms. She couldn't wait to get away."

"Hmpf," Edie said. "Probably a big disappointment to them. They probably expected her to stay and help, then take over when they retired. Keep it in the family."

"I wouldn't be surprised," Clare said. "I got the distinct impression that there was a rift there. And I don't think they ever spoke to the media after she died."

"Well, you can't blame them for that," Anna said.

"That's for sure," Maggie said, at the same time Victoria spoke.

"No, you can't," Victoria said. "They do try to insert themselves into people's grief,

127

don't they?"

"Just imagine losing not only a daughter, but your grandchildren, too." Anna's sadness at the mere thought suffused her face and her voice. Tears dampened her eyes.

"Did she have any brothers or sisters?" Maggie asked.

Clare shook her head. "She was an only child. Kenny was, too. That's why they were so tickled to have twins. Kate said she always wanted a sister, and she thought a twin sister must be a wonderful thing."

In the moment of silence that followed, Maggie was sure that they were all remembering the beautiful little Upland twins. She said a short prayer for the repose of their souls, knowing that such sweet innocence would be rewarded in heaven.

It was Anna's soft voice that brought them from their quiet reflection. "We mustn't forget Kate's neighbors. If a man was at the house playing with the children, neighbors might have seen something."

Louise grinned at Anna. "An excellent idea, Anna."

"That might be just the place to start," Maggie said. "If nothing comes of it, then we just forget about Kenny and let law enforcement handle it. It seems likely that if there was a stalker, one of the neighbors might have seen something."

"This is the perfect time of year to ask around, too," Louise said, "with things relaxed after the bazaar and lots of people gossiping in the break room every day."

Clare perked up immediately. "Oh, thank you." She looked around the frame, smiling at each of the others in turn. "I *knew* I could count on all of you. I'm sure the neighbors will know something, and that can take us to the next step."

At the other end of the frame, Maggie, Victoria and Louise all looked at each other with raised brows. Clare definitely had a case of selective hearing.

Then Edie surprised them all with a suggestion of her own.

"I think we should do an online search on all the people and businesses involved before we go any further."

"Online?" Clare seemed disappointed at such passive activity.

Edie nodded. "It's what real private investigators do. They say almost all of private investigatory work is done on the computer these days. Of course, we don't have access to the special sites real private investigators use, but we could still learn a lot. For instance, we could probably find out who runs the preschool — see if there are any men there. I've never heard of a male preschool teacher, but there could well be men on the administrative side."

"And definitely at Nature's Best," Victoria said.

"Okay," Clare said, bringing the conversation back where she thought it belonged. On finding information to support Kenny. "What about K.C.?"

"There's sure to be a lot online about him," Louise said.

"This will be an excellent start," Maggie said. And it would give them all a chance to decide for themselves whether or not Kenny was innocent.

"Does Kenny have a lawyer?" Louise asked.

"I don't know." Clare's eyebrows came together as she debated the importance of this. "He should have one, shouldn't he? If he wants to prove his innocence. I can't believe I didn't think to ask him."

Victoria pondered this, finally nodding thoughtfully. "A lawyer might be required to give the authorities information on his whereabouts, if he knows. Because they're officers of the court," she added. "But Kenny could probably speak to a lawyer on the phone without revealing where he's hiding. Maybe Hal would know about that,

Maggie."

Maggie nodded, an indication that she would ask her son.

But Edie had something else in mind as regards Kenny retaining a lawyer. "A good lawyer is essential if he ever plans to turn himself in — after Kenny gathers his evidence, of course," Edie added, responding to Clare's angry look. "He'll need advice beforehand once he's ready, and the lawyers usually negotiate some kind of deal ahead of time."

Clare looked impressed at Edie's knowledge. "How do you know that?"

"I just read the papers," Edie replied. "And I watch those true crime forensic shows on cable. I like to keep up with what's happening in the city and the country, too. You can't be too careful these days."

Clare took a deep breath and released it, reminding Maggie of someone doing relaxation exercises. The corner of Louise's mouth twitched, and Maggie had to hide an answering grin.

"Okay. Then let's all get online tonight and see what we can learn." Clare nodded in satisfaction.

Maggie thought it would be interesting to see just what information was available to the general public over the internet. She wasn't sure how expert any of them were on the computer, but they could all do Google searches. Even Anna, so old-fashioned in many ways, used the computer for email, to keep in touch with her out-of-state sons and their families.

Maggie looked thoughtfully at Edie, whom she suspected had fairly advanced computer skills. She knew that Edie had computer programs on quilting design and belonged to online groups that chatted about quilting. Still, whatever they were able to do, or not do, they'd feel like they were helping. And it would placate Clare for the time being.

"How do you plan to keep in touch with Kenny?" Edie asked. "To let him know what we learn?"

"I don't know." Clare looked stricken.

Another thing she hadn't thought of. *Poor Clare,* Maggie thought. She'd thrown herself wholeheartedly into this investigation for Kenny, and she didn't even know how, or even if, he planned to keep in touch. Once again it showed his cunning. If she didn't know how to reach him, she couldn't tell anyone else — like a 9-1-1 operator or police officer Michael Browne.

Still, Clare had been through enough.

"I'm sure he'll find a way to keep in touch

with you, Clare. He'll want to know what you learn." Maggie felt better when Clare beamed a smile at her.

16

As they drove home, Maggie and Victoria couldn't help discussing Clare's bizarre theory. *Or perhaps we should call it Kenny's theory?* Maggie thought.

"I know you didn't know the Uplands as well as some of us, but can you imagine shy little Kate having an affair?" Maggie asked.

"And bringing a man into her home with her little girls?" Victoria shook her head. "One thing I do know about Kate, she was very protective of those girls. If she *was* having an affair — and I do find that hard to believe — she would have been very discreet. She would *not* have conducted it in her own home with her children present. So if the girls told their father about a man visiting them, I'm sure it was innocent."

Maggie agreed. "First thing Monday, we'll talk to Gladys and Fran. Gladys lives across the street from the Uplands, and Fran directly behind them. Remember? Fran said she watches her granddaughter after school and she used to play with the twins. One of them will know what was going on."

"Meanwhile," Victoria said, slowing the car as she approached Nature's Best, "I have a hunger for a nice fresh salad. Let's stop here and have a look at that excellent produce people mentioned."

The produce *was* excellent. Both Victoria and Maggie quickly filled baskets with fresh greens and plump, colorful fruit. While Victoria tried to chose between a basket of strawberries (for spinach, strawberry and pecan salad) or blueberries (so high in antioxidants), Maggie worked her way over to the pharmacy.

Once there, she didn't have to pretend an interest. The shelves were filled with more vitamins and supplements than Maggie even knew existed. As she stood before the selection of calcium supplements — who knew there were so many? — a young woman restocking a bit farther along asked if she needed help.

"Thank you, no. I was just looking, but I'm overwhelmed by the number of choices."

The young woman laughed. "We get that a lot. Mr. Sandoval — he's our pharmacist

— he can explain the advantages and disadvantages of the various brands if you want." She gestured toward the pharmacy counter. "Just take the bottles up to the 'ask the pharmacist' window, and he'll be glad to help you."

Maggie thanked her again and returned to her contemplation of the calcium supplements.

Just as Victoria joined her, saying she'd decided to splurge and get both types of berries — "and why not, they're both loaded with antioxidants" — she made up her mind.

"Did you know there were so many ways to take calcium?" she asked.

Victoria glanced at the overflowing shelves. "Yes, I did. I like the calcium citrate myself. I think it's easier on the digestion."

Maggie looked surprised. "Why, Victoria, I didn't know you took a calcium supplement."

Victoria responded with a solemn nod. "My mother and grandmother both suffered from osteoporosis, so I started taking calcium when I was in my forties. You should really look into taking a calcium supplement. Every woman should."

Maggie contemplated the bottles for a moment longer, then chose two and made her way to the pharmacy counter.

A handsome, olive-skinned man came forward almost immediately. Maggie was impressed with his dark good looks. There was a kind of old world charm about him, and she was surprised to find he did not have an accent. It would have seemed the appropriate thing; overall, he had the look of a dashing swashbuckler from one of those old black and white movies. Perhaps it was just the dark mustache, or maybe the cleft in his strong chin.

"May I help you?"

His smile was appealing, and Maggie and Victoria both returned it with pleasure.

"Ah, I see you're looking at the calcium supplements. All women should take one. Calcium's such an important ingredient to good health and strong bones."

"So my friend was telling me," Maggie said. "I wondered if you could recommend something. I have to admit there are so many choices, I don't know where to begin."

Once again, his smile warmed her.

"There are so many choices because everyone reacts differently to the ingredients. Some are made from fish bones, and anyone who is allergic to fish cannot take that. Some combinations are easier on the digestive system."

Here Victoria nodded. "Yes, I find the calcium citrate most agreeable myself." She leaned close to Maggie's ear and whispered, "Some of the first ones I tried gave me terrible gas."

Politely, Mr. Sandoval pretended not to hear this latter comment, but from the way his lips gave a slight twitch, Maggie thought he probably had. She liked him more than ever.

"Okay, so this one then?" She held up a bottle that said "calcium citrate" on it.

Mr. Sandoval, who quickly asked them to call him Tony — "everyone does" — led them back to the shelf as he explained the pluses and minuses of the various combinations of ingredients for another five minutes. Maggie, who would have usually found such a discussion mind-numbing, listened with rapt attention. In the end, she put one of the bottles in her basket while Tony beamed, commenting on the healthy selection of foods they had chosen.

"You have a wonderful produce department," Victoria said.

"Thank you." Tony seemed delighted at the compliment. "I'm hoping to buy into the store, so I take your comment personally. Even if I don't select the produce myself," he added with a grin. "But fresh food products, made without chemicals, are the best way to keep healthy. It's the reason for the existence of Nature's Best."

"You're hoping to buy into the store?" Maggie said. "That's amazing. Nowadays, it seems that all the stores are owned by big conglomerates. It seems strange to think of an owner actually working in his store."

"Presently, there are four owners, all pharmacists, and they all work in the stores. The idea is to provide the kind of food that can keep people healthy. That's the idea behind the first store."

"The first store," Maggie repeated. "This isn't the only Nature's Best then?"

"No. There are three stores in Tucson, and another in Phoenix. This is the most recent addition to the line."

"Well, I wish you much success with it. This is my first time shopping here, but I'll certainly be back."

"Me, too," Victoria said. "Your fruit is beautiful, and I love fruit."

"That's why you have such beautiful skin," Tony said.

Maggie almost giggled at the expression in Victoria's eyes and the pink blush that stained her cheeks. She knew the compliment from the attractive pharmacist had embarrassed her friend, even as it gave her a bit of a thrill.

They said their goodbyes, made their purchases, and headed home.

"What a nice man," Victoria said, as she pulled out of the parking lot.

"I wonder if he's married," Maggie said, giving her friend a speculative look. Unlike Maggie, who was a widow, Victoria had never been married. She didn't talk about it, but Maggie had gotten the impression that there was a very serious relationship at some point in her younger years, but that the young man had died in the service of his country. In Vietnam, probably, the bane of their generation.

"Don't you be silly," Victoria said. "Besides, didn't you notice the ring on his finger?"

17

Clare had the same idea of stopping at Nature's Best. However, she returned home first to have lunch with Gerald who had not arranged a golf match for the day. While they ate their meal of ham sandwiches and melon slices, Clare told him that her friends had been talking about Nature's Best and what excellent produce they had there.

"I thought I'd go over and see for myself," she said. "Maybe get something nice for dinner."

Gerald offered to clean up the lunch dishes, and she left immediately, glad he had not suggested going with her. He almost never went to the Senior Guild meetings, even though he knew most of the men there, but he'd actually wanted to drive her over that morning and attend — in order to be there to drive her home again. But Clare had put an end to that plan. She didn't think she could handle that kind of kid-glove treatment, even though she was tickled that he was so concerned about her.

Clare had to take a moment before she entered the store. She was so excited to actually be doing the work of an amateur sleuth she feared her blood pressure might soar. Her heart was certainly racing and she didn't think that was a good thing. So she forced herself to slow down, to take several deep breaths. She remembered a speaker at the Senior Guild a year or two ago who'd talked about relaxation and de-stressing. She'd talked them through several exercises. Clare remembered her recommendation about deep breathing. "Take deep, cleansing breaths," she'd said. This required breathing deeply through the nose, then holding the air in the lungs for a moment before releasing it all through the mouth.

Clare tried it, then repeated the exercise several times as she sat in her car. She realized that she did feel much calmer. Her heart beat was regular again, and the lump in her throat had receded.

This really works, she thought, as she finally exited her car. *I'll have to remember to tell the others.*

But, once inside, all her good work was as nothing. Her heart speeded up again, and she wished she could take a few more of those deep, cleansing breaths. But everyone would surely think her deranged if she did that inside the store. Or think she was having some kind of an attack.

Willing herself to relax through sheer will power instead, Clare stopped just beyond the door to look around and get her bearings. She didn't shop here often, and it had been a while since her last visit. To her far right, Clare saw what she was looking for — the customer service counter.

Clare smiled happily as she approached the young woman working there. She appeared to be of an age with Kate, so she might have known her. Excellent.

"Hello," Clare said, trying hard to inject an air of desperation into her inquiry as she continued. "I hope you can help me. You're too young to know, of course, but my husband is retired now, and he's just driving me crazy at home."

At the bewildered expression on the face of — Clare dropped her gaze down to check her name tag — Heather, Clare wondered if she was laying it on too thick. But what the heck, playing the helpless old lady had come in handy before. Old ladies were so unthreatening, people were more than willing to talk to them.

"I was hoping you might have some part-time positions here. If I could get him out of the house a few hours a day it would be so helpful — for my mental health, you know."

"Oh." Heather's expression cleared, as she finally seemed to understand what Clare was after. She smiled. "Yes. The store often hires part-time people." She lowered her voice to confide in Clare. "I think they prefer that, because, you know, they don't have to provide benefits and all."

Clare nodded solemnly. Personally, she thought that was terrible, but the owners probably considered it smart business tactics. "Oh, good. I'd heard something like that. Someone I knew at church had worked here part-time. In the offices, I think. She was good at accounting and such. And of course, my Gerald was a CPA." Clare hoped Gerald would forgive her outright lie. He'd been in banking, though, and that was close to accounting, wasn't it? Clare's voice lowered somewhat, and it wasn't hard to put some of her grief into it. "Of course, Kate is gone now, so I couldn't ask her about it. Or how it was to work here."

It took a moment. Then Heather's eyes widened and her mouth formed an O. Clare was beginning to think Heather wasn't too bright; she wasn't sure if that would be good

144

or bad for her purposes.

"Oh, my. Do you mean Kate Upland? Were you a friend of Kate Upland?"

On this subject, Clare could be completely truthful. "Well, we weren't close friends. The age difference, you know. But I knew the whole family. I always work at our big Fall Bazaar — at St. Rose?"

Everyone knew about the St. Rose Fall Bazaar, and Heather was no exception. She nodded eagerly.

"I *love* the St. Rose Bazaar! We always go — me and my whole family," she added.

"We always saw Kate and the twins at the bazaar," Clare said. "She and her husband were very active in the church. Always keen to help out."

Heather retained her wide-eyed look. "Wasn't it awful? I never knew anyone who was murdered before. I couldn't stop watching the news reports about the house and everything."

Clare nodded sympathetically — not a difficult thing, as she had done the same.

"Did Kate like working here?" Then, realizing that might sound like sheer voyeurism, Clare quickly added, "Do you like it?"

"Oh, sure." Heather shrugged. "It's good for me, convenient to my house and all. I have good hours, too. That's the same thing

Kate used to say. She and I are — were," she corrected herself with a grimace, "about the same age. I have a little girl, too. Only the one though."

"That's good. I wouldn't want to send my husband down here to apply if it wasn't a good place to work. And since I can't ask Kate . . ." Clare let her voice trail off.

"Oh, I know just what you mean." Heather looked around, as if checking to see if anyone might be nearby, then lowered her head closer to Clare's. She lowered her voice, too. "Actually, Kate told me she was going to quit. She wasn't very happy the last few weeks she worked here, but she never told me why. She said it wouldn't be right to accuse someone until she was absolutely sure."

Clare let her face show her concern. "She was unhappy? Are you?"

"Oh, no." Heather seemed to cheer up again. "I love working here. You get to meet so many people and most of them are really nice." She giggled like a teenager when she admitted that she liked all the young, athletic men who patronized the store. "It's because Mr. Sandoval is an athlete, too, and he carries all kinds of supplements and things that the athletes like. We have the best selection in the valley. Mr. Sandoval runs marathons, you know."

"No, I didn't," Clare said. "So you don't know what Kate meant by her comment about accusing someone."

Heather shook her head, her face solemn. "She worked in the office. She only worked out here when a lot of people were out sick, like with that flu last year. She said she didn't care for it. Too much people contact I guess. She really liked to be in back, working with numbers. She called it number crunching. It was such a shock for everyone here when we heard about her death. Mr. Sandoval went home when he heard, he was that upset. We all were, but we couldn't all leave and close down the store."

It was at this point that Clare's luck ran out. Another customer approached the counter, so Clare thanked Heather for her help and took her cart over to the produce section. But she left with a satisfied smile. Heather had provided some wonderful information — perhaps even a vital clue!

18

On Saturday, Clare dragged Maggie over to Gilligan's Car Lot. K.C. had a great deal of presence. He was a big man, who had once been an athlete in excellent shape, but now had the pudgy look of a gone-to-seed football player. He was a little younger than the Quilting Bee ladies, with his brown hair just beginning to gray at the temples — which made a man look so distinguished, but a woman just look old.

One thing K.C. had in abundance was charisma. *Which is probably how he became so successful in the car business,* Maggie decided. As she knew from her online research, he'd started many years ago with just one used car lot, and he now had several dealerships and a number of used car lots as well. He wore dark slacks with a neat polo shirt that featured the dealership name and logo embroidered on the left chest. The soft golden color made his hazel eyes appear striking, though somewhat feral. *Tiger eyes,* Maggie couldn't help thinking. And tigers could be very dangerous, even tame ones. Just ask Roy Horn of Siegfried and Roy.

"Hello, hello."

K.C. walked toward them, his hand already outstretched, his smile wide and welcoming.

"It's good to see you, Mrs. Patterson." He glanced around as though looking for someone else. "I don't see Mr. Patterson. Are you thinking of getting a car of your own?"

Clare, flattered that he remembered her, returned his smile. "No, no. One car is just fine for Gerald and me. Since we were bringing it in for servicing, I talked Maggie into coming with us."

Clare quickly jumped in with an introduction — which K.C. brushed aside.

"I know you from the church, of course, Mrs. Browne." He shook her hand. "You and the other women do a great service for the parish with your fine quilting. I purchased one of your quilts at this year's auction, you know. Thought it would look good in my guest room."

Maggie nodded modestly but had to admit she was flattered. She had no idea he knew who she was, much less what she did to help out at St. Rose.

"We were talking about gas prices and alternative fuel cars at the Quilting Bee," Clare said, using the story she'd concocted the evening before. "Maggie expressed an interest in a hybrid car, so I told her to come along with us today. I ran off the road up north and even though the car started up just fine, Gerald is worried there might be damage we can't see."

"An excellent idea to have it checked out," K.C. agreed.

Then he surprised Maggie and Clare with an additional comment to Clare, his expression somber. "I heard about your experience during the storm. You actually saw Kenny Upland!" He shook his head. "Such a tragic thing. Sometimes, coming back to the real world is too much for soldiers after combat."

"Oh, but Kenny is okay," Clare protested. "He didn't do it."

K.C. seemed startled at Clare's outburst, but he didn't immediately protest. Maggie assumed that if he knew she'd seen Kenny, he also knew that she thought him innocent.

"You didn't happen to notice anything odd about Kate just before she died, did you?" Maggie asked him.

K.C. pinched his lips together, his eyes on

the floor. As the minutes stretched out, Maggie wondered if he would answer at all. But he finally did, shaking his head as he spoke.

"Kate was a good worker, and I dealt with her often. But not enough to have a real idea of her state of mind. I used to visit her while Kenny was overseas, you know, take her and the twins out to one of those pizza places where the girls could play games. I think it was hard on her, having Kenny gone. But I didn't notice anything in particular after he came back. I'm sure the adjustment must be difficult. Is there a reason you ask?"

Maggie looked at Clare, not sure if she should explain. Maggie thought it might sound strange, but apparently Clare had no such qualms.

"After he saved my life," Clare began — a bit overdramatically, Maggie thought — "he told me all about how he was away when they died. And I believed him. You should have seen how upset he was, just emotionally distraught! So I thought we could ask around a little, to find out if there might be someone who wanted to see Kate dead. And naturally, we thought of coming to the places where she worked."

Maggie thought she saw something flash

in K.C.'s eyes, but whatever it might have been, he was quick to cover it. And when she saw a pretty young woman pass alongside them, she thought perhaps he'd just been looking at the legs below a skirt that was much too short for office wear.

"I don't know," he said again. "Kate was an excellent worker, but her socialization skills were not well developed. I don't think she had any particular friends here, or I'd let you speak to them. She was shy," he added, as though that explained everything. And, unfortunately, it did.

With that, K.C. turned to Maggie.

"So, you say you'd like to look at a hybrid?"

Maggie would have preferred being at home with her sewing and Barbara Rosenblatt reading to her. But she nodded.

"I've been hearing about these new hybrids, and they sound almost too good to be true. I like the idea of saving fuel and helping the environment. But I wonder how they drive. Are they as good as a gasoline fueled car?"

K.C. beamed at her. "Come right this way, Mrs. Browne, and you can check them out for yourself. I have two different models on the lot you can try. Beautiful cars, and excellent for the environmentally aware person."

Maggie followed K.C., with Clare trailing along behind her. She had no intention of replacing her car at this stage; it still ran well and had a couple of years left on its extended warranty. But she *was* interested in the hybrids she'd read about. It would be interesting to look one over, and especially to go on a test drive. She wondered how it would handle. She comforted her conscience by telling herself she wasn't wasting her time, or K.C.'s. This way, when she was ready to purchase, she'd be closer to an intelligent decision.

19

"I heard your friend was found okay, Ma," Hal said.

Hal was the oldest of Maggie's four sons. With his wife and two sons, he lived in the house they had all grown up in, now surrounded by a mere five acres instead of the fifty plus of years ago. While their father had been a rancher and run cattle on the property, Hal was a successful lawyer who just kept family pets. These included Maggie's faithful old mare, Chestnut, whom Maggie still took out for long desert rides, and a frisky Golden Retriever named Goldie.

As on every other Sunday morning, the family had gathered at the old ranch after mass for the Browne family brunch. Everyone brought a contribution, and they often ate out on the back patio. They sat there now, listening to the wind stir the leaves of the eucalyptus trees into a kind of natural symphony.

Maggie smiled at Hal's mention of Clare. Despite Clare's notions about Kenny Upland, Maggie was happy that her friend was back, bruised but safe.

"Yes. She wasn't actually 'found,' she just turned up at the church for the Quilting Bee meeting. And what a story she had to tell."

The entire family had to hear the story first hand, of course. So while they ate, Maggie recounted Clare's tale. She took her time, enjoying their reactions when they heard who was responsible for Clare's rescue. When Maggie finished, carefully eliminating the part about Clare offering their help in proving Kenny's innocence, Michael was frowning at her.

"What are you getting involved with now, Ma? Did Clare call the FBI? Kenny Upland is wanted on a fugitive warrant."

"Of course she called them." Maggie did her best to look indignant. "She told me at church this morning that she was waiting to hear back from them. She was very excited about it."

"Don't get involved," he said.

"I don't plan to. Clare is convinced he's innocent, and she wants to prove it . . ."

Before Maggie had a chance to finish, Michael interrupted, telling her again not to

155

get involved. Maggie knew he was just concerned for her welfare, but she did dislike being told what to do. After all, she was the mother, and he would always be her baby. So she let him rant on for a while about her talent for getting mixed up in dangerous situations, then promised him solemnly to be careful.

"Isn't it interesting that he's stayed so close to Scottsdale," Sara said. "I would have thought he would run as far as he could manage. Makes you wonder if maybe he is innocent."

Now Michael frowned at her.

"Come on now, Michael," Hal said, feeling he should defend his wife. "You knew Kenny, too. We all did. Admit it, when you first heard what had happened, did you think of Kenny right away as the culprit? Or perp, or whatever you might call it?"

"No, I didn't," Michael admitted. "Not at first. And we don't call them perps," he added, somewhat disgruntled. "That's TV stuff."

Frank laughed. "Don't ask him what the cops really call them." He glanced toward the children's table. "It's not suitable for mixed company."

Amid the laughter of his brothers, Sara complimented Maggie on her contribution to the family brunch.

"Ma, this fruit salad is delicious." Sara's pretty face remained serene, so the guys couldn't accuse her of changing the subject. Or perhaps they, too, had tired of it. Maggie did notice that Hal smiled as he looked down at his plate. "Where did you find such wonderful fruit?"

"At Nature's Best," Maggie told her, "near the church. We were talking about it at the Quilting Bee, and Victoria and I decided to check it out on the way home. They specialize in organic food, you know, and everything is fresh and chemical free."

"I'll have to stop there," Sara said. She looked over to her sons, who were eating enthusiastically from the fruit salad their grandmother brought. "I like to have some healthy choices for the boys. And it's all organic, you say?"

"It's kind of far for you, isn't it?" Michael asked Sara. But she merely shrugged.

Then he turned an intense look on his mother. "I didn't know you shopped there, Ma. I've never heard you mention it before."

"It's one of the places that Kate Upland worked, so Victoria and I decided to check it out."

She laughed then, relating how Clare had gone in, pretending to be scouting the place so that her husband might apply for a part-time job. "She told them he was driving her crazy since he retired and she wanted to get him out of the house."

Everyone laughed except Michael, who continued to frown at her as he worked at emptying his plate of its waffles, ham and fruit.

"And what's this I hear about you getting a new car, Ma?" Frank asked.

The others were instantly interested.

"Honestly, for a big city, word sure does travel quickly. How on earth did you hear that I was looking at cars?"

"One of my old high school friends works over at Gilligan's. He called to tell me he saw you test driving a hybrid."

Maggie nodded. "I did. It drove very nicely, too. I hadn't planned to replace my car for a few more years, but with gas prices what they are, I'm debating it."

There was some talk of cars and mileage until Michael asked a question that silenced everyone.

"Didn't Kate Upland work for Gilligan's, too?"

Michael gave her one of his stern cop looks, but it didn't faze Maggie, who took another sip of coffee before gazing back at her youngest son.

"What are you up to, Ma?"

"It's nothing, really. Clare has a bee in her bonnet about this case. She says Kenny saved her life and that he's innocent. And she's not going to let it go until we try and learn something that might help prove that. She and Gerald were taking their car in to be checked and Clare wanted me to go with her to talk to K.C."

"Ma . . ." Michael began.

Maggie held her hand up in a "stop" position, her head tilted to one side. "I'm just trying to look out for Clare, Michael. I don't want her to put herself in a dangerous situation. She can be naïve about things, and she gets carried away thinking she's like an amateur sleuth in a novel. That's why she's so excited about the FBI coming to question her, you know. She thinks she'll be able to tell them all about Kenny and his alibi, and that will make some kind of difference to their investigation."

Michael laughed. Hal and Sara looked surprised.

Maggie nodded. "It looks like you all have the same idea I do about that. I don't think anything she has to say will influence their perception of the case."

"Good. Then you'll be practical and stay out of this," Michael said.

"Don't worry, we merely promised to talk to the Uplands' neighbors at the Guild tomorrow."

"Ma, that's not staying out of it," Michael argued.

"Of course it is. After Clare's experience, everyone will be gossiping about the Uplands anyway. We'll just be eavesdropping, basically."

Maggie put her fork down. She'd had enough to eat and wanted to concentrate.

"Michael, do you have any inside knowledge about the Upland case?" she asked.

Michael stared at his mother.

"You don't have to tell me what all is involved, or any specific details. I understand that it's an open case. I just want to know if you have any idea why they're so convinced Kenny did it. You heard what I said about Clare's disappearance. She says Kenny saved her life, that he was polite and kind and absolutely devastated about losing his family. But especially at being blamed for the whole thing."

Maggie stopped for a moment while she gathered her thoughts. She wanted Michael to understand what it was she yearned to know — no, *needed* to know.

"A lot of us at the church had trouble believing Kenny capable of what he's been accused of. You boys just said the same thing." She glanced over at Hal before returning her gaze to Michael. "So that's why I wondered . . . Do you know anything about the case against him?"

Michael picked up his spoon and stirred his coffee.

"I don't know a lot about it," Michael finally said. "But I have talked to some of the guys who worked on the case. Because it was close to home," he admitted.

Maggie nodded. She knew that her son took a particular interest in any crimes that occurred in "her" part of town. And, as Hal said, they had all known Kenny to some degree. Because the youth minister liked to have an authority figure present, Michael often volunteered his help chaperoning the youth trips, so he had contact with Kenny, too.

"There is some evidence that is highly incriminating."

"Real evidence?" Maggie asked. "Like DNA or fingerprints or something irrefutable like that? Or just circumstantial things?"

"Oh-oh," Frank said. "You did it now."

"You — and everybody else in this country — have been watching too much television." Michael put his spoon aside. His voice was strong, his face set. "All those programs about DNA and forensic evidence are making people want all that stuff at real trials. Circumstantial evidence used to be the norm in most criminal cases. Now juries want DNA for a simple convenience store robbery." His lips drew down in disgust.

"So all the evidence they have against Kenny is circumstantial?"

Michael stared at his mother in frustration. "I can't say for sure, but probably. Interviews with his friends and family, reasoning over what his life was like, what probably happened. And the lack of any other evidence linking the killings to anyone else. These kinds of crimes usually involve a disgruntled or mentally ill family member." His expression turned bleak. "There just isn't any motive for anyone other than Kenny to have done it."

Maggie thought this over. "Clare is intrigued with the whole post traumatic stress disorder thing. She seems to think it absolves him in some way, but to me, post traumatic stress is another strike against him, not the other way 'round. I think it's possible for a man suffering from it to get violent during episodes."

Maggie listened as the young people discussed PTSD. She was surprised to hear how many people they knew had served in Iraq. And more than one had problems that could be blamed on PTSD.

Maggie found it all very interesting, and listened carefully to what they had to say. When the conversation wound down, she decided to broach the topic that was causing problems among the Bee women — Kenny's theory on why his family was gone.

"Do you know if there was any evidence that Kate was having an affair?"

Michael's eyes widened. "Kate Upland?"

Hal and Sara echoed his incredulous question. Even Bobby and Merrie expressed surprise.

Frank commented in a droll voice. "Hmm, from Michael's reaction, I'm thinking the police didn't find anything about an affair."

Maggie merely nodded. "I thought it was ridiculous, too. We all do. But Clare claims that Kenny thinks Kate had an affair while he was gone, that she was acting strange and seemed to be afraid of something. He's working on the assumption that someone was stalking her, and that's who killed her. And he seems to have decided all this because the twins mentioned a man coming to the house, and because his marriage just wasn't the same."

Sara laughed. "I'd be surprised if it *was*

the same, after him being gone for so long. A lot of families are having real difficulties because the main breadwinner is gone."

"That's what we told Clare." Maggie sighed. "We're hoping that talking to the neighbors will help convince her this whole idea of an affair is crazy. Though she told us the twins said something to Kenny about a man who would come and play with them. He thinks that was some kind of proof, but we think the opposite — that Kate would never have brought someone to the house if everything wasn't perfectly legitimate. In fact, K.C. mentioned yesterday that he used to pick up Kate and the girls and take them out for pizza when Kenny was overseas."

"I think part of PTSD is paranoia on the part of the patient," Sara said.

Maggie nodded. "Louise said as much on Friday, but I don't know if Clare was listening." She sighed. "I don't know what to think, I really don't. I always liked Kenny. He seemed like a family man who truly wanted to help kids. His experience in Iraq was tragic all around, for him and for his family. Not necessarily because he killed them during a bout of PTSD." She stumbled over the initials, but it was quite a mouthful to say post traumatic stress disorder over and over again.

"The real tragedy here is the deaths of three lovely people. And the destruction of a fourth because of the accusations. Whatever happened, it seems to be connected somehow to Kenny's service overseas. Either he's just ill and paranoid, or something really happened when he was gone. But I still can't imagine anything Kate could have done that would have brought about her death — and the death of her children."

Michael pushed away his coffee cup. "If Kenny is innocent, why doesn't he come to the police and explain where he was? If he'd done that, he could have gone to the funerals." He shook his head. "Sounds pretty slim to me."

Maggie might have her doubts about Kenny, but this part she did understand.

"Honestly, Michael. If you'd been out camping, and, on your way back to town, you heard that your family had been murdered and left in a house that was rigged to explode and burn . . . and the news reports made it clear that the police wanted to talk to the missing husband . . . Would you turn yourself in?" Maggie shook her head. "I wouldn't. He would have been in handcuffs and downtown in the Fourth Avenue Jail so fast his head would have been spinning. Everyone assumed he was guilty because he was missing. But he was just out of touch."

Michael remained skeptical. "It's hard to be out of touch these days."

"But it *is* possible. Not everyone carries a cell phone everywhere. And there are areas that are not covered by cell towers. Just look at how no one could get hold of Gerald when Clare was missing. One of the men from the Senior Guild had to go out to the lake and tell him. Some places in the mountains where people go camping would probably have spotty coverage because of the landscape. The mountains interfere with signals, and there wouldn't be a lot of towers in unpopulated areas. And since he was trying to get away from it all — like Gerald and his friends — he probably didn't even take a phone."

Michael conceded that point. Then something seemed to occur to him. He glared at his mother. "Ma, do you know where Kenny Upland is right now?"

"No." She answered quickly, but she could see that Michael was debating whether or not to believe her. "I wouldn't lie to you about that, Michael. I truly don't know where he is. I don't think Clare knows either. Her description of where she ran off the road was rather vague. She described a burnt out cabin some distance from the crash where Kenny took her to recover, but she said it didn't look like he'd been living there for six months. And she figured it wouldn't matter if she could find it again because he'd be long gone if she did."

Everyone agreed with her. Someone who had successfully eluded the police and the FBI for six months would know enough to move after an encounter like that — even if the encounter was with a person friendly to his cause.

"Kenny is an expert at surviving in the wilderness," Frank said. "I'm not surprised they haven't found him in six months of looking. Remember that guy in . . . where was it, North Carolina? Bombed a bunch of abortion clinics and then hid in the woods for years? He was a survivalist, too."

"Eric Rudolph," Michael said. "They called him the Olympic bomber — the 1996 Olympics in Atlanta. He was on the run for five years."

His brothers had to rib him about such esoteric knowledge, but it was all done in fun. Still, it wasn't enough to distract Michael from his purpose.

"Don't you get involved with Kenny Upland, Ma, you hear me? Whether he's guilty or not, he's a wanted fugitive. There's no telling what someone like that might do

167

if he feels he's cornered."

"That's exactly how I felt about Clare going after him. Don't you worry about me, Michael. I do have both feet on the ground," she added, implying that the flighty Clare did not.

"If he is suffering from PTSD, he's already paranoid. Geez, this is not a good situation, Ma," Michael finished, running his fingers through his hair.

Maggie gave her son a stern look. "My friends and I only talk about these things. It makes for something interesting to discuss while we quilt."

"Yeah, sure." But he couldn't continue to glare at her. She wouldn't be his mother if she didn't care so much about other people.

"You know, Ma, I heard someone recently mention that he liked to listen to audio books. He listens in the car when he goes on trips, and he said his wife listens while she does needlework. I was thinking that you and your friends could do that — listen to a book together while you sew at the church. Keep your minds occupied."

Keep us from trying to help Clare, Maggie couldn't help adding. But only to herself. And she didn't bother telling Michael about the CD player and the audio book that she kept next to her favorite sewing chair.

The others, however, laughed at Michael's blatant attempt to keep Maggie's mind otherwise occupied.

"Sounds like a good Christmas present, Michael," Frank suggested.

The brothers roared.

20

Clare was late. It was very unlike her, and especially on this Monday when they had all agreed to an early start. Everyone was worried. It was too soon after her disappearance, for one thing. And they couldn't help thinking of her wholehearted support for Kenny Upland. Could he have contacted her? Kidnapped her? Worse? While they all wanted to think the best of Kenny, not everyone was convinced of his innocence.

"Clare is never late," Anna said. Her brows almost met over her nose her forehead was so crinkled with worry.

Louise put an arm around Anna, squeezing her shoulder. "I'm sure she's fine. Probably just running a bit late. It happens to all of us from time to time."

"Let's just get on over to the kitchen and see what we can learn about Kate Upland. After all, that is why we planned to arrive early today," Maggie said. "Everyone is sure to be talking about Clare and gossiping about the Uplands."

Louise agreed. "Good idea. Clare will probably show up while we're over there and join us."

"And we'll have some news for Clare when she arrives," Anna added.

Besides that, it was an unseasonably cool morning, so the thought of warming themselves with hot drinks was appealing. But their main motive was to learn all they could about the Upland family, especially Kate. And everyone at the Senior Guild knew that Gladys, who lived across the street from the former Upland home, always started the day with a cup of coffee — and a bit of gossip with whoever might be in the kitchen.

Their expectations were met immediately upon entering the community room; the first sentence they heard supported Clare's view of the Upland case.

"You know Kenny wasn't even supposed to be there that day."

Maggie turned toward the voice and recognized Jack Banderly, Fran's husband. They lived directly behind the Upland house, and Maggie knew they had feared for their home in the conflagration following the explosion. Luckily, the fire department was able to keep the flames from spreading to any adjacent homes, but it had been a near thing.

Both Banderlys sat at one of the large round tables along with Gladys and another man from their neighborhood whose name Maggie thought was Will.

"That's what Clare said." Edie stepped forward, pausing at the table while the others approached the counter with the coffee urn and the hot water.

Jack admitted he hadn't been to the Guild meeting on Friday. "So I didn't hear Clare's story," he said. "But I heard all about it from Fran."

Maggie was sure he had. Everyone at St. Rose probably knew the story by now. It would have passed from spouse to neighbor to acquaintance. Look at how K.C. Gilligan had known, and that was even before Sunday masses.

Steam and a delicious scent of peaches rose from the mug in her hand as Maggie moved toward the table. "What do you mean, he wasn't supposed to be there? Did you tell the police that back in May?"

"Sure," Jack said. "Both the police and the fire inspectors. Kenny told me that he was going off for a few days, on a special camping trip. We used to visit when we were both out doing yard work," he explained.

172

"Nice, friendly guy, though he was a little less forthcoming after he got back from Iraq. More private like. More nervous."

"I think he had inner demons from his war experience," Fran said.

The Bee members, cups in hand and choosing seats for themselves, exchanged knowing looks. Clare was sure the PTSD played a big part in all that had happened, and here was one small validation that Kenny's condition had changed. But it still didn't absolve him.

Meanwhile, Jack continued. "He didn't give too many details about where he was going or what he was doing, except to say that it was one of those survival-type trips. I know he was an expert on survival in the wilderness, and I figured he was doing something on that. He used to do segments for the people from TV stations about desert survival — how to do things like collect water and find shade and all that, if you got stranded in the desert."

"That's right," Will said. "I remember seeing him on a news show once, giving advice about how to survive if your car broke down out in the desert. Some real interesting stuff."

Another of Kenny's former neighbors nodded. "I even heard that he was working with the FBI and Homeland Security on something. Top secret. Really made me wonder when I heard about the explosion."

The man sitting beside him nodded solemnly. "With the terrorist threat these days, they need patriots to sacrifice. Kenny was the kind who would do that, too. He's probably off working on some top secret terrorist thing right now. I'll bet the government knows where he is, and they just want us all to think he's in trouble. He could get in tight with some of our country's enemies that way."

Maggie stared in amazement at the man who had a thick Texas accent. She didn't know him, but there were many people in the Senior Guild she didn't know. He could be a new member, or perhaps a friend of one of the members who was here visiting. He seemed to be tight with the man beside him — who was speaking in his turn.

"Some of those survivalist groups can be dangerous. They store arms and train and all. Saw a program on the cable channel about them. Kenny would be just the person to infiltrate a group like that. You know, one of them moles they call it. I'll bet he and his family are all okay — probably living with some crazy group out in Montana or Idaho. Gathering information for the government."

The women all stared at him, stunned by such a bizarre theory. Jack and the other men had apparently heard it all before; they barely reacted.

"Goodness." Maggie didn't know what to say. She knew there were always conspiracy theorists around, but she hadn't known some were sitting right here at Senior Guild meetings. "What about the bodies they found in the house?"

The Texan dismissed this with a wave of a beefy hand. "Staged. Put dummies in the body bags. With the explosion and all, none of the relatives was going to insist on seeing the bodies."

Not knowing what to say to this, Maggie busied herself with her tea, dunking the bag in and out of her mug before taking it out and putting it on a napkin. She noticed the other women all seemed very interested in their mugs, too. Even Edie, she was glad to see, seemed unable to come up with a response. And Edie was full of conspiracy theories herself.

The two conspiracy theorists rose while Maggie was having a sip of her tea. It had a rich peach flavor that was somehow comforting. And definitely warming.

"Well, we're off. Taking inventory in the

supply closet today . . ."

With a polite nod to those still in the break room, they walked out, mugs in hand. Jack and the few other men in the room followed them out.

21

The women exchanged glances afterward, several of them fighting grins. No one commented, however, just in case the men were still close enough to overhear. They were a tolerant bunch at the Senior Guild and didn't want to hurt anyone's feelings. But Maggie thought they all felt as she did. Those two men were crazy!

Very softly, Louise said, "Survivalist camp in Idaho."

And that was it. Everyone broke out laughing. It felt good, too.

Once they had the absurdity out of their system, they settled back down to their drinks. Gladys and Fran got up to replenish their cooling coffee.

"Well, that was certainly interesting," Victoria said.

"But we know Kenny isn't undercover in some survivalist camp," Anna said, "because Clare saw him right here in Arizona."

"It's a good theory," Edie said, "just not true in this case."

"Wouldn't it be nice, though, if Kate and the girls really were safe in Idaho." Anna released a sigh.

The thought sobered them all. Of course it would be nice. Better than nice. But they all knew that, for the Uplands, there was no chance of such a fairy tale ending.

For a moment, each woman pursued her own thoughts. Until Maggie broke the silence. Someone had to do it, she thought, or they would be there all morning.

"I heard Kate had some trouble making ends meet when Kenny was on active duty," she said.

"She never said so, not in so many words," Fran said. "She was shy, and very private about her personal life. And she was proud, too. She wouldn't have wanted to admit that she needed financial help. Like that would be some kind of shortcoming. But I know she took some bookkeeping jobs. She was a whiz at bookkeeping. That's how she could stay home with the kids, you know, because she was so good with managing their finances."

"The poor girl was having a hard time with Kenny gone," Gladys said. "But I know K.C. was a big help. I was out getting my mail one day, and I saw her getting into his car with the girls. She told me later that she was doing some work for him and he'd sometimes take them out for pizza. Must have been quite a treat for the girls. They really missed their dad. I think it was very hard on Kate, having Kenny gone for so long. They were always very close, doing everything together as a family."

"I felt the same," Maggie said. There were nods of agreement from the other Bee members.

"I thought of post traumatic stress right away," Edie said.

"I thought it made no sense when they said he did it in those early reports," Louise said. "Though they said it on the news so much, I came to half believe it."

Gladys nodded. "Kenny was a great one for doing things as a family. Except for those times he would go off on his own to camp. Kate told me about that once — how he'd take himself off for a couple days. That's how I knew it must have really bothered her because that wasn't the kind of thing she usually shared. Not such intimate things, if you know what I mean. But she said that he had nightmares after he got back from Iraq. That post traumatic stress disorder thing. She said it frightened her something awful,

179

the way he would thrash around in his sleep, and he'd cry and scream sometimes. She worried that he would hurt himself — or her. I think that must be why the police are so sure he did it. They must have found out about that."

"That has to be a big reason behind why the police think he did it," Edie agreed. "That post traumatic stress can make men do awful things."

"Even still, I don't see how they can think Kenny capable of killing his family. They're all he lived for," Gladys said. "It wouldn't surprise me one bit if he does away with himself, in fact, even though it is against the church's teachings."

Anna shook her head at the thought of such drastic action.

But Fran agreed. "You're so right about Kenny Upland," she said. "The twins used to play with my granddaughter, and they were wonderful little girls. Kenny and Kate would invite my granddaughter over there, and they would set up games for the kids to play — wonderful, fun games. Chloe just misses them something terrible. Kenny built this marvelous playhouse for them. It was destroyed in the fire, of course." She sighed at the pointlessness of it all. "Chloe still talks about that playhouse and how wonderful it was. She's been after her grandfather to build one for her in our yard."

"It makes you wonder just who the police talked to, doesn't it?" Victoria mused. "Almost everyone here at the church knew the Uplands, and they all seem to feel that they were a couple devoted to their family. No one seems to think Kenny capable of killing his family. And yet, the police seem certain of his guilt."

"Because he wasn't there when it happened," Louise said. "And he's family. That makes him the prime suspect."

"That's another thing," Maggie said. "Jack said he knew Kenny was supposed to be camping out alone that weekend. If he knew, others must have, too."

Fran nodded at once. "He told the police that. You heard him. He told everyone that day that Kenny was camping and that they had to get in touch with him and tell him what happened to his family."

"Someone could be trying to frame Kenny," Edie suggested. But even she didn't sound convinced.

"I just hope he doesn't do something drastic," Fran said, "because I agree with what Gladys was saying. Wouldn't surprise me at all to hear about Kenny's suicide. He lived for those kids and for Kate. Doesn't matter how good a Catholic he was, without them he might not want to go on living."

"Clare says he's intent on finding the real killer," Louise said. "At least that's what he told her. He's trying to get together some evidence that he can take to the police. She saw a lot of newspaper clippings. She thought he was reading everything he could to look for clues."

"Well, then that would give him a reason to go on living, wouldn't it?" Fran said.

"Did you ever see anyone hanging around the house?" Maggie asked. "During that time Kenny was gone, I mean. Or even afterward."

"Kenny told Clare he thought someone was stalking Kate," Louise said. "Did you ever see a man hanging around, looking suspicious, or like he didn't belong?"

Gladys thought for a moment, her forehead creasing into a deep frown. "I don't think so."

"I saw K.C. Gilligan there a few times," Fran said. "But he wasn't acting suspicious or even just hanging around. I'd see him in the yard with Kate and the twins, barbequing usually. He'd play games with them, too, and supervise them in the swimming pool. I always thought it was real nice of him to come over while Kenny was gone. I told

Jack we have to go to K.C. for our next car. That was such a nice thing he did to help out someone in the parish." She ended with a definitive nod.

"Do you know K.C.?" Maggie asked.

"No, I don't know him," Fran replied with a smile. "I just feel like I know him, I guess. I see him around the church. He always comes to the bazaar, and the last few years he's been donating a car for the raffle."

They all nodded. Everyone at the church knew that K.C. Gilligan donated a car for the raffle every year. The church made hundreds, perhaps thousands of dollars on the ticket sales. Maggie, not as altruistic as some others, thought it a good move on K.C.'s part. He got a lot of good will that way, and probably a lot of customers from the parish. And a nice tax write-off as well.

"How did Kate get the job at Gilligan's?" Maggie asked. "Do you know?"

"Someone at church told her about a position at Gilligan's," Gladys replied. "I think Kate liked the fact that K.C. is a parishioner. He advertises in the bulletin every Sunday, you know."

"How did Kate feel about working there?" Victoria asked.

"It was the oddest thing," Gladys said. "At first she seemed very happy. I thought that working was bringing her out of her shell. Her hours were set up so that she only worked while the girls were in school, so she thought it was perfect. But around the time Kenny got back, she stopped talking about work. I thought it was the readjustment — having him home again after all that time. But a few weeks before she died, she was so tense I thought she might be ill. But when I asked, she just dismissed me with a few words, like 'everything's fine,' or something like that. But she looked really stressed."

The Bee women exchanged glances and nods. This could tie in with Kenny's theory, passed on to Clare, that she was having an affair with a man she worked with. She wouldn't have wanted to let her elderly neighbor know about that. Still . . .

"Kate was so good with the kids," Fran said. "I told her once she should look into providing day care at her home. That play area in the yard would have been ideal for a day care."

"What did she think of that?" Maggie asked. It did sound ideal for Kate.

"She said it was a good idea, and she would consider it. But after Kenny came back from Iraq she never mentioned it. We all knew he'd changed, and once she even told me about the terrible dreams he had. I think she was afraid to have kids around in case he went off the deep end."

Maggie noted the understanding look on Louise's face. Sympathy for Kate, no doubt. Personally, she hadn't heard anything so far to support Clare's contention that Kenny was innocent. The more she heard, the more unstable he sounded. And someone like that could be capable of almost anything.

"I heard she worked at Nature's Best, too," Victoria said. "That's a very nice store."

"Pricey, though," Gladys said.

Fran was nodding. "Kate never told me she worked there, not until I was over to pick up Chloe one day and saw the Nature's Best bags on her counter. I was surprised, I'll tell you that. I agree, they're expensive over there, even though they have real nice produce. And I knew she had to be struggling with Kenny overseas. That's when she told me she was working there. They were real good to her, used to let her take some groceries for nothing. Some of the older or bruised produce, you know, or dented boxes and cans — thing that didn't look so nice on display. With what they charge there, the stuff has to look real good."

"I think she was embarrassed about having to work," Gladys said.

"I wonder why." Louise appeared puzzled. "Most women work these days. It's not like the 1950s when women were expected to stay at home with the kids. You'd think she would have been more embarrassed about *not* working."

"I think it had something to do with her parents, and with the fact that she was so shy," Fran said. "I think she had self-esteem issues. If the house had exploded while Kenny was in Iraq, I would have suspected suicide."

Gladys nodded her agreement, surprising the Bee women. Suicide was considered a major sin by the Catholic Church. Anna, especially, was shocked. She tried to hide it, but Maggie could tell by the unnatural look to her jaw; she was gritting her teeth.

"How can you say that?" Anna said. "Kate was serious about her faith. I can't believe she would do such a thing, especially if it meant harming the twins."

Gladys nodded again. "You're right, she would have provided for the kids — sent them off to visit her parents, perhaps. But if I'd heard she'd swallowed a bottle of pills, I wouldn't have been shocked."

"If she'd swallowed a bottle of pills," Maggie said. "But her home exploded in spectacular fashion. Even if she was suicidal, women rarely use such dramatic means. But that's beside the point. I don't think the possibility of suicide on Kate's part has ever come up, and the police and the fire department did extensive investigations."

"I think," Victoria said, "that she would want to keep herself going for her children. It is the motherly thing to do, and Kate was a very good mother."

"I'm sure that's why she made herself get out of the house — get those jobs and all," Fran said. "For the good of the twins. Otherwise, she would have preferred to stay in and keep to herself. But she wanted the girls to have a normal life. Kenny wanted them homeschooled, you know, but she stood up to him about that. It was rare for her to do that. She took her wedding vows seriously and she always said they used the old-style 'love, honor and obey' form. She didn't oppose him often."

Maggie was beginning to wonder if she'd known Kate at all. The woman her neighbors described was not the young woman Maggie *thought* she knew.

"She always seemed like a typical modern woman — confident in her motherhood and her place in the world. I guess you never know." Maggie shook her head at her own foolishness. No one really knew another person, and Kate had been, at best, a casual acquaintance.

"She tried hard to appear that way," Gladys said, making Maggie feel better. "I'm not sure she succeeded, though from what you say perhaps she did. I always thought I saw an uncertainty about her, as if she was never sure she was doing the proper thing." She tipped her coffee mug toward her, decided there wasn't enough for another sip and put it aside.

"Clare said Kenny told her the girls mentioned a man who spent time at the house. From what you've said, that must have been K.C." Louise looked around at the other Bee members. Maggie knew where she was heading and nodded a tacit agreement. "He thought it meant she was having an affair."

The reaction all around them was the same — shock. No one could imagine Kate having an affair, even if her husband was half a world away in a war zone.

"An affair?" Fran repeated. "I find that very hard to believe. Impossible, in fact."

"And Kenny himself said that?" Gladys asked. "You'd think he, of all people, would know her well enough not to believe such a thing."

"Sometimes it's the quiet ones who really surprise you," Diane said.

Maggie had noticed that while Diane had listened avidly to everything being said, she'd made few comments.

Fran shook her head. As far as she was concerned, Kate was as she appeared. "Like I said, I would see K.C. over there, playing in the yard with the girls. He loves kids, always says his great regret was that he and Rosemary never had any. I've heard that he did that kind of thing with other employees who had kids."

"And I saw him taking them out that time," Gladys added. "For pizza, Kate told me later. That may be what the girls mentioned to their father."

"K.C. seems like a real nice guy, and she was working there at his place. He probably knew Kenny, too, from church activities. K.C. is involved in all kinds of things here at the parish. He's on the parish council you know."

"We keep telling him we can't wait for him to retire and join the Senior Guild." This from one of the women in the Sewing Circle. "But he says he's still having too much fun selling cars and making commercials to retire."

"That's because he loves being around all

189

those pretty young things working for him."

Maggie frowned at Diane, wishing she'd kept her thoughts to herself. Even if this particular comment was of interest in regard to Kenny Upland and Kate. Diane loved the lowest kind of gossip, and her stories often verged on slander. She liked all those television shows that gossiped about celebrities, too. Still, if K.C. had a history of harassing female employees, it could have a bearing on Kenny's theory. Shy as she was, Kate would not have appreciated someone, and especially a boss, who made inappropriate comments. But would she be brave enough to complain? Not from what these women said about her personality. Not if she had serious self-esteem issues. Still, Maggie found it impossible to believe she would have a relationship with someone who abused her. Or — more importantly — allow him access to her children.

So Maggie asked, "What do you mean?"

"You know DeLinda, who does tole painting? Her daughter worked for him the summer she finished high school, and she quit after three weeks. Said she couldn't take any more of his ogling her. You could ask DeLinda yourself, but she went back to Chicago to spend Thanksgiving with her son's family. That daughter goes to North-western now, so she's there, too."

"Is that all K.C. did?" Edie asked. "Leer at her?"

Diane's eyes twinkled at being able to share even juicier gossip. "Well, I heard she asked a few other women who worked there, and they all said he was a problem. But they also said the pay was good and the hours flexible, so it was worth putting up with some leers."

"Oh, my." Anna was shocked.

"Hmpf." Edie's reaction was halfway between a snort and an admonition. "Men like that should be horsewhipped. Those women should all get together and leave en masse. See how he likes that."

Diane merely shrugged. "There would be plenty of other women ready to take the jobs."

Too true, Maggie thought.

"If he was acting that way with Kate, I doubt she would have invited him to her home." Louise was always practical, the voice of reason. "And I'm sure she would not have allowed him to associate with the twins."

"He does have a lot of charisma," Maggie said.

"Oh, he can charm the bark off a tree if he wants to," Diane said, making Maggie

191

wonder how she knew that.

"K.C. is a great guy," one of the women not previously heard from said now. "A real asset to the St. Rose community. Don't you go maligning him." She shot a stern look toward Diane. "That girl probably just wanted to take the summer off so she could hang out with her friends instead of working."

"No, she took a waitressing job at the Olive Garden instead. That was a lot more work than ferrying cars around a lot or taking them through the car wash there." Diane's voice had a "so there" aspect matched by her smug look.

"Carl Squires's wife works at Gilligan's, and she's going to be retiring real soon," Diane said. "She's worked there for twenty years. Carl says she'll be joining the Senior Guild, too, so then you'll be able to ask her yourself. What it's like working there," she added, as though an explanation was necessary.

22

As they headed back to the Quilting Bee room, all talk was of the still missing Clare.

"I'm going to call her," Louise decided, pulling out her cell phone the moment they returned to their room.

But before the call had a chance to connect, Clare herself walked through the door.

"Where have you been?" Edie's question came close to sounding like a command.

Louise flipped her phone closed and tucked it back into her purse. "I was just trying to call you, to see if everything was all right."

Clare seemed surprised at the concern she saw in her friends' eyes. She looked from one Bee member to another. "Sorry I'm late. I didn't mean to worry you."

But she couldn't keep the excitement from her voice when she explained *why* she was late.

"I was interviewed by the FBI," she said.

"Oh, my." Anna paled considerably. "It's about Kenny, isn't it?"

"Well, it's about time," Edie said.

"I'm surprised it took this long," Maggie said, seating herself and picking up her needle.

"So, what was it like?" Anna asked. "Did they want you to work with their sketch artist? To get a drawing of what Kenny looks like now?"

"That would certainly be very interesting," Edie said. "Describing someone and having a picture made. Very tricky, I would think."

But Clare was shaking her head before Edie even began to speak. "No, there was nothing like that. It was very disappointing, actually. Not at all what I'd expected," she added with a sigh.

"Well, sit down and tell us about it," Maggie said. "It would be nice to finish up this quilt before the day trip to Laughlin." Once the Fall Bazaar was over, the Senior Guild arranged a day trip to Laughlin, Nevada, on the Arizona border. Everyone enjoyed the visit to the casinos, and riding on a well-appointed bus made the trip easy.

Clare stored her bag in the closet and sat at her usual spot, picking up a threaded needle. As she pushed the needle down into the quilt sandwich, she told them about the special agent who had knocked at her door just as she was ready to leave for the church.

"It was a woman," she said. "She was very attractive."

"And I thought that was just Hollywood, making the female FBI agents so good looking," Louise commented with a smile.

"What did she wear?" Anna asked.

"A dark suit," Clare replied. "She looked very nice. Very professional. Not anything like Jodie Foster, but she could have been an actress playing an FBI agent. She was that good-looking."

There was an indecipherable noise from Edie, but Clare didn't seem to hear it. She merely continued with her recitation.

"But she wouldn't even sit down. I asked her to. I even offered her some coffee. But she just stood there by the door and asked her questions and then left. She was there all of fifteen minutes." Clare's voice reflected her disappointment. "Maybe not even that long."

"I understand they're very busy with issues of homeland security these days," Maggie commented.

This seemed to mollify Clare, who had been looking forward to her interaction with the FBI and couldn't believe her interview had been so brief.

"It was still exciting," Clare told them. "Just not at all what I'd expected." She heaved another sigh as she rocked her needle through the quilt, producing another set of lovely, even stitches. "I thought there would be two men in dark suits — like on television. And that they would sit down and ask lots of questions."

"What did she ask you?" Edie said.

"Just where I'd seen him, both here in the valley and then later. Of course, I couldn't say for sure where we were in the forest, but I did my best."

"What did she say about his alibi?" Louise asked.

Clare looked completely frustrated as she left her needle for a moment and looked at the others. "She wasn't at all interested in what he told me. I tried to tell her that he said he was innocent and all, but she just dismissed it."

"The jails are full of innocent men," Maggie said with a small smile.

"You actually tried to tell her you think Kenny is innocent?" Edie said.

Maggie couldn't tell if Edie thought this the height of foolishness or if she was impressed by Clare standing up for Kenny when faced with the authority of the FBI.

Clare, however, had righteousness on her side. "Of course I did. I saw him, she didn't. I heard his story, heard the emotion as he talked about his lost family. Saw the tears in his eyes." Clare was close to tears of her own.

Anna nodded solemnly. Edie continued to stitch, but her mouth pulled to one side in an expression Maggie could not interpret. She wondered if Edie too questioned Kenny's innocence.

"And of course, I knew Kenny before all this happened. I knew what he did here at the church to help the young people and all. So I think I can judge what he could and couldn't do better than a stranger, even if she is a special agent of the FBI."

Clare finished with a flourish, pulling her needle though the last few stitches and cutting the thread with a loud snip of the scissors.

"Do you think she was a profiler?" Louise asked.

This put Clare into a thoughtful mood. "I don't know. She didn't say anything about that. I don't know if there's any way to tell, is there?"

Louise had to admit that she had no idea.

"Was it frightening?" Anna inquired. "Having her there?"

Clare thought for a moment. "Yes, I guess it was. But in an exciting kind of way, if you know what I mean. I felt like the heroine in a novel, being able to tell her Kenny's side of the story. How much he loved his family and how he'd never do anything like that to them."

"How did she react to that?" Maggie asked. She was all too sure she already knew the answer.

Clare sighed. "I don't think she liked my theories very much. She barely listened. That part of it wasn't at all like a novel."

No, Maggie thought. In a novel the agent would probably have listened attentively to the amateur, then taken action based on what she'd learned. Much as Maggie enjoyed reading cozy mysteries, she didn't confuse them with real life.

"I think she just wanted to find out if I knew where he was so they could go arrest him." Clare took a few stitches, then abandoned her needle.

"They have a theory of what happened, and they're going with that." Louise's voice was matter of fact.

Edie nodded her agreement.

Clare suddenly looked confident and strong. Her spine was straight, her shoulders pulled back. Her lips tightened into a firm line. "Then it's up to us to prove them wrong."

23

"We've been talking to the others in the break room," Anna told Clare. "Remember, we planned to be in a little early today so we could talk with some of Kate's neighbors."

"We didn't get any new information on Kenny Upland," Edie said, a sour expression on her face. Her needle, however, kept up its steady even movement, creating a row of beautiful even stitches.

"Oh, no," Anna said, contradicting her. "We did hear something. Jack Banderly said he and Kenny used to talk while they did yard work, and Kenny told him he was going to be out of town that week."

"Oh," Clare said, excitement infiltrating her voice. "That's just what we need. Did he tell the police that?"

"He says he told them, Clare," Maggie said. "Back in May." Her needle, too, moved steadily through the quilt sandwich as she spoke. Their current project was a pieced maple leaf, done in bright fall colors. The quilting stitches outlined the pieced leaves and created "ghost" leaves scattered across the beige background. "Fran said he told everyone, over and over, that Kenny was away camping and they had to get in touch with him and let him know what happened."

Clare looked surprised. "I wonder why no one ever heard about that? It seems as if they just decided right away that Kenny did it and didn't mention anything that might have helped prove him innocent."

"And we learned more about Kate working," Victoria said. "That's what we really wanted to know right now, isn't it?"

Together, they recounted to Clare what they'd learned from Fran and Gladys. It gave them a chance to review the information as well. And for Clare, Maggie and Victoria to recount their recent experiences.

Eyes twinkling, Clare told them about her visit to Nature's Best. "I already told Maggie about this when we went to Gilligan's on Saturday, but I had the most wonderful adventure on Friday. I went to Nature's Best."

"It's a nice store, isn't it?" Victoria said. "Did you get some fresh produce? Maggie and I stopped there on Friday, too." She

201

clipped a thread as she looked across the table at Clare, waiting to hear her answer before she threaded it through the eye of the needle.

Clare reddened. "I, uh, I did get some very nice strawberries. I made shortcake for dessert."

"My fruit salad was the hit of the family brunch," Maggie said. "You were right about the pharmacist there, Louise. I was quite impressed with him. He's very knowledgeable about natural substances, and very willing to share what he knows."

Clare was suddenly impatient with this discussion of the store, anxious to tell them about her brilliant ploy to get information from a staff member. So she explained what she had done.

Louise listened, puzzled. "Just what were you trying to achieve, Clare?"

"I wanted to see what an employee would say about Kate," Clare explained, exasperated. "And if there might be any rumors there about her and another employee."

"It seems all we've learned is what we already knew," Maggie said. "The same things we heard here this morning. Something happened to change Kate just before she died."

"No," Edie said. "Clare just said the

young woman at the store told her Kate planned to quit her job. That's something we hadn't heard before. At least, I haven't."

"No," Clare said, her voice insistent. "She said Kate said she didn't want to accuse anyone until she was absolutely sure. That's got to be important."

"Accuse anyone of what?"

"That's what we have to find out." Clare's frustration grew. She knew the information she'd obtained from Heather was important. Why couldn't the others see that? "Maybe Kate knew who the stalker was, or suspected she knew. But didn't want to say anything until she had proof." Clare smiled, satisfied with this explanation.

Maggie considered this theory but decided it was too vague to lead anywhere.

"Both Gladys and Fran agree that something was bothering Kate in those last few weeks before her death," Maggie said. "They say she barely spoke at all and seemed upset about something."

"The stalker!" Clare suggested.

Maggie sighed. Clare was much too focused on the idea of a stalker. She herself was withholding judgment until they could come up with something more concrete than Kenny's suggestion that it was a good possibility.

"That's another thing," Maggie said. "Neither Gladys nor Fran ever noticed anyone hanging around the house. It seems that they should have done — if there had been anyone to see."

Clare seemed distinctly unhappy now. She pulled her thread slowly through the fabric layers, then smoothed the line of stitches with her index finger before looking back up. "So you think everything Kenny told me is wrong?"

Maggie wasn't sure what to say. But she was saved temporarily by Victoria, bless her.

"Clare, this situation isn't as black and white as you seem to think. There are so many factors involved, and Kenny's illness complicates things."

"That's right," Maggie said. "It's possible that Kate may have just been upset about Kenny and the PTSD that didn't seem to be improving. That would certainly bother me."

"From what they said, Kate seemed to enjoy her jobs, at least until those last few weeks when she seemed almost ill and didn't say much about anything," Victoria said. "Fran thought working was helping to bring her out of her shell, at least until she got so stressed out there at the end, about something she wouldn't discuss."

Clare nodded, as though this explained something she'd suspected all along. She wasn't stitching, just listening and reacting. "Since her relationship with K.C. seems to have been very open, we should probably concentrate on Nature's Best and the preschool," Clare said. She decided not to use the word *stalker* again, as it seemed to stir up the others. "Are there any men at the preschool offices?"

Maggie, however, caught the reference even if it was merely implied. "But we don't even know if there was a stalker!" she exclaimed. Clare's blind faith in Kenny was wearing on Maggie's nerves.

"It does seem unlikely there was a stalker, if her neighbors never saw anything suspicious." Victoria's voice was much cooler than Maggie's.

But Clare's reaction remained the same. She set her mouth at a stubborn slant. "Kenny seems sure there was."

Victoria caught Maggie's eye, winking in an attempt to make her smile at Clare's obstinacy. But Maggie merely exhaled heavily, frustrated by the whole thing.

"Diane claims K.C. Gilligan harasses his women employees," Edie said.

"No!" Clare was shocked. "K.C. is such a nice person! He's a really good man who donates to Catholic Charities and St. Vincent de Paul. Donates a car to our raffle every year . . ."

"Yes, Clare, we know," Louise interrupted.

"He may seem that way," Edie said, "but it bears checking out. Also, there's a Tyler Gilligan listed as a top salesman at the dealership. Since K.C. doesn't have any children, who is this Tyler? A nephew? Cousin? There was a photo, and he looked rather young for a brother, though that's always a possibility."

Maggie was glad to leave discussion of the stalker behind.

"You know, I saw that name, too, but I didn't think anything of it," Maggie said. "I just assumed it was some relative of K.C.'s."

"Yes, I noticed that, too." It was Victoria's turn to chime in. "I thought it was nice that he had a relative there with him since he'd wanted a family so much."

"When I Googled the name Tyler Gilligan, I found some references to a Tyler Harris-Gilligan. With a hyphen, you know." Edie's voice let them know what she thought of *that* little gimmick. "He called himself that when he first started working at the dealership, then dropped the Harris somewhere along the way. When I looked up Tyler Harris, I found a young man from the

California Bay area who looks like the same person. There were some sports references. He was a track star at his high school and at a community college."

"Oh, my," Clare said. "Do you think it's a long-lost son?"

Clare didn't seem to notice the strange looks she got from the others. She was already plunging into a story about a book she'd read.

"I read a book this summer like that. The man in the book had fathered a son when he was only a teenager, and the baby was adopted by some relatives of the teen mother. Then, when he was eighteen, he started looking for his biological parents. The biological father was a rich man, and the long-lost son claimed he just wanted to get to know his real father, that he didn't care about money. But, of course, as soon as he was recognized by his father and added to his will, he killed him. Poison," she announced with a nod of her head, her lips pursed tightly together.

Edie just stared at Clare. "Poison?" she said. "That's odd. Poison is usually a woman's weapon."

Clare shrugged, undeterred by Edie's theory on poisoners.

"I know who Tyler Gilligan is," Louise

said. "K.C. told the youth group about him, and Amanda told us. She was surprised about the story, but not in the way you'd think."

"Oh, I can't wait to hear it," Clare said, making herself more comfortable by wriggling in her chair.

"Like your book, Clare," Louise began, "it's about a baby who was adopted at birth."

Clare sat up tall, her fingers holding her needle but not stitching as she gave her full attention to Louise and her story.

Louise sighed. "It seems Rosemary became pregnant as a teenager. Her family was embarrassed and sent her out of state to stay with a relative, and she had to finish high school somewhere else. But she had the baby there — in California, I guess — and then gave him up for adoption right away."

There were several surprised exclamations at that. While everyone at the church knew K.C., Rosemary had been somewhat of a shadow beside her charismatic husband.

"Goodness," Edie said. "How come the whole parish doesn't know about this? It sounds like the kind of juicy gossip Diane would enjoy spreading."

Louise could only shrug. "I don't know

why it didn't get all over the church, but Amanda told us about it over a year ago."

"What was it that surprised Amanda about the story, Louise?" Maggie remembered Louise's cryptic comment before she began the story.

"It bothered her that K.C. told this story as an example of how you should forgive others. It seems he told them that he forgave Rosemary for this early episode in her life. Because he loved her so much. That bothered Amanda a lot. She didn't see why Rosemary needed forgiveness, for one thing. She also asked me how anyone could give up a baby."

"Things are very different now," Maggie said. She remembered how people talked about young girls who "got in trouble" many years ago. She was glad some of these things had changed.

But Edie had other ideas on the topic of change.

"That's not necessarily a good thing," Edie said. Her lips drew into a tight, prim line. "Teenage girls raising babies!" She clicked her tongue and shook her head. Disapproval flowed from her. "They're barely out of babyhood themselves."

But Anna was more sympathetic. "Poor Rosemary," she said. "I'm sure it's very difficult to give up your baby, even when you know he'll have a better life with others."

Louise nodded. "I did try to explain that to Amanda, but I'm not sure she got it. It's a completely different mindset in our young people these days."

"Poor Rosemary," Clare agreed. "And then she never was able to get pregnant again. I wonder if there's a connection."

"A connection to what?" Anna asked.

"You're not trying to imply that God punished her for getting pregnant before she was ready for motherhood, are you?" Maggie couldn't believe Clare would feel that way.

"No, no, not at all."

Clare's raised eyebrows and appalled expression told Maggie that she was way off base.

"I just meant that if that first birth ended in a C-section, then something could have gone wrong that might have prevented more pregnancies. My sister-in-law had that trouble," Clare went on, not giving anyone else a chance to interfere before she finished her explanation. "Not that she got pregnant as a teenager, but she had her first child by C-section and there was some kind of damage to her Fallopian tubes. It was an emergency delivery, so I guess the doctor was rushing and wasn't as careful as he might have been. But she was never able to get pregnant again."

Louise agreed that such a thing could happen, though it was more unlikely these days.

"So, did Tyler just show up on their doorstep one day?" Edie asked.

"Apparently," Louise said. "K.C. told the youth group that Tyler decided to find his biological parents when he came of age, and he found Rosemary. His biological father died in his twenties, in a car accident, and Rosemary was able to tell him that."

"Did K.C. know she'd had a child before they met?" Anna asked.

"No. That was how he got into the whole forgiveness thing. I guess he felt he had to forgive her for keeping the entire episode a secret. He told the kids his wife wanted to get to know her son, so he took the young man in, offered him a job at the car dealership, and let him stay with them until he could get established. That's probably why he did the hyphenated name thing," she said, turning toward Edie. "As a tribute to K.C. I understand he had to work his way up, but Vince recently heard that he'll take over the whole thing when K.C. retires."

"Probably inherit it eventually, too," Edie said.

Clare grinned. "So it *is* like that book I told you about."

"Except," Maggie reminded her, "it's not K.C. who is dead."

"And the Uplands didn't have enough money to make killing them worthwhile," Victoria added.

Clare nodded, but she couldn't help frowning.

24

Michael entered the house, took a deep breath that produced an appreciative grin, and kissed his mother on the cheek.

"Pot roast." It wasn't a question, just a statement of recognition. Grateful recognition.

"Mmmm." Deeply appreciative of the trouble she went to for their weekly dinners, Michael added a kiss on her other cheek, then removed his jacket and draped it over a chair.

Maggie kept a few beers in the frig for her sons' visits, and she fetched one as he walked in to join her. As she put the finishing touches on their dinner and Michael relaxed with his beer, she told him what Clare had said about the morning's interview with the FBI. And how upset she was that the woman never even sat down, much less listened to her theory.

"She tried to tell her that Kenny is innocent. Told her how he'd saved her life when her car went off the road and she lost consciousness." Maggie shook her head in wonder at Clare's temerity. "She told her how sincere he was about his innocence, and how broken up over the loss of his family."

Michael's eyes sparkled with amusement. "I'll bet that went over well."

They both laughed.

"Clare was the only one who was surprised that the FBI woman wasn't interested in Kenny's story. Or perhaps what I should say is that Clare was indignant that she wasn't listened to."

Maggie brought the pot from the stove, setting it down on the quilt patterned tiles she'd placed in the center of the table. When she removed the cover, the rich aroma of beef, onions and spices tickled her nose and made her mouth water. She had a small dining room in the condo, but she mostly used it as a sewing/quilting room. She and Michael enjoyed their Monday night dinners in her cozy kitchen.

She passed the plates to Michael and returned to the stove to remove a pan of biscuits from the oven. Michael filled their plates while Maggie poured them each a glass of iced tea, then spread butter on a biscuit. Butter might be out of fashion, but there was nothing like it to melt over a biscuit fresh from the oven. She smiled as Michael took two, breaking them open and slathering both with butter. That artificial stuff might be okay for some people, but Maggie had raised her boys eating *real* food — sugar and butter, whole milk, marbled beef. They'd turned out well, too, all of them tall and lean and strong. She'd never had any problems with her weight either, though she'd noticed that she could no longer overindulge without consequences. The problems of aging, she thought, but without rancor. She'd had a good life, and still did. Her only regret was losing her husband so early, but that was not something she could have changed by her actions. Apparently, God needed Harry more than she did.

They ate in silence for a while, getting the edge off their hunger, before Maggie spoke.

"So, were you able to learn whether there's any good evidence against Kenny? Is he really guilty?"

Michael paused with a biscuit halfway to his lips, spearing her with one of his probing cop looks. What he didn't realize was that it had no effect on Maggie. She was his mother. She'd changed his diapers and kissed his skinned knees. He didn't intimidate her at all, even now that he was six inches taller and outweighed her by at least seventy-five pounds.

"I don't want you and your friends poking into the Upland case, okay? It's still an open case, and he's a wanted fugitive."

"Michael," Maggie said. "I told you we were just talking to a few people — to get Clare off our backs."

"Is she still insisting that Kenny is innocent?"

"Oh, yes. She's worse than ever."

Michael sighed. "I talked to a friend who's on the case."

His face looked troubled. *Ah-ha,* Maggie thought. There might be room to doubt Kenny's guilt after all. If they had incontrovertible evidence linking Kenny to the destruction of the house, Michael would be looking smug.

"He said that they're all sure it's Kenny, all right. They couldn't find anyone else with a motive. Everyone loved that family. It's the kind of crime that is usually tied to a family member, and with Kenny's PTSD, he's the only one they can find who might have done it. And this isn't for public release, but they were all shot with a military issue gun."

It was Maggie's turn to sigh. She wanted to believe the best of Kenny. She'd always liked him, as she'd liked the entire family. But she knew the Scottsdale Police Department did good work, and they were convinced Kenny did it. The gun evidence was hard to dispute, but she wouldn't be able to tell Clare about that since Michael had told her about it in confidence. There had been speculation about how the family died, but, amazingly, nothing official had ever come out.

"Let me ask you something." Maggie toyed with a bit of meat on her plate, pushing it around with her fork. "Have you ever heard anything about K.C. Gilligan harassing the young women who work at his dealership?"

"No, but that probably wouldn't be a police matter. Maybe a civil suit if the woman wanted to take it there. But that kind of thing is hard to prove. It usually comes down to a he-said, she-said thing — who the jury believes." Hoping to get off the subject of crime, he asked how she'd spent the afternoon. "Have you looked into those audio books I told you about?"

Maggie smiled. "Michael, I've been listening to audio books for years. Lots of quilters do. I've purchased a few favorites, but I usually get them from the library."

Noticing that Michael was finished with his meal, Maggie rose to get the dessert from the counter. She smiled as she sliced into the apple pie.

"I was going to make pumpkin, but then I thought you'd be getting enough of that next week. So I made apple."

"Love them both," Michael said, grinning at her. He watched avidly as she looked to him for an okay on size. "Is there ice cream?"

"Of course. Just let me finish with this and I'll get it."

But Michael got up. "I can get it. Want yours a la mode, too?"

As they settled back at the table with their dessert, Maggie told Michael that she had gotten the apples for her pie at Nature's Best.

"Remember, I told you yesterday that I've recently discovered them and they have the best produce."

Michael merely nodded, his mouth full of pie, but she noticed his brow furrow.

"I was reading about them online. It's a very interesting story. A group of men from Arizona who attended pharmacy school together decided they wanted to encourage a healthy lifestyle and started the first

Nature's Best in Tucson. Besides regular prescriptions, they do a lot of homeopathic things. I talked to the pharmacist at the local store last week, and he's a very personable man. He said he's hoping to buy into the store himself. It's unusual to have the owner working in his store these days, but he said all the owners do."

"I hope you don't buy too much there, Ma."

Seeing his mother's odd look, Michael quickly added. "It's quite expensive from what I've heard."

"I do know how to budget, Michael." But Maggie had to smile. It was a tender and loving thing, for a son to be so worried about his mother's finances.

25

Clare called as Maggie finished cleaning up the kitchen. Michael always offered to help, but she usually sent him on his way. She had a routine that worked for her, and she didn't mind the solitary time. She turned on the radio and sang along to the oldies as she worked. She always made up frozen dinners with the Monday leftovers, then shared them with Michael. She'd just stored hers in the freezer when the phone rang.

"Has Michael gone?"

Clare's voice came clearly through the line. Quite a change from that whispered call she'd gotten on Wednesday.

Hearing that Maggie was alone, Clare jumped straight to her reason for calling. "I couldn't wait until tomorrow to hear. Did he have anything to say about the Upland case?"

Clare might be anxious, but Maggie really could have waited until the morning to discuss this. She pulled out a chair and sat down.

"Michael did talk to someone on the case. He thinks that they've settled on Kenny because they can't find any motive at all for anyone else. He said everyone loved Kate and the twins. And in a case like this, it's usually a family member that is responsible."

Clare sighed, an action Maggie had almost succumbed to herself.

"Kenny thinks that's why they've settled on him, too," Clare said. "I heard from him this evening."

"What?" Maggie was surprised. Or perhaps stunned was a better description. "He called you?"

"Yes."

Maggie could hear the excitement in Clare's voice. Pride even. She was living some kind of dream, helping a fugitive find justice.

"Remember when you all asked how we would keep in touch? When I offered to help him? I guess this is the way."

Maggie heard a titter of a laugh. Almost a giggle.

"He wondered if we'd learned anything helpful."

Maggie shook her head, glad Clare

couldn't see her. "Did you call that FBI agent?"

"No." Clare seemed puzzled. "Why would I do that?"

"To tell her that he called, of course. You have to remember that he's still a wanted fugitive, Clare. You could get in trouble for helping him. We all could."

"But I don't know where he is. I'm not helping him physically. I don't see how investigating something that has the police stymied could be a problem. It's like those college classes you hear about, where they look into a case and end up proving the person was innocent all along."

Maggie wasn't sure Clare wasn't thinking of some book she'd read, or a TV show. Maggie seemed to recall a television movie with Dick Van Dyke that sounded somewhat like that. Still, she had to agree that they were not doing anything illegal — at least she didn't think so. But she'd always been a strictly law abiding person, and it seemed wrong somehow not to let the authorities know that a wanted fugitive had been in touch.

"I think those classes look into cases where someone has already been convicted," Maggie said. "But I just thought the FBI would be interested in the fact that Kenny called you. They might want to tap your phone," Maggie suggested.

Clare couldn't help the excitement in her voice. "That would be something wouldn't it? But I doubt it would help anyway. Kenny's smart enough to use one of those disposable cell phones you hear about on TV."

Maggie had to agree with that, too. There were so many forensic shows on TV these days, all the criminals knew exactly what to do and not do. "Well, you'll have some exciting information to share with everyone tomorrow," Maggie said. She knew Clare would be pleased.

26

Victoria enjoyed her evening with the bunco group. The women were close to her in age, and most of them were teachers or former teachers. The game was fun, and spirits ran high as they played. Unfortunately, there wasn't much chance to talk during the play — at least not about what interested Victoria. And she could find no way to bring up Kate during the refreshment gab session afterward.

So Victoria volunteered to help Eleanor with the cleanup.

"So many of the others have someone at home, waiting for them. I don't," she told Eleanor, when her hostess suggested she could take care of it the next day. "Besides, you don't want to wake up and find the place a mess. It's always better to clean up right away."

Not that the women made much of a mess. Tidying up was more a matter of plumping pillows and checking for stray cups and napkins.

As they worked their way around the living room, Victoria felt the time was finally right to broach the topic she was really interested in.

"How are things at the preschool?" she asked, hoping to gently lead up to the subject of Kate.

"Good. I enjoy the children."

"Do you ever think of retiring? I know you're younger than I am . . ."

"Oh, I wouldn't be too sure of that." Eleanor laughed. "I go through phases where I'm sure I'll retire next month. Next week sometimes." She straightened up, rubbing at the small of her back. "Those are the weeks when things aren't going well of course."

"I had weeks like that back in my teaching days," Victoria said.

"After what happened to Kate Upland I was sure I would give it all up. I felt so bad about those little girls. It's really hard to read about something like that when you actually know the people involved."

"Wasn't that terrible?" But wasn't it wonderful that Eleanor herself brought up Kate's name. "I knew Kate, too, a lovely young woman."

At the quizzical look from Eleanor, Victoria elaborated. "I quilt with my neighbor, over at St. Rose, and I work at their bazaar every year. That's where I met her. She and her family always came."

Victoria retrieved a crumpled paper napkin from behind a small accent cushion, carefully avoiding Eleanor's eyes, giving her time to say something she might not say if too closely watched. People were always more willing to share when the talk seemed mere trivialities.

Eleanor sighed. "Kate was the nicest person imaginable. I don't know how that husband of hers . . ." She broke off, giving herself time to bring her emotions under control. "She was a whiz with accounting. I still miss her." She shook her head. "She had a lot of trouble when Kenny was over in Iraq. Being a whiz with financial matters doesn't help if there's no money coming in."

Victoria chanced a glance in Eleanor's direction. Eleanor stood unmoving, staring off into space. "I understand that happens to a lot of military families."

"Poor Kate. She was such a shy little thing. She apparently let her husband handle almost everything for her. Then to have him gone like that. She had to take

226

other part-time jobs to make ends meet. I tried to tell her to find something full time and more permanent, but she wouldn't even consider it. She wanted as much time as possible at home with her girls."

"She was a good mother," Victoria agreed. She sensed that Eleanor was mostly remembering now, not really conversing. And she was glad to allow it.

"She took office jobs at Gilligan's and at that organic grocery." Eleanor smiled. "She was horrified the first time they asked her to help out at the pharmacy counter there because they were shorthanded."

Victoria smoothed her hands over a sofa cushion, ironing out the wrinkles caused by recent sitting. "It is hard to imagine her working with the public like that."

"I know. She said that she never did enjoy it, but she did get used to it after a while. They only asked her to help out when they were really strapped for people, so it wasn't every day. But then shortly before her death, she got kind of odd. Even more introverted. And she didn't talk at all. I don't know what it was, but she seemed very upset, kind of worried and agitated. I asked if she was ill. She claimed to be fine, and I remember wondering if there were problems in her marriage. That happens quite often when a partner returns from a war zone. After what happened, I guess that was it."

Victoria affected surprise — not difficult as she was surprised. "Trouble with her marriage? I understood she and Kenny were devoted to each other and to the twins. They certainly seemed that way whenever I saw them."

"I know. That's what I thought, too. But after she died, there was a lot of talk. I think most of it came from the questions the police asked. We all got the impression that there was trouble between the two of them, and that's why he finally exploded."

"I've heard there was post traumatic stress involved."

Eleanor nodded vigorously. Neither of them was even pretending to clean up any longer. "I thought so! Kate was very private about her home life. Except for talking about the kids, of course. So none of us knew for sure about problems. But we wondered about post traumatic stress, especially after what happened."

They moved into the kitchen, taking the few stray cups and bits of trash they'd found for disposal.

"Kenny was quite active at St. Rose. He worked with the youth group, and by all accounts the kids loved him."

Eleanor nodded. "I'm not surprised. I saw him with the twins often enough, and he was wonderful with them. He'd talk to the other kids in their class, too, which many of the fathers don't do."

"One of the women at St. Rose claims that she saw Kenny recently. That he saved her life when her car ran off the road up along the Mogollon Rim. She also says he told her he didn't kill his family and that he's trying to discover who did."

Eleanor's eyes widened, and Victoria knew she was anxious to hear more. Grateful that the bunco game had not gone too late, Victoria accepted a cup of tea and sat down with her hostess at the kitchen table.

"Was it really Kenny?"

"She's sure it was. She was even interviewed by the FBI about it."

Eleanor leaned forward. "Did he tell her who did it?"

"That's the odd thing. Kenny seems to think Kate had an affair while he was in Iraq. And that this man was stalking Kate once he returned. He thinks that if he can pinpoint the man, he'll be able to figure out what happened. But all of us who knew Kate find the whole thing very hard to believe. That she would have an affair, that is."

Eleanor nodded her assent. "I could never believe that of her. She was so shy, and really quite naïve. Prim almost. He might just be trying to muddy the waters, bring in someone else to take the blame."

Victoria shrugged. "He said something about the girls mentioning a man who would come over to the house, who would take them out to eat and play with them."

Eleanor dismissed that with a wave of her hand. "It was probably just someone being kind, a family friend or a neighbor who knew their dad was gone."

"My thoughts too," Victoria said, taking a sip of her tea. She didn't see why she should explain about K.C.'s visits to the Upland house. Even when Eleanor almost asked.

"I wonder who it could have been." Eleanor stared off toward the kitchen window, though it was impossible to see anything but a reflection of the room there.

Victoria saw her chance to probe. "I guess there aren't any men at the preschool who might have befriended her and the girls."

Eleanor took a moment to respond, as though she was running possibilities through her mind.

"I wouldn't think so. Perhaps someone from the car dealership. So many more men there."

"Or the grocery store, I guess," Victoria suggested. "It's right in the neighborhood, and if she worked at the counter she might have made friends with a neighbor."

"I suppose." Eleanor appeared less certain. "I know she seemed to be making friends with the pharmacist there. She used to talk about him sometimes. But then, a few weeks before her death, she pretty much stopped talking — about anything. She really turned in on herself. She seemed to be fretting over something important, but something personal. She never said what."

"That's interesting. I've seen the pharmacist in the store of course. He's quite personable."

"Oh, yes," Eleanor agreed. "Tony Sandoval. He's quite active in the area, donates to all the local charitable events. He's been generous to the preschool during our fund raisers. Because we're neighbors of his, he says."

"That's very nice. I've heard that he belongs to St. Rose."

Eleanor nodded. "I didn't know that, but I have assumed he's a member of St. Rose, just because of his Mexican heritage." She laughed, a little embarrassed. "I guess I'm responsible for racial stereotyping. And here I am always lecturing the teachers about

231

avoiding it."

Victoria thought it best not to comment. "I wonder if that's how Kate got the job. If she knew him from the church, I mean."

"No, I happen to know that she got that job from a referral. One of the teachers at the preschool was getting a prescription filled and heard him saying how he really needed someone to do his books. Apparently he was doing them himself, but the store did so well it got to be too much."

"One of the other quilters told me it's a compounding pharmacy, which is a rarity these days. That might help his business, too."

"It is a very nice store, but on the expensive side."

Victoria knew that Eleanor led a comfortable life, but she supposed she could afford to do that because she was frugal in other areas.

"He does seem to draw a lot of the local athletes," Eleanor commented. "I often see them going in and out late in the afternoon. Such good-looking men, and not all high school and college age."

"Really?" Victoria wondered if this could have any significance. "I suppose they go there for the wide selection of vitamins and supplements. I was told that the pharmacist mixes up special combinations for various age groups and lifestyles."

Eleanor finished the last of her tea, putting the cup back in its saucer with a sigh. "Maybe I should check that out. I wonder what he has for mature women too foolish to consider retirement."

Victoria laughed, picking up her empty cup and taking it to the sink.

"You do that. It might be just what you need for a little pick-me-up."

The two women exchanged warm good-byes at the door. Victoria was glad she'd been asked to talk to Eleanor. She'd forgotten how much she enjoyed her company. She was already looking forward to the following Monday evening.

27

The women continued with their online research, but there were no "ah-ha" discoveries.

"Of course, we may have found something but not know what it is," Clare suggested. "We aren't going to stumble on an entry somewhere that says that K.C. Gilligan harassed Kate Upland. Or any of the other people she worked with."

"That's a good point," Victoria said, "and one of the reasons this kind of thing needs to be left to real investigators. They have ways of getting at information that we can't access."

"But the police and the FBI aren't really investigating anymore," Clare protested. "They've all decided that Kenny in guilty because they can't find anyone else to blame. They aren't looking for anyone, only Kenny."

Maggie had to admit that Clare had a

point. The justice system was supposed to be open minded about suspects, but in this case that particular principle was being overlooked. So perhaps it was a good thing that Clare had embraced Kenny's cause. Innocent or not, he deserved to have someone on his side. Maggie just hoped he was innocent because she didn't know what would become of Clare if she had to admit his guilt.

"Kenny called me last night."

After the mundane accounts of frustrating online searches, Clare's report of a phone call from Kenny created some excitement. Maggie couldn't believe Clare hadn't blurted out her news the moment she walked in the door.

"What did he say?" Louise asked.

"Well . . ." Clare's fingers stilled momentarily as she thought. "He asked how I was after the accident, if I'd had any problems. I thought that was really nice of him."

The others agreed that it was nice of him to inquire after her health.

"Then he asked if my friends had agreed to help him out. Remember, I told him about how we all managed to identify two other killers by talking and everything," she added proudly.

"Did you tell him that some of us weren't

real happy about being drawn into aiding and abetting a fugitive?" Edie asked.

"Of course not," Clare said. "The poor man's self-esteem is bad enough right now. I could tell he expected me to say that not everyone wanted to help him. I couldn't do that to him. And besides, none of you did refuse to help."

Clare pulled her needle through and snipped off the thread. "He was hoping for some good news, but I didn't have any for him." Clare sighed as she unwound thread from the spool. "I told him we've been discussing his case ever since I got back. And that we talked to his neighbors and all."

Clare cut a new length of thread and inserted it through the eye of the needle. As soon as she pulled it through, she continued, forming the knot at the end by rote as she spoke.

"I told him what Diane said about K.C. Gilligan. He knows K.C., of course, but he had never heard about the harassment thing. He seemed very interested though." Clare pushed her needle into the quilt and popped the knot through the surface, allowing it to embed itself in the batting between the fabric layers. "I don't think he knows Diane," she finished.

"Oh, Clare." Louise frowned. "I'm not

sure you should have told him about K.C."

"Or Diane," Edie added.

Maggie, too, felt apprehensive. She realized that in talking to Clare the previous night, she'd never learned what was said during the exciting phone call. They'd gotten off on a tangent when Maggie mentioned calling the FBI.

"What if he decides to go after K.C.?" she asked now.

"We don't really know what his state of mind is," Louise added.

Edie seemed to agree. "Well, if K.C. dies in a house explosion, then we'll know." She nodded, a solemn inclination of her head.

The others, however, looked at Edie as though she might be half out of her mind, finally giving tentative, nervous laughs.

"Don't be silly," Maggie said.

Clare looked stricken by Edie's comment, but her face quickly cleared. "He's not guilty. I'm sure of it."

"I hope so," Louise murmured.

"Me, too," Maggie added under her breath. She kept her head down as she worked on one of the quilted maple leaves. The variegated quilting thread made the stitches forming the leaf appear to shimmer in the room's bright light.

"I had to ask him not to call me at the

house again." Clare heaved a heavy sigh. "Gerald didn't like it at all."

"Can't blame him," Edie declared. "He probably isn't as convinced as you are that Kenny isn't a murderer."

Clare sighed again. "I've talked to him about it. Reminded him that Kenny saved my life. But he's not sure of his innocence, he says. He doesn't want me getting involved with him while he's still a fugitive."

"He's being sensible, because he loves you," Victoria assured her. "You're looking at things more emotionally. You met Kenny in person, and he helped you after your accident. You're grateful."

Clare seemed uncertain but nodded a tentative agreement. Her eyes sought Victoria's across the frame. Victoria's eyes were filled with warmth. Comforted, Clare's eyes sparkled with her silent thanks.

"So, did you learn anything interesting at your bunco group last night, Victoria?" Louise popped a knot into the quilt, throwing a quick glance at Victoria before she began to stitch along the edge of a pieced leaf.

"Nothing terribly interesting, no," Victoria replied. "Eleanor liked Kate a lot and said she almost retired after what happened to her. But she often says she's going to retire. She'll probably be working at the preschool until she's well into her seventies, maybe her eighties."

Clare slumped down in her chair, leaning over the quilt in a way that was sure to leave her with a backache.

"One thing, though," Victoria continued. "She did know how Kate got the job over at Nature's Best. It seems that one of the preschool teachers was there having a prescription filled and heard Tony say that he needed someone to do bookkeeping, that it was getting to be too much for him. She's the one who told Kate about it."

"Well, it's one more piece of information," Edie said. "Investigating is like a quilt — you have to have all the pieces before you can put them together and see the pattern."

Anna smiled at Edie. "That was nice."

Edie mumbled her thanks, looking somewhat abashed at the compliment.

"Other than that, all that Eleanor said was what we've heard from everyone. She can't believe Kate would have an affair, and Kate was stressed to the point of illness just before she died."

Then Victoria seemed to recall something else.

"Except for one thing, which may or may not mean anything. She knows Tony at the pharmacy and likes him. She said he's very generous with all the local charities and always helps out when they have a fund-raising project. She commented about the athletic men of all ages who are constantly coming and going over at Nature's Best. It's probably nothing . . ." Victoria shrugged. "But, as Edie says, it's another piece of the puzzle. And we've noticed that ourselves about the Nature's Best customers."

28

"It might be time to have a talk with Kate's family."

Maggie's suggestion was met with general approval, though also with some doubt.

"That would be great," Clare said. "I'd love to hear what they have to say. But how? They don't live here in the valley. Do you think they'd talk to us over the phone?"

Maggie shook her head. "They might. But that isn't what I was thinking of. We all signed up for the Laughlin bus trip with the Senior Guild. What if we could stay at their bed and breakfast overnight? We'd have to drive up, rather than take the bus . . ."

"What a great idea, Maggie." Clare looked happy enough to applaud. "We can use my car if someone will share part of the driving. It's been fully checked out since my accident, and it's in fine shape."

Maggie, Victoria and Edie all said they would help with the driving.

"I'll have to stick with the bus," Louise said, adding that she sure would like to try the bed and breakfast though. "But I'll never hear the end of it if I don't sit with Vince on the bus as planned. He might agree to stay over, but that would ruin the girls' night out atmosphere."

Anna preferred not to stay overnight. "It's enough for me to do the one-day trip. That alone will be exhausting."

"Do you think there will be a vacancy at such short notice?" Victoria asked.

"All we can do is ask," Maggie said. "It's the middle of the week, which should be in our favor." The Senior Guild trip was scheduled for that Thursday, so if they decided to drive they would have to leave the next day.

"Do any of you know Kate's parents?" Victoria asked.

"I met them once," Maggie said, "when they were visiting Kate. They came with her to bring the twins to religious class, and then picked them up afterward. The twins seemed very fond of them."

"I never met them myself," Clare said. "So maybe you should call, Maggie. Their names are Earl and Penny Montgomery." Her eyes sparkled. She couldn't wait to get up there and see if Kate's parents knew anything about her death. Or about an affair she may have had while her husband was away serving his country.

Maggie could see the eagerness in Clare's eyes and warned her. "We'll have to be careful. Her parents won't want to hear about this theory of Kenny's. I'm sure the whole idea of her having an affair would turn them right off and we wouldn't get another word out of them. We'll have to try and get information about Kate without mentioning that."

"I still can't believe Kate would have been unfaithful to Kenny. They were so in love." Anna sighed. She believed in love and loyalty and commitment.

"Still, we should try," Clare said. "Kenny was her husband. He should know what she might be capable of."

Maggie didn't understand why Clare wouldn't let go of the whole affair idea — Clare seemed determined to prove Kenny correct — but she offered to go to the church office and check in the phone books there for the bed and breakfast number.

As soon as she returned, Maggie made the call.

"Hello, Mrs. Montgomery? This is Maggie Browne, from the St. Rose Quilting Bee in Scottsdale. We met when you brought your grandchildren to their religious class last year."

"Mrs. Browne. Yes, I remember you." Her voice warmed up a bit from her initial hello but remained guarded. As though she expected Maggie to ask her how she felt about losing her daughter and grandchildren in such a horrific manner.

"May I say I'm very sorry for your loss. I still want to cry whenever I think of poor little Kelsie and Kerrie."

"Thank you." Penny's voice sounded thick and choked. There was an audible swallow. "I appreciate it."

"Our church group has a day trip planned for this Thursday, but four of us from the Quilting Bee thought we'd like to stay over — maybe see a show."

"That will be nice for you after all the work of the bazaar. You've just finished with that, haven't you?"

Maggie was flattered that she recalled the timing of their bazaar.

"Yes, we have. It's always such a relief. I guess this is terribly short notice, though. Would you have anything available?"

"How many did you say?"

They spent a few more minutes making the arrangements.

As it happened, there were four rooms

available. Maggie had looked up the bed and breakfast online after Clare first mentioned it and knew the entire house offered only four suites.

"You're empty right now?"

"Yes, until the weekend. So I can give you each your own room, and I'll even offer a discount. It's nice to have some business come in so unexpectedly. And people who knew Kate," she added, in a voice so soft Maggie almost didn't catch it.

"Why, thank you. That's very nice of you."

Maggie ended the call, then told the others about Penny's generosity.

"Oh, this is very exciting," Clare said. "Just think, we can combine business with pleasure. And each with our own room. Not that I minded sharing," she added quickly, in case Edie might be offended.

Edie, however, seemed more interested in the discount Penny had promised.

Maggie remained uneasy about poking into an open case.

"I still think this whole affair isn't really our business, Clare." She winced at her inadvertent pun. "We're actually just being nosy Parkers."

"No, Maggie. We aren't. We're helping our friend Kenny, who is being accused of a heinous crime. That he didn't commit,"

Clare added with a particular emphasis.

Maggie was impressed with Clare's erudition. And altruism.

That taken care of, they returned to Quilting Bee business.

There was only a little left to quilt in the center of the maple leaf quilt, and it was time to roll in the sides of the frame. They used an old-fashioned system of four two-by-fours covered with muslin to create their frame, the same kind of basic frame used for quilting bees in the old west. The quilt top, batt and backing were attached to the muslin with safety pins. Specially made stands for the four corners of the frame held the quilt at the correct height — an improvement over the kitchen chair backs used in pioneer days. The system was ideal for group quilts, as the women could quilt from all four sides. Once they could no longer reach into the unquilted area, they rolled up two sides and stitched until they could once again no longer reach where needed. This would be their final roll. They would be able to finish the center of the quilt from the new position.

They arranged themselves around the newly positioned quilt and began to work. Tired of the constant discussion of the Uplands, they called a temporary truce and discussed their plans for Thanksgiving next week. No one had company coming in this year; they all planned to be in town for the holiday.

Edie was sharing a recipe for sweet potato casserole when Clare's cell phone rang.

It was unusual for one of them to get a call during the morning. All their friends and family knew they quilted then. So there was instant apprehension.

"Oh, dear," Clare said, fumbling for the phone. "I hope Gerald and Samson are okay."

There was no sewing for the minute it took her to say hello, after which Clare became excited, rather than despondent. So it was not bad news. It was, however, surprising news.

"Kenny!" Clare looked around at the others, her face happy. "What a coincidence! We were just making arrangements to stop at the Montgomery's bed and breakfast."

"Why would you want to do that?"

He answered with such vehemence that Maggie, seated beside Clare, easily heard every word.

Clare's smile vanished. "We want to talk to them," she said. "The Senior Guild is sponsoring a one-day trip to Laughlin this week, and we thought it would be a good

247

time to see them. We just made arrangements to stay overnight."

"They hate me."

Maggie frowned. She could hear him clearly, even the petulance in his voice. He sounded like an immature teenager.

"They think I killed their daughter. How can they think that?"

On the other side of Clare, Louise leaned forward, catching Maggie's eye. She raised her eyebrows. "Stress," she mouthed. "Paranoia."

Maggie nodded her understanding.

Then, as quickly as it started, it was over. Maggie could hear his voice apologizing, though she was unable to catch every word. His tone was sincere.

"I'm sorry, Mrs. Patterson. I was calling to apologize to you about last night. I know your husband was upset about my call, and I didn't mean to cause any problems between you."

Clare visibly relaxed.

"That's all right, Kenny. Things are difficult for you right now."

"I know you're at the church in the morning, so I'll try to catch you then. I'm checking up on K.C. and I may have some interesting news."

Before Clare could inquire about that titil-

248

lating disclosure, he disconnected.

Clare put her phone back into her bag. Maggie noticed that her hand trembled a bit as she attempted to open the flap of the bag.

"He sounded different this time," Clare told them. She gave a jittery laugh that had nothing to do with humor. "He made me nervous, the way he snapped at me about the Montgomerys. I wanted to hang up, but I was almost afraid to."

The others stared at Clare, offering what silent comfort they could without actually getting up and giving her a hug. A "hmpf" came from Edie, but her expression was supportive.

"He can't harm you over the phone," Anna assured her.

The absurdity of the situation did make them all smile, and Clare thanked Anna for her comforting observation.

"The thing is, it made me think about something else that happened between us. Something I didn't tell you about," Clare said. "Before." The final word was almost a whisper.

"Something that happened while you were with Kenny?" Maggie asked.

"Yes." Clare swallowed, taking a few more stitches before pulling the needle through and then looking around at her friends. "I wasn't sure myself how I felt about it. Ambivalent, I guess. And I was afraid you would all think it was not a good thing and hold it against Kenny. And I believed him . . ."

As though just realizing what she'd said, Clare stopped for a moment. Then she rephrased. "I believe him. I don't think he killed Kate and the girls." Her voice had grown softer, and Maggie wondered if she did still believe it — at least as truly as she had last week.

"So what happened?" Louise asked.

"It was just a little thing actually. I told you that he gave me some ibuprofen when I first woke up after the accident. And I was so sore, I was glad to have it. I slept real well after that and didn't wake until the next morning. That was when he told me that he'd slipped a sleeping tablet in with the ibuprofen."

"Without telling you." Maggie's words were a statement, not a question.

Everyone was shocked. They were even more surprised that Clare had not mentioned it.

"But that's terrible," Louise said. "Clare, how could you condone that? You made him sound like a saint for helping you, and now you say you were drugged?"

"What if you'd had a bad reaction?" Edie asked. "He couldn't know about your allergies or about what other medications you take and how they might interact with what he gave you."

Clare looked uncomfortable. She wriggled in her chair a bit, trying to feel more relaxed. "It did bother me. But his explanation was so good. He said I really needed the rest, to heal. I was so sore from the accident, I just hurt all over. And I did feel a lot better after I slept all that time. I slept very well."

"Still . . ." Louise said.

"Hmpf." Edie definitely did not approve. "You're lucky you woke up."

"You're looking at it in a different light now, aren't you?" Victoria said. "With him having a tantrum on the phone, you're wondering if he's as sane as you thought."

Clare nodded slowly. "I guess that's it. I don't see how he could be so nice and so helpful, and yet turn so strange so quickly." Clare shivered slightly at the remembrance.

"It could be the paranoia that comes with the PTSD," Louise told her. "I've been reading up on it recently. From what you've said of your time with him, he does seem to exhibit the classic symptoms."

Clare stared glumly down at the quilt top.

"Clare," Victoria said. "Why don't you tell us again about your meeting with Kenny. Right from the beginning, when you first saw him in Big-mart. The police always have people tell their stories over and over again. I suppose they're often looking for a discrepancy so that they can accuse that person, but sometimes the person remembers something new."

"What a good idea," Anna said. "It will let us look at it from a new perspective, too, since we have a lot more information now."

"That's true, Anna," Maggie said. "It's a good idea. Do tell us again, Clare."

"Okay." Clare paused for a moment, getting her thoughts in order. Then she suddenly recalled something. "Oh! I just remembered. As Kenny was saying goodbye just now, he said something about checking up on K.C. Then he said 'I might have some interesting news.' What do you think he meant?"

No one knew. After going around in circles for a minute or two, they returned to their original plan, and Clare began her story. This time they did not listen in stunned surprise to her recounting of events. There were numerous questions as she went along. Louise, especially, was interested in his demeanor, as well as his physical condition. She explained that she was trying to get a handle on his PTSD and just how much it might affect his behavior. Clare finished her story at their usual quitting time.

"Do you think Kenny was taking things like sleeping pills and anti-anxiety meds before Kate died?" Louise asked Clare.

"He said he needed them, but I'm sure he just meant now." Clare's voice broke. "Since the explosion and fire. Since he's been on the run."

"Are you sure?" Louise asked. "With the PTSD, he may have been using them before. People can have strange reactions to sleeping pills. There's been a lot said recently about that, even in the popular media outlets."

"That's right," Edie said. "There was that congressman who had an accident near the capital. He was asleep but driving his car. And people sleepwalk to the refrigerator and eat whole meals while they're sleeping and don't remember afterward."

As they covered the quilt frame, Edie continued with the tale of a Canadian man who killed someone while sleepwalking.

Maggie was happy to get away.

29

Clare, Maggie and Victoria made a quick stop at Nature's Best after the Bee meeting.

"I'm very excited about this trip, aren't you?" Clare asked.

"It will be pleasant, I'm sure," Victoria said.

"Maybe not," Maggie said. "Kate's parents might not want to talk to us, especially about Kenny. And please don't mention his theory about her having an affair either."

"But it makes so much sense . . ." Clare began.

"As a plot in a romantic novel," Maggie said. "A romantic suspense novel," she added. "You know we've all said it's inconceivable to picture Kate with another man. Her family would be terribly hurt to hear such a suggestion. I don't see how Kenny could even consider such a possibility."

"But he knew her better than anyone," Clare said.

Victoria, ever ready to play the part of mediator, chimed in. "There could have been a stalker without an affair. I think the problem here may be in Kenny's logic." She seemed to think it over for a second. "Didn't Louise say the PTSD would make him paranoid? That might account for it."

"But what about K.C. Gilligan and the sexual harassment?" Clare persisted. "He could have done something to Kate while she was working there. Kenny sure seemed to think it possible."

Maggie realized they had stopped at the vitamin aisle and saw Dr. Sandoval standing there with a clipboard in his hands. Two men in tennis clothes stood conversing with him, white pharmacy packages already in their hands. Both had heads thick with white hair but youthful, toned bodies.

Tony's supplements do have a good effect on aging bodies, Maggie thought. She recognized the man closest to her from the church, and he had to be at least seventy years of age. Probably seventy-five. She knew that he'd lost his wife to cancer a few years ago, and she had been seventy. He looked terrific, actually, much younger than he'd seemed during her illness. Of course, that kind of devastating illness could have an effect on a person's relatives as well as on the patient, but this was a truly dramatic change in appearance. Perhaps he'd decided to do something about his own health after his wife's terrible illness. Tony appeared to be something of a miracle worker.

As the men nodded to Tony and moved away, he greeted the women from St. Rose with a smile.

"Can I help you with something today, Maggie?" he asked.

Maggie found herself smiling back, then introducing Tony to her friends. He greeted them with the same delightful smile, and Maggie could see that Clare was every bit as taken with him as she herself was. *And Clare still had a husband at home,* she thought with a smile. It had to be that illusion of old-world charm. There was something about him that reminded her of the actor who played Zorro in those old black-and-white movies. All he needed was a Spanish accent and a sword at his side.

"Our quilting group is planning a little getaway," Clare told him, "to Laughlin."

"Ah, it sounds like just the thing. A few days away from the requirements of daily life. You will all return new women."

"And a little richer, let's hope," Clare said with a laugh.

"Just an overnight trip," Maggie corrected

him. "We're going on the day trip with the Senior Guild, but we thought we'd stop overnight in Bullhead City. A little girl time."

"We thought we'd check out your sample-size products," Victoria said. "I'd like to get some natural products, and the smaller the better. Even when I'm not flying, I try to pack as little as possible. At my age, I can't handle large suitcases."

As he led them around the end of the aisle to a section along the back wall, he discounted Victoria's words about age and disability.

"You all appear young at heart. You just have to take your vitamins to keep your bodies looking young, too."

He gestured toward the sample bins. "Here you go. We try to have some products that aren't available at your average drug store. For instance, this deodorant is made from all natural products and does not contain any aluminum. Excess aluminum has been linked to Alzheimer's, you know."

He mentioned the good properties of the shampoo and conditioner as well and suggested they try the aloe vera lotion.

"They keep those casinos cold, and the artificial atmosphere will dry out your skin. Be sure to take facial moisturizer, too."

Ten minutes later, as they got back into the car, Victoria commented on the personable pharmacist. "Did you notice the sad look in his eyes?"

"Not really," Maggie said. "But he's a good salesman." She looked at the supplies she'd bought, things she didn't necessarily need. "He's turning us all into environmentally aware consumers."

"And that's a good thing," Victoria said.

30

The drive to Bullhead City was uneventful. The women reviewed what they knew and what they wanted to know. They discussed how they might approach the Montgomerys for information without causing problems. They were sure to be leery of too many questions after the media blizzard that had surrounded their daughter's demise.

Once they'd talked that subject to death, Clare began to tell them in detail of a book she'd recently read about a housewife who helped prove the innocence of a fellow member of the PTA — one who had been falsely accused of murder.

Maggie only half listened, though the story sounded like one she would enjoy. She knew Clare was trying to make a point by choosing this particular story, but she had other things on her mind. Were they making a big mistake? Was Kenny Upland guilty? Michael certainly seemed to think so, and he'd talked to people who were actually working on the case.

She let out a sigh. Victoria glanced at her, raising her eyebrows in a silent question. *Are you all right?*

Maggie shrugged. She didn't want to get into the discussion of the pros and cons of their actions. Again. She just wished she could be as certain as Clare that what they were doing was right. As certain as Clare that the PTSD had not driven Kenny into familial abuse of the worst kind.

They arrived at the bed and breakfast as the sun began its descent into the western horizon, splashing the sky with coral tones. They received a pleasant welcome; Penny and Earl were friendly, if a bit cool.

Once the introductions were over, Earl said point-blank that they would not talk about Kate's death or about Kenny. "The memories are too painful for my wife," he added. And Penny did look close to tears from the short mention.

"I understand," Maggie said.

Clare, however, looked stricken. How could they learn anything that might help Kenny if they wouldn't talk to the Montgomerys?

"But perhaps you'd like to share happy

memories of Kate," Maggie suggested. "We enjoyed visiting with Kate and the twins at our bazaar every year."

Penny smiled at this, though Earl retained his stoic expression. He was tall, with a wiry build and the leathery skin of a man who spent a lot of time outdoors.

"I'd like that," Penny said. "Most people don't talk about Kate at all. They're afraid I won't be able to handle any mention of her, so they don't say anything. But I don't mind talking about the happy times. In fact, I'd enjoy it."

She shot a challenging look toward her husband, as if daring him to object, as she directed her guests into the large dining room.

"Come on in here. I thought you might be hungry after your drive, so I prepared a cold supper. Nothing fancy."

But the Bee members were eager to demur after seeing what she had ready for them. Nothing fancy indeed! The spread would have been perfect for an afternoon tea at a women's club fashion show. Tiny finger sandwiches of egg salad, cucumber and salmon; fruit salad; green salad; two kinds of pasta salad; four kinds of cookies — the bite-size ones that did not invoke the guilt brought about by eating the saucer-sized

261

cookies bakeries made. There was freshly made lemonade and iced tea, as well as hot coffee and tea.

"I made decaf since it's late," Penny told them, checking on the coffee pot.

Maggie and Victoria urged Penny to sit with them.

"Tell us about Kate as a girl," Victoria suggested. "Was she much like the twins? I always thought they looked like her."

Penny smiled, and her eyes lit with pleasure as she spoke.

"Oh, Kate was the prettiest little girl. She loved to play dress up, and she loved dolls. I still have some of her dolls here."

She looked over to the adjoining room where Maggie could see a glass-fronted cupboard that contained a dozen or more collector dolls and a pretty china tea set.

"She could play for hours with her dolls," Penny continued. "And with her tea set. She particularly liked that the tea set was real china, just like what we used with the guests." She sighed at the sweet memory. "She loved baby dolls, too, and loved to change their clothes and pretend to feed them bottles. I just knew she would make a great mother someday."

"And she did," Victoria said quickly, hoping to stave off the tears she could see shimmering in her hostess's eyes. "Kate was a wonderful mother. We looked forward to seeing her and her daughters at the fall bazaar."

"One of her neighbors told us she suggested Kate open a day care facility at her home," Maggie said, "because she was so good with the kids and she had such a nice play yard right there at the house."

"They did have a nice yard," Penny said. "You know, I recall Kate mentioning something about that. She was giving it some serious thought. I didn't know it was a suggestion from a neighbor."

She took a deep breath, and Maggie wondered if she, like Fran, was thinking of the problems Kenny's condition created for such a plan.

"We'd really hoped Kate would want to take over this place one day. After we retired, you know. She was thinking about that when she started out at the community college, taking business courses. She was very good at accounting and bookkeeping. She told us that one of her professors said she had a natural aptitude for it." Penny smiled proudly.

Her thoughts however, seemed to linger much farther into the past. "She was so cute when she had her tea parties. She'd serve all the things I did for the guests. Finger sandwiches and petit fours. Fruit and nut breads. She'd pretend that she was the hostess of a bed and breakfast. It wasn't until she was a teen that there was any indication she might not want to take over here." Penny sighed.

"That's a rebellious time for young people," Edie said.

"What were her friends like when she was a teenager?" Victoria asked.

"She was a girly girl, always was," Penny said, a sweet smile making her look years younger. "She didn't go in for sports, like so many girls do now. She was a bit of a nerd, I guess. She was in the Spanish club and the National Honor Society. Her friends seemed to have similar interests. They liked to listen to music and play games on the computer."

"She doesn't sound very rebellious," Maggie commented.

"Oh, she wasn't rebellious in the way you're thinking. She didn't act out, or get into serious trouble, or even drink. She just decided the place here was way too much work and complained endlessly about helping out."

"I suppose she wanted to date and hang out with friends," Edie suggested.

"I guess that was part of it, though she didn't date much. That was a sore spot with her and her girlfriends, I know. I often heard them complain that the guys didn't want to date brainy girls."

Everyone agreed this was a problem that had carried on through many years of teen relationships.

Penny began to looked tired, and Maggie realized she would have to clean up before she could go to bed. So she thought it time to suggest they retire to their rooms.

"Come on, let's call it a night," she said, rising from her place at the table. "We want to head over to Laughlin first thing in the morning, to meet the others arriving on the bus."

As Penny escorted them upstairs to their rooms, they had a short conference about when breakfast should be ready.

Once they were alone in the hall outside the guestrooms, Clare leaned in close to Maggie. "Are we really going to go to the casino in Laughlin?"

"Of course," Maggie replied. "We signed up for the day trip, so we planned to come anyway."

"It's our cover story," Edie said. "We have to follow through. Besides, it will be fun."

"Why, Edie, I didn't think you approved

of gambling." There was a teasing note in Victoria's voice.

"I don't. And I don't plan to do any, thank you very much. But I will do some shopping. And I'll look around. People watching can be highly entertaining."

"Educational, too," Victoria said.

"I'm so disappointed that they won't discuss Kate's death," Clare said.

"Can you blame them?" Victoria said. "Just imagine what they must have endured back in May."

Clare blushed. "You're right. But how can we learn if anyone wanted to kill Kate if we can't ask about her life before she died?"

"We can learn a few things obliquely," Maggie said. "For instance, an old boyfriend is unlikely because Penny said she didn't really date."

"Oooh." Clare perked up at that. "I see."

Before closing her door, Maggie noticed that Clare seemed to be moving down the hall in a daze, a faint smile on her lips. Maggie suspected she was once again visualizing herself as the intrepid amateur sleuth.

31

There was no question that Penny was a whiz in the kitchen. Her breakfast was every bit as good as the cold supper the night before. There were eggs, pancakes, breakfast potatoes, ham and bacon and sausages. She had homemade bread to eat plain or toasted. There were buttermilk biscuits, three kinds of muffins, and a coffeecake. Even the jams and jellies seemed to be homemade. The Quilting Bee women praised the meal so much, Penny actually looked embarrassed.

"Now I know what a compliment it was when Kate purchased my muffins at the bazaar every year," Maggie said. "She always said they reminded her of yours."

Victoria smiled. "Maggie spends a whole day making her muffins for the bazaar bake sale."

"We all bake for it," Edie said. "Do you ever share your recipes? Because I would love to have one for this coffeecake."

"It is wonderful, Penny," Victoria agreed. "It reminds me of the one my Aunt Jane used to make. She was the best baker in the family and would always make her coffee-cake for holidays and special occasions." Victoria smiled at Penny. "I haven't thought of her for years. It's a shame because I have some very pleasant memories of Aunt Jane."

Penny's cheeks turned pink with pleasure. "I don't mind sharing my recipes, but I have to tell you I often make impromptu changes, so your results might not be the same."

The women assured her that was fine.

"I'll have a copy for you when you get back," she promised. "I have all my recipes on the computer. Kate taught us how to do so much with it. She set up a simple book-keeping system and organized my recipes for me." She smiled, proud of her talented child.

"Don't you and Earl eat breakfast?" Edie asked, helping herself to more of the straw-berry jam.

"Oh, we ate over an hour ago. Earl likes to get an early start and then have a long walk with the dogs. He used to run, but his knees can't take that anymore."

"You have a dog?" Clare asked, always eager to swap stories with another dog lover.

"Yes, two beagles." Penny smiled. "We always had a dog when Kate was growing up, too. We keep them back in our apartment so they won't bother the guests."

"Kate had a beagle, too," Clare said.

Penny's eyes clouded, but she quickly recovered. "Yes, that was Snoopy. The twins named him. We have him here with us now. Luckily, he gets on well with our old dog."

"So that's what happened to him!" Clare seemed delighted to hear that Penny and Earl had taken in the dog. "Kenny wondered what had become of him. He worried that he might have died in the fire."

Penny turned a puzzled look toward Clare. "Kenny? But . . . Kenny's been missing ever since . . ."

"How could you know what Kenny's wondering?"

Earl's voice thundered into the quiet room. He must have returned from his walk just as the subject of the dog came up. It was also obvious to Maggie that he was the one who didn't wish to speak of Kate. Penny had been happily reminiscing about her last night and this morning.

Clare looked earnestly into the faces of Kate's parents.

"A week ago, I drove off the road in a bad storm and ended up unconscious in a ditch.

Kenny saved my life. He was camping out in a burned-out cabin below the Mogollon Rim. He told me that he was innocent."

"Well, what else would he say?" Earl sounded exasperated.

Despite the man's intimidating frown, Clare didn't give up. "He also said that Kate was acting strange after he came home from Iraq and that he thought there might be a man stalking her."

Maggie silently thanked the Lord that Clare had not proffered Kenny's theory of an affair. She could imagine what Earl would think about *that.*

Still, there was an audible gasp from Penny at the mention of a stalker.

Clare looked right at her as she continued. "He said she was nervous and seemed to be afraid. He thought it might have been someone she met on one of her part-time jobs."

Penny and Earl exchanged a puzzled look. It was obvious even to Clare that they had no idea what she might be talking about.

"Anyway, Kenny is convinced that's who killed Kate and the girls, and he's been trying to find proof to take to the police."

The couple's faces remained stonily set. They could have been posing for Grant Wood's *American Gothic.*

"She might have been afraid of *him*," Earl finally said. "Going to war changes a man. I saw it happen in 'Nam . . . You see things, do things. It changes you. I was lucky with Penny here, but a lot of my buddies had their marriages break up after they returned. And with Kenny, he had PTSD. Kate told us," he added, glaring at Clare. It was as if he wanted her to know that he knew about Kenny and his problems and he wasn't going to let her persuade him of his innocence.

"It frightened her," he continued. "And it turned out she was right to be frightened."

Without another word, he turned and left the room. The quietness of his exit had a greater impact than if he'd stomped out of the room and slammed the door. The solemnity of his departure emphasized it and highlighted his despair.

Her mouth tight with emotion, Penny apologized for her husband.

"There's no need to apologize," Maggie said. "He's upset about losing Kate, and that's as it should be."

"Did you see Kate much when Kenny was away?" Clare asked.

Penny didn't embrace the topic. She answered in a dull voice.

"We tried to get Kate to bring the girls and come stay with us. We thought it must

271

be hard for her, being alone. We didn't even think about the financial repercussions. I could tell she was feeling a lot of stress, but I thought it was from being alone with two little ones to care for. I knew she must be lonely and starving for adult company. She never was one to make friends easily, and I know she didn't have close girlfriends. She was so taken up with Kenny and the twins."

"She was a wonderful mother," Clare said.

Penny barely seemed to hear. Now that she was speaking about Kate's more recent past, she seemed almost trancelike.

"And Kate didn't want to come here with the girls?" Maggie's voice was gentle, almost reluctant to ask a question where the answer might be painful.

"She didn't want to leave her home. She was afraid they might lose the house. That's why she took those jobs, to try to help out. She loved that house."

Maggie shook her head. *That poor girl,* she thought. So much was happening to her, she must have felt unable to cope.

"Kenny told me he thought someone was stalking her. She never said anything to you about that?" Clare still hoped to prove Kenny's theory correct.

"No. She did say that Kenny was beginning to act jealous — which he never had been. Also that he was getting extremely paranoid. I guess the two went together. It bothered her as much as the dreams he would have that disturbed their sleep."

Clare nodded. "He said that he would go off to camp out on his own when he had too many of those episodes. Because he was afraid he might hurt her."

"She worried about that, too."

"Do you know if he ever signed up at the VA for treatment of the condition?" Maggie asked.

Clare jumped in. "He said he did."

"I asked Penny." Maggie's voice was firm. She wanted an answer from Penny.

Penny shook her head. "She said he didn't. That she kept getting after him to go in, but that he didn't want to. I guess he had gone down a couple of times. But there's a lot of paperwork, and the lines are so long everything takes hours. The first time, she said he waited for five hours and still wasn't called in to see someone. So he left. He said it was the same the second time, that he waited four hours. But that's what he told her. I don't know if it's true."

"I think it is," Maggie answered. "Our friend Louise has been doing a lot of reading about PTSD since Clare had her run-in with Kenny, and she's learned the VA is heavily understaffed. So many of the returning vets are having problems and they've been slow to respond. She said four- to five-hour waits are not unusual."

"The one thing we've discovered in talking to people who knew Kate," Victoria said, "is that they noticed a change in her a week or two before she died. They describe her as looking ill. But no one seems to know what the trouble was."

"A woman who worked with Kate heard she was going to quit her job," Clare said. "The one at the pharmacy. Kate also made a strange comment to her about accusing someone — that it wouldn't be right to accuse someone unless she could be absolutely sure."

"Do you have any idea what Kate might have been referring to?" Maggie asked.

"No." Penny looked upset. "I have no idea. I didn't know . . ."

Without another word, she hurriedly left the room, taking the same path Earl had used.

32

The women enjoyed their day in Laughlin.
As Dr. Sandoval had promised, getting away
helped them relax. Clare and Maggie specu-
lated about whether the vitamins and
supplements he'd recommended were helping them feel better physically. Or just
providing that illusion.

They all felt good as they headed back
across the river. In fact, Clare was lobbying
for another quick trip the next morning,
then leaving for Scottsdale after lunch. Edie
mumbled about addictive personalities and
gambling compulsions, though she didn't
seriously oppose the plan. She'd had a good
time shopping, and praised a show she'd
seen.

"I seem to have more energy since I've
been taking those supplements from Nature's Best," Clare said. "And I won that
two-thousand-dollar jackpot. I still can't
believe it. Wait until Gerald hears," she said

happily. "It must be an omen, don't you think? That other good things will happen? Things always happen in threes."

"Except when they don't." Edie's dry tone caused a bit of laughter.

They were still smiling when they entered the bed and breakfast. But a "breaking news" report changed everything. Penny and Earl were in the sitting room, the large television on. Earl's face was grim, Penny's streaked with tears.

"Watching a sad movie?" Victoria asked, smiling at the couple. The happy group of women bore a stark contrast to their host and hostess.

"They cut into my program with some breaking news," Earl announced. "It's a house explosion, in Phoenix."

Penny's already pale face lost even more color.

As one, the women turned toward the television screen. They had been concerning themselves with another recent house explosion, and they didn't happen that frequently, even in a large city.

Victoria saw a tea pot on the coffee table and poured out a cup, stirring in two teaspoons of sugar. She placed the sweet tea into Penny's hand. The cup rattled in its saucer, and Victoria reached out, placing

276

her hand on Penny's arm. She hoped to offer comfort and was encouraged to see the other woman bring the cup up to her lips. It had only been six months since she'd lost her entire family in an explosion.

"It's Scottsdale," Clare said, reading the place name showing at the bottom of the screen.

"Oh, my." Maggie leaned forward, staring hard at the television, as though that would make it spew out more information. "It's K.C. Gilligan's house."

Victoria could no longer ignore the report. This was too much of a coincidence. She gave Penny a last quick look, to be sure she was all right, and shifted her attention to the television.

Penny, looking a little better, turned to Maggie when she identified the home. "Do you know him?"

"He belongs to our church," Maggie said.

"And Kate used to work for him," Clare said. "He has a large car dealership in Scottsdale and is very active in the parish. We heard that he used to stop by and take her and the kids out while Kenny was in Iraq."

If possible, Penny's face became even paler. Victoria turned her attention back to her, worried that she might faint.

"Oh." Penny suddenly appeared to realize who it was they referred to. "I remember her saying that her boss would take them all out for pizza sometimes. He didn't have children of his own and liked to visit with the girls."

Victoria nodded. "K.C. regretted not having any children. He apparently takes an interest in the children of his employees."

"It's that Kenny," Earl suddenly said, his voice thundering through the quiet room. "I'll bet he's involved in this."

It didn't take long for the media to make the same connection. Then they were replaying footage from the Upland tragedy. Happily, Penny had left the room by then, escorted out by a disgusted Earl.

"They should have caught him by now," he muttered, as they left for their private quarters.

The newscasters continued to detail the particulars of the two episodes, mentioning the wanted fugitive. But to Maggie and Edie, the differences were more apparent than the similarities.

"There's no fire," Maggie said. "Or if there was, they put it out quickly." Her clearest memory of the May disaster was of flames leaping from the damaged house.

"And there are no bodies inside," Edie said.

"What about K.C.?" Clare had gone almost as pale as Penny. "They haven't said if he was there."

Victoria leaned in toward Maggie's ear, keeping her voice very soft. "Remember when Edie said that if we heard K.C. died in a house explosion, then we'd know?"

Maggie nodded. She'd been thinking the same thing, and Edie probably was, too. She didn't know about Clare, who seemed able to keep facts limited to what she wanted to hear.

Reporters were broadcasting from in front of Gilligan's car dealership, showing the employees looking concerned about the owner's whereabouts. But no one seemed to know where K.C. was. Maggie began to fear that he might have been inside the house after all.

33

The Quilting Bee women decided to stay in front of the television through the entire news program, as there was often an update on the big story at the very end of the broadcast. There was still no word on the whereabouts of K.C. Gilligan. Neither was there a report of a body in his home. The women all knew they would not release a name without notifying relatives first. Edie, however, felt sure the news media would have relished reporting the presence of a body, had there been one.

"That kind of thing is hard to keep secret when so many people are involved in a scene. It would have leaked out by now."

Her confident tone convinced the others, who instantly felt better. None of them wanted to think another death had occurred.

At ten-twenty, Clare's cell phone rang. Wide-eyed, she turned to the others after answering, mouthing "Kenny" to them. She didn't seem to know what to do, so perhaps she was no longer so convinced of his innocence, Maggie thought.

"Put him on speaker phone," Maggie suggested.

Clare fumbled with the small keypad for a moment, then held the phone awkwardly in front of her. They all heard the tinny voice coming from the small phone.

"Are you still willing to talk to me? Did Kate's parents poison you against me?"

"What?"

Clare couldn't hide her surprise, even though Kenny had already told her something to this effect in his earlier call. To Maggie, it was just another sign of his paranoia.

"Of course I'll talk to you," Clare said. "The Montgomerys have been excellent hosts. Your mother-in-law is a wonderful cook," she added.

There was a momentary silence from the other end, though Maggie was sure she could hear some deep, almost panting breaths. As though Kenny was trying to get himself under control. Victoria must have heard it, too, because she raised her eyebrows as she met Maggie's eyes.

Finally, in a thick, resigned voice, Kenny

said, "They think I did it."

"Of course they think that. Now. What else can they think, with the police and media convinced of your guilt. It's up to you to prove them wrong. And we're doing what we can to help."

Maggie was pleasantly surprised by Clare's tough, businesslike tone of voice. And Kenny seemed to listen. He mumbled something that sounded like "I guess."

But enough of the same-old, same-old, Maggie decided. The timing of this particular call was no coincidence.

"Kenny, it's Maggie Browne. What do you know about the explosion at K.C. Gilligan's house this evening?"

"I know I didn't do it," he replied. "I want you to know that. I don't want him dead. I want him alive to answer for killing Kate and my girls."

Maggie, Victoria, Edie and Clare exchanged looks. They all knew that felons usually claimed innocence. There were no guilty men in prison; everyone knew that. Yet his statement about wanting to see K.C. pay — that held a ring of truth.

"Where are you? Can you prove you weren't in Scottsdale today?"

A heavy sigh preceded his words. "Of course not. I'm a fugitive on the run. I can't have people seeing me."

"Did you get a lawyer?" Edie asked.

"No. I wouldn't trust a lawyer. He'd turn me in."

Edie persisted. "But to prove your innocence, you're going to have to turn yourself in eventually."

"I'm not turning myself in until I can prove someone else did it."

Stubbornness was evident in his voice. Maggie almost expected him to hang up on them.

"I thought I was getting close with K.C. and that stuff you told me about the sexual harassment," Kenny continued. "I've been doing some investigating myself, and it's true. He likes pretty young women around the place. There's a real high turnover among women between twenty and thirty."

"Tell us where you were today," Edie said. "Then we can know that you're telling the truth."

There was silence for a moment, before they heard a heavy sigh.

"Okay. I'm in Phoenix, in an area with a lot of homeless veterans. They know what it's like, coming back and having your whole life destroyed, so they aren't likely to turn me in. I was trying to see what I could learn about K.C. and I did find out a lot."

"So these other veterans you saw today are independent sorts, who aren't likely to vouch for you with the authorities," Maggie said.

"No. They don't go near authority figures. But there are other vets who help me out, and they would be more likely to be believed. But I'm not giving out names until it becomes absolutely necessary," he added, as though he knew what the next question would be. "Are you still in Bullhead City?"

"Yes," Clare replied. "We had a nice day at the casino with our friends. The Montgomerys have a great place here."

"Did they try to poison you against me?"

"Earl isn't too happy with you," Maggie said dryly.

"They always hated me. That's why it was so easy for them to blame everything on me."

The man is whining, Maggie thought. It was not an attractive feature in a grown man, especially one who was expecting you to take his word concerning some very serious issues.

"So K.C. is your main suspect in the fire at your house," Maggie said. "Though I don't see how you can extrapolate from a tendency to ogle young women and ratchet up to murder."

"Especially the murder of children," Edie said. "K.C. is fond of children in general and seemed especially close to your daughters."

"Also, it doesn't seem logical that he would destroy his own home just to frame you. Not without some knowledge that you were at least in the vicinity." Maggie shook her head, unable to see the sense in his argument.

"But that's where you're wrong."

In protesting her statement, Kenny's voice steadied into a firmness that commanded their attention.

"K.C. is having financial problems. He decided his empire wasn't big enough and opened another big dealership — over in Gilbert. You know he already has car lots in north Scottsdale and Mesa in addition to the place on McDowell. But it takes a lot of money to expand, and the economy hasn't been great. Plus gas prices keep rising. He's losing a lot of money. Cars aren't selling as well, and people are keeping the cars they already have a little longer. Going for the more fuel efficient models, instead of the big gas guzzlers. One of those new franchises he opened was for Humvees."

"So you're thinking that he could have burned his own home to collect on the insurance," Edie said.

"Sounds good to me," Kenny said. "And if he could do it in the same way they say I destroyed my house — well, why not implicate me further?"

"I don't think they ever released the details of how the explosion happened at your house," Maggie said.

"Just that the gas was left on," Edie said. "But something had to ignite it to cause a fire like that."

Leave it to Edie to know that, Maggie thought.

Kenny definitely sounded defensive now.

"K.C.'s house didn't burn. There was just a gas explosion."

Now how on earth did he know that? Maggie wondered. They'd seen it on television — over and over again. But Kenny claimed to be in a homeless camp. How had he learned so much already?

"Did you see the report on television?" she asked.

"No, there's no TV here. But I went to the library and checked the internet."

Interesting, Maggie thought. Wanted by the Scottsdale PD and the FBI, and he can just wander into a library and sign up for computer time.

"If K.C. did destroy his own house," Edie

said, "not having it burn afterward could save a lot of his belongings."

"It's something to consider," Maggie agreed.

"Kenny's house burned," Clare said. They all recalled the leaping flames captured by a neighbor's video camera. They didn't need the replays they'd seen this evening to remember that. "How could he have a gas explosion without burning down the house?"

"I don't know," Kenny said. "I don't know about explosives."

"You didn't learn anything about explosives while you were in Iraq?" Edie challenged. "They seem to be everywhere over there."

There was a brief silence. Maggie noted that no sounds came from his side of the line. It wasn't anything like television, where there was sure to be a train whistle, or ambulance sirens, or some other unique noise to help pinpoint where the call originated.

"I drove a truck in Iraq," Kenny finally said. "We delivered supplies. Mostly, we had to figure out how to avoid being killed by IEDs."

There was a short moment of silence while they digested this.

He didn't exactly answer the question, Maggie thought. And the look Victoria sent her way told her that her friend noticed the omission, too.

Clare, as usual, remained oblivious.

"Do you know anything about Tyler Gilligan?" Clare asked.

"Tyler Gilligan?" he repeated. "Ah, yeah, that was that son of Gilligan's wife that turned up. He talked about it to the youth group one time. He was real proud of the fact that he'd forgiven his wife, and then accepted her illegitimate child as part of his family."

"Did Tyler volunteer at the church, too?" Clare asked.

"No, I don't think so. I never saw him there. I don't think he's a Catholic."

They heard a murmur from Kenny's side of the line, as though someone were calling out to him.

"Look, I gotta go. I hope you don't believe all this bad stuff about me, that's all I wanted to say."

And with that, he broke off the connection.

The women weren't sure what to think. They sat in silence for some time after the call ended.

"Do you still think he's innocent?" Edie

288

asked, looking at Clare.

Clare answered right away, but her lower lip seemed to tremble. Just a bit.

"Kenny saved my life. Yes, I'm sure he didn't kill his family."

"We haven't been able to find a motive for anyone else to kill Kate," Maggie said. "Or the children. It's the brutality of killing the children that points to passionate emotion and so to a family member. Or to mental illness. Kenny is still the best possibility, just because of the PTSD."

Clare shook her head. "He saved my life." Her head was set at a stubborn angle. "I just know he couldn't have killed Kate and the girls. He saved my life," she repeated, "and it must have been a danger to him, being out there on the road helping me when there's a reward out for his capture." She took a deep breath. "There must be something we can do to help him. He's not the horrible person people think."

The others knew she would not be talked out of her belief in him.

"You've already helped others see that, Clare," Maggie told her. "By telling everyone how he helped you."

This made Clare smile a little, for which Maggie was grateful.

34

Any possible plans to return across the river were scrapped in light of events in Scottsdale. The women awoke early, partook of Penny's excellent breakfast, then listened to the television news before starting the drive back. They were relieved to learn that K.C. had turned up in good health. He'd driven to Tucson for a dinner meeting the night before, then listened to CDs on the drive north. He was unaware of what had happened to his house until he arrived home around midnight.

Still, the women kept the news/talk station turned on as they debated the importance of Kenny's information about K.C.'s business and financial situation. There was speculation about issues that might factor in to what had happened. They couldn't argue with the fact that the whole country was in an economic downturn. Gas prices were sky high; raises were slow in coming.

Many businesses were closing, some of them long-established and with good reputations.

"Gerald liked to get a new car every year when he was still working, but not very many people do that anymore," Clare said.

"I don't know," Victoria said. "While all of that makes a lot of sense, I don't see how K.C. could imagine that the insurance company would just pay him if he's in financial straits. It's such a cliché to attempt to get out of business troubles by torching a business for the insurance. If his business is in financial trouble, that should be the *last* thing an intelligent man would do. And K.C. is smart."

"But if he can pin it on Kenny," Clare said. "Don't you see how he could think that? It didn't take the TV stations long to decide it was like the Upland fire and start talking about the similarities."

"True. The insurance company is going to look hard at him before parting with any money. He'll have to have an alibi for the time that they think the device was set."

"But he could have hired someone," Edie said. "That's what I would do."

The others laughed uneasily.

"But who set the fire?" Victoria asked. "Kenny thinks K.C. set the gas to explode at his house. But it doesn't make sense that K.C. would do the same thing to his own house."

"It has to be him," Clare said, passion in her voice. She'd given her loyalty wholeheartedly to Kenny, even though she professed to like K.C. At least she had before Kenny saved her life and started her looking into his case. "He's still trying to frame poor Kenny. You heard the reporters on TV last night. They all mentioned him right away, saying it was just like the Upland fire, and Kenny is still missing. They may not have said outright that it was Kenny, but they sure implied it."

"If they continue to blame Kenny, K.C. should be able to collect the insurance easily enough," Edie said. "Probably has a lot of it, too. That was a nice house."

35

The Browne family had a perfect early November day for their brunch that Sunday. As they gathered after mass, temperatures hovered in the mid-seventies, with highs expected to hit the low eighties. The sun shone comfortably warm on the lawn where they set the picnic tables.

Maggie's sons teased her about the Laughlin trip and whether she'd won enough to assure their inheritance.

"So, how come you decided to drive up?" Hal asked.

"We thought it would be a nice relaxing trip if we could stay overnight."

"Girls gone wild!" Frank suggested, causing his brothers to laugh.

"Also, Clare wanted to talk to the Montgomerys," Maggie added. She'd considered not mentioning this part of it, but she didn't like keeping secrets from her sons. And she wanted to see if they had any useful information.

"I should have known," Michael muttered.

"The Montgomerys?" one of Maggie's daughters-in-law asked.

Maggie explained about the couple who ran the bed and breakfast and who they were related to. "It's a very nice B&B," she finished. "And Penny is an amazing cook."

"So, did Clare learn anything from them?" Hal asked.

"Not much," Maggie admitted. "They don't like to talk about Kate, and especially not about her death."

"That's to be expected," Sara said, and Maggie nodded her agreement.

"Earl, especially, got very upset whenever Kenny was mentioned. We did some reminiscing with Penny, however, recalling happier times with Kate. And we learned that it was unlikely there was an old boyfriend in Kate's past who could have turned up at this late date and killed her."

"I guess you heard about the Gilligan house," Hal said.

Maggie nodded. "We watched the coverage on TV."

"It was hard to avoid." Sara stopped short of rolling her eyes.

"So you heard that they suspect Kenny

294

Upland," Frank said.

"Kenny told Clare he didn't do it." Maggie took a sip of her iced tea, not noticing Michael's sharp look. "And the explosion was different. Both may have been caused by leaving the gas jet on and dousing the pilot light, but there was a huge fire at the Uplands. It's what everyone remembers from the news coverage, the flames leaping from the remains of the house. None of the footage I saw of Gilligan's house showed any flames. Just a large hole where the wall of a room had blown out."

"Wait a minute!" Bobby's brows drew together as he looked at his mother. "Clare saw Kenny last week. How could he tell her he didn't do it?"

"Ma . . ." Michael had that warning tone is his voice. At six foot two and 200 pounds of solid muscle, it was sometimes hard to remember that he was her baby. He took the "guard and protect" aspect of his job seriously, especially when it came to his mother's well-being.

Maggie took her time answering. She wanted to give him her mother's stare for a moment — the one that would make him feel guilty for yelling at the woman who birthed him.

"He called. While we were still watching

the news reports, in fact."

"He calls her?" Michael asked.

Maggie nodded. "This is the third time that I know of. He called her at home the first time, and Gerald got pretty mad."

"As he should," Michael said. "No matter what Clare says, Gerald can't be sure it's safe for her to associate with a wanted fugitive."

Maggie nodded her understanding. "He's called on her cell since then. He wasn't happy to hear we were going to Bullhead City. He thought the Montgomerys would poison us against him — I think that's how he put it." Maggie shook her head. "I know Clare believes firmly in his innocence, but he can sound like a whining child sometimes."

Michael sighed. "So you talked to him, too?"

"Not exactly. Clare put him on speaker phone so we could all hear."

"You realize I'll have to report this?"

This was something Maggie had not thought about, but she realized now that she'd put Michael in a difficult position by telling him about the phone calls. Of course he would have to report it. She hoped Clare would understand that she hadn't done it on purpose.

She nodded. "I don't know how much good it will do. I assume he's using those throwaway phones you hear so much about on television detective shows."

Clare would claim she'd said too much, revealing the phone calls from Kenny, but Maggie didn't think anyone would be able to find him from such vague information. She didn't understand everything about how the technology worked, but she knew there would not be someone in a basement with a tape recorder and earphones — like the phone taps portrayed in old movies. A cell phone would be harder to trace, and she thought it could only pinpoint the particular tower the signal came from. That had to encompass a wide area.

And what if they did find Kenny? Wasn't it about time he turned himself in anyway and tried to work within the system to prove his innocence? With information from him, the police might be better able to discover what really happened back in May.

But, on the off chance the police were able to find Kenny from the information that he was making cell phone calls . . . she hoped Clare would forgive her.

"Kenny did tell us something interesting," Maggie said. "He started looking at K.C. as a suspect in the deaths of his family after

Clare told him she'd heard rumors of sexual harassment. And he claims K.C.'s business is in financial trouble. He suggested K.C. destroyed his own home in order to collect the insurance."

"And what?" Michael's skepticism launched his question. "He tried to frame Kenny for it by using the gas explosion?"

"Well, that's obvious, isn't it?" Sara said. Maggie silently blessed her for coming to her aid.

"K.C. is financially strapped at the moment," Hal said. "I've heard that from more than one source. He chose the wrong time to expand operations. He got good deals on the land for the new dealerships in the east valley, but his biggest expenditure is on inventory. Car dealers have a great deal of money tied up in inventory. And then the housing market crashed, and gas prices soared. The economy is hurting, and people aren't spending. They figure a new car is the least of their worries right now."

"That's what Edie said." Maggie looked down at her plate and decided she'd had enough breakfast. She pushed it toward the middle of the table and rested her arms on the cleared space.

"It makes a lot of sense," Sara said. "Except for the part about K.C. doing it for the insurance money. Surely he's too intelligent a man to try something as obvious as that."

"People can be pretty dumb," Michael said. "Especially when money is involved."

Merrie, who had taken the baby inside to nap, returned just then. "Did you get these baby greens at Nature's Best?" She gestured at the salad Maggie had provided as she helped herself to more. Not having been privy to the most recent discussion, she didn't realize she was changing the subject.

But Maggie thought it was probably time. She admitted that she had done her shopping at Nature's Best.

"It's delicious," Merrie said. "The sprouts give it such a nice nutty flavor. Did you get the greens packaged this way, or put it together yourself?"

"It was packaged," Maggie said. "I was talking to the produce manager there, and they actually put together their own combinations. That's why it's so fresh and so different."

"You seem to be spending a lot of time over there," Michael said with a frown.

"Better there than poking herself into your investigations, huh?" Bobby said, then laughed along with his other two brothers.

But Michael continued to frown.

36

After the trip to Laughlin, the Bee women were ready to get back to work. Senior Guild meetings in November and December were casual, more social than work oriented, as the various craft groups reviewed their projects and looked at the successes of the recent bazaar. There were last-minute expenses to tabulate and profits to tally. Final figures were usually not ready for Father Bob until December, but he always said it made the best Christmas gift of all, to have that money available for the aging parish's many needs.

So on the Monday after the Laughlin trip, many of the Senior Guild members lingered in the break room, or visited in the courtyard, discussing the past year and making plans for the coming one. However, in the Quilting Bee room, work continued at a constant level throughout the year. The quilters sewed continuously; as soon as one quilt was completed, it was wrapped in cotton muslin and stored in their closet. Every August, they made up an inventory with descriptions of all the quilts that were ready and sent it off to the agent who conducted the auction.

So while other groups relaxed until after the holidays, the Bee women pulled out their needles and thread and got on with it. Not only with their quilting, but with their exploration of Kenny's story. As Clare told them often throughout the morning, things were sure to improve; how could they not, with the auspicious way the day began?

There were two incidents, actually, that Clare slotted under "auspicious." First, Gladys brought in a quilt top for them, a beautiful string quilt — hundreds, perhaps thousands, of tiny strips of fabric sewn together in a wild swirl of color. Because they used the smallest of scraps, string quilts had been big in 1930s America. For the most part, those were utilitarian quilts, meant for everyday use by the families who made them, so most had not survived. But there were some extant in museums, and viewers oohed and aahed over them. How could they not, when the work involved was considered? Modern quilters still enjoyed the challenge of making string quilts; taking

301

the smallest bits of fabric and turning them into something big and beautiful was hard to resist.

"Gladys, that is a wonderful top," Victoria said, as she spread it over one side of the quilt frame so they could all admire it.

"Gorgeous," Anna agreed. "That's called the Spider Web, isn't it?" In the Spider Web pattern, the small pieces of fabric were sewed over a triangular paper foundation, then sewed into an octagonal block. The result resembled a spider web, hence the name.

"What a lot of work you put into it," Maggie said, running her fingertips gently over a block.

"I didn't know if you would be able to quilt it for the auction." Gladys's eyes shone at their praise, even as she wondered about the appropriateness of her choice.

"I don't know that it's a good top for hand quilting," Victoria, ever the diplomat, suggested. She said it slowly, as though it was something they had to consider. But she knew, as did the others, that it was not something they would want to hand quilt. For one thing, there were too many seams to stitch over. Also, it was too busy a pattern to show off the quilting stitches. Still, they didn't want to hurt Gladys's feelings.

Maggie was glad Gladys realized it was problematic.

"I can machine quilt it," Edie offered. "An overall pattern, with a variegated thread. Something curved and swooping, I think, to contrast with the straight lines of the design. It will turn out very well."

Everyone relaxed.

"Oh, I'm so glad to hear that," Gladys said. She knew that Edie did exquisite work. "I don't need any more quilts myself, and I've made a lot of them for my children. I'm not sure they appreciate them the way they should, either. So I've decided to make them for the church from now on. I wanted to work with all my bits and pieces, but it wasn't until it was finished that I worried about the quilting of it. Since I don't hand quilt myself, I hadn't really thought about it until I was almost ready to bring it in."

While they were still admiring the top with Gladys, a new woman appeared at their door. She was of medium height and perhaps twenty pounds over her ideal weight. Her hair was still a deep, rich brown, but Maggie was sure it had some help in that regard. There were lines around her eyes and lips that told of age — and of laughter.

Anna rushed over to meet her, pulling her into the room to introduce her around.

"You all have to meet Theresa. Theresa Squires — her husband is Carl Squires, who does woodworking," she added, introducing her to the others one by one. "We sat together on the bus going out to Laughlin last week, and we had such a good time we sat together coming back, too."

Anna and Theresa exchanged smiles at that point, and everyone could see that they had indeed struck up an immediate friendship.

"I've just retired," Theresa told them. "On the thirty-first of October," she added with a little scrunch of her nose. "Halloween. There must be something ominous about that. But I've been looking forward to joining the Senior Guild for such a long time, Carl told me to come along on the Laughlin trip. Then I was mad because he went to sit with his friends on the other bus and left me all alone. But I'm so glad he did because then Anna got on board and asked if she could sit with me." She smiled at her new friend again. "And Anna encouraged me to come right in and join you all. I used to quilt years ago," she added. "But I'm afraid I'm more than a bit rusty. I don't know if I should really work on one of your fabulous quilts."

They all dismissed her concerns, welcoming her to the group.

"I've got to get going," Gladys said, welcoming Theresa to the Guild as well, then turning toward the door, only to be halted by Edie's voice asking her to wait.

"I brought in a top today, too," Edie continued. Reaching into her tote, she brought out a simple nine-patch in blue and white — *simple* being a relative word in association with a quilt like this one. It might look plain in its present state, with the solid white-on-white squares in between the blue nine-patch ones, but once the quilting stitches were added, it would be a thing of rare beauty. Edie had penciled the quilting stitch pattern — a feathered heart — onto the solid squares.

"Very nice," Anna said.

Gladys agreed. "I like blue and white quilts," she said, "even though I usually make scrap quilts myself. The blue and white ones have such serenity. They give a room a calmness just by being there."

"Oh, but it is a scrap quilt," Edie said. "You'll notice there are at least a dozen different blue fabrics comprising the nine-patch blocks. I decided to clean out the blue fabrics in my stash," she added, referring to the collection of fabric most quilters kept on hand.

"Perhaps we can work on this one next," Victoria suggested. "It is a calming quilt, and we could use that right now, don't you agree?"

"Good point," Louise said.

"Can you believe what happened to K.C.'s house?" Gladys said. "It was just like Kenny's. What do you think, Clare? Did he do it?"

"Of course not." Clare's reply was prompt. "He even called to tell me that, that night, right after the news report."

"He called you?" Theresa seemed stunned by this news. "My goodness, he's a fugitive, no one has been able to find him in the past six months, and he's calling you."

"He did save my life," Clare reminded her. "He knows that I believe his story that he didn't kill his family. I promised to help him prove it, too, but it's not easy."

An understatement, Maggie thought, as they began to take their seats around the frame. As Anna gestured Theresa over next to her, Maggie caught her trying to hide a secret smile. *Just like a cat who'd gotten into the creamer,* Maggie thought. She didn't have to wait long to find out why.

"Theresa just retired after twenty years with her company," Anna announced, as they settled into place around the frame.

"You'll never guess where she worked," she added, unable to hide her grin any longer.

And that was Clare's second auspicious event. Or perhaps even the third. In later retellings, she sometimes counted both of the quilt tops that were brought in that morning.

"Gilligan's," Maggie said immediately.

Gladys had been heading for the door, but turned at that, and pulled up a chair.

Anna's grin faded. "Oh, I didn't think you'd guess so quickly."

Which made Maggie sorry she'd shown off that way. But, really, there wasn't any other choice. The grocery had only changed ownership a few years ago, and the online articles on the company said they started up a few years previous to that. And Maggie had never heard a preschool referred to as a "company."

She explained her reasoning to the others, even as she apologized to Anna.

"Maybe you can help us, with your insight into K.C.'s character," Clare said. "Did you work with him?"

"I was a cashier, in the service area," Theresa said. "K.C. is very hands-on. He likes to know all his employees personally. He knows almost everyone by name, and there are a lot of people working at the various dealerships." She took the threaded needle Anna offered and followed her instructions on how to make a proper quilter's knot. "But I don't understand. What does K.C. have to do with it?" Theresa asked. "Other than having his house destroyed, I mean. I don't understand how they reached the conclusion that Kenny did it, other than the fact that there were explosions in both cases."

"It's a little complicated," Clare said.

"A little!" Edie said. She jabbed her needle into the quilt top so hard Maggie was surprised it didn't go in all the way to the top of the eye.

"Kenny told me that he suspected Kate had an affair," Clare said.

"But we've pretty much abandoned that idea," Louise said quickly. "None of us believed it, and everyone else we've asked is shocked by the very notion."

"I'm not surprised," Theresa said. "I didn't know Kate very well, but she was the most shy and conservative young woman I've ever met."

Theresa held the threaded — and now properly knotted — needle in her hand, looking uncertainly at the quilt top. There was only a small amount of work left to be done on it, and she seemed reluctant to add her amateur stitches.

Anna noticed, and took a few minutes to help her start. "Here you are," she said, showing her how to pull her knot through so that it settled in the batt, between the layers of fabric. "You can just stitch along the pieced leaf here. It's a nice straight line, and that will let you practice before we get to those beautiful feathered hearts in Edie's nine-patch."

As though she was just waiting for Theresa to get settled, Clare began to speak.

"Kenny said he came to the conclusion that Kate was having an affair because she had changed so much in those last weeks before she died. And he said the girls talked about a man coming around to the house while he was gone." Clare nodded, as though it was the only conclusion he could have reached.

"That's a man for you," Edie said. "Mention a male visitor and the first thing he thinks is she must be having an affair."

"It was probably K.C. visiting the kids while Kenny was gone," Theresa said.

"How did you know that?" Clare said. "That's what we found out, after talking to some of their neighbors, like Gladys here," she said, nodding toward Gladys, who listened avidly. "But you knew immediately.

Do you live near the Uplands?"

"No. After Carl retired we moved into those condos out on Hayden. But that's just the way K.C. is. He used to come over to our place all the time when I first started working there, when the kids were young. And I wasn't even a single mother." She noticed Gladys's start of surprise and added, "I know Kate wasn't either, not really, but she was effectively a single parent while Kenny was gone. I started working there right after my youngest started school, and K.C. would often come over after work, bring pizza, and take them to the park. He just loves small children. Once, he took us all out to the Wildlife Park. It's just such a shame that he and Rosemary never had kids."

"I wonder why they never adopted," Anna said, "because everyone says the same thing about him and children."

"I asked him once," Theresa admitted. "After I'd been there a while, and I knew him well. He said that he and Rosemary just kept thinking they would have them on their own. Then it got too late to adopt. They frown upon older parents, you know. And Rosemary insisted on a baby, and there just aren't many babies available. The girls keep them these days. There isn't the stigma attached to unwed motherhood, not like back in the fifties and sixties. And then, once Rosemary got the cancer, that was it. They don't let anyone with a terminal illness adopt."

"I guess that's why he took in Tyler," Maggie said.

"Oh, that was something!" Theresa said. She stopped sewing to tell them all about it; it was difficult for her to stitch and talk at the same time.

"Tyler had been adopted as an infant, out in California. But as soon as he was eighteen, he started searching for his real parents. He was twenty-one by the time he found Rosemary. K.C. told us all about it later. It was quite a shock, not only for her, but for him. As you can imagine. She'd had the baby when she was in high school, only fifteen or sixteen. And her parents had sent her off to a relative in California until she had the baby and had it adopted."

"My granddaughter told me that K.C. talked about it to the youth group," Louise said. "How these things happen and how he'd forgiven his wife and taken in her son."

Edie sniffed. "Forgiven his wife. Honestly. Why should he have to forgive her for something that happened so long ago, probably years before they met."

"That's the way a lot of men feel though," Victoria said.

"Did he take Tyler into the business right away?" Clare asked. "We all knew he didn't have children, so we were surprised to see Tyler Gilligan listed among the company employees. And Edie found him listed in some earlier papers as Tyler Harris-Gilligan."

"I suggested we try looking into things the way real private investigators do," Edie told Theresa. "So we all tried checking on the places where Kate used to work, to see what kind of information we could come up with."

Theresa nodded, as though it all made perfect sense. Personally, Maggie thought the poor woman looked a bit overwhelmed. Not necessarily from the stitching, though she was nervous about it, but from the personalities of the Bee women and the unusual subject matter.

"The thing that really bothered K.C., and the reason he probably phrased it that way . . ." Theresa stopped, as though planning how to best form her sentence. "It wasn't just the shock of discovering that Rosemary had a son from her teen days. He learned that she'd always feared that the reason she couldn't have children was that something had gone wrong when she had that first baby. She was in labor for a long time, and the fetus went into distress, so she had to have an emergency C-section. So when she married K.C. and then couldn't seem to get pregnant, she worried about that being the cause. She was so embarrassed about being pregnant so young, she'd never told K.C., so how could she mention it to the doctor? She was afraid the doctor would tell him."

"She never told her doctor she'd already had a child?" Louise was startled. "But that could have had major ramifications for her and her health. Especially if she had gotten pregnant, and had an RH factor problem. They have to know about previous pregnancies. For a lot of reasons."

"Louise is a registered nurse," Victoria told Theresa. She thought that would explain her vehemence. And Theresa's strange expression did soften once she heard this.

"We also heard that K.C. has a problem with sexual harassment," Edie said.

Whoa, Maggie thought. *Nothing like a rapid change of topic.* Didn't Edie realize that Theresa was a friend of K.C.'s? And a good friend, from the sound of it. She hoped Edie didn't cause Theresa to resent them and stay away in the future. Theresa seemed like

313

a nice woman who would be a good addition to the Bee.

But Theresa was not offended. In fact, she chuckled.

"Oh, that." She waved a hand in dismissal. "That comes up all the time with K.C. He definitely appreciates a beautiful woman. Some of the young women don't like it, and leave. But, as far as I know, it's never gone beyond that. He was faithful to Rosemary, I'm sure of it. I did hear that when he was younger he liked to slap people on the rear, but he apparently matured enough to know he couldn't do that and stay in business — at least with the sterling reputation he likes to maintain."

Clare frowned, but it was with frustration, Maggie knew, not anger or unhappiness at Theresa's words.

Gladys said goodbye, but had one parting remark. "Kenny should have known that nothing was going on with Kate if the girls talked about a man coming over. If she was fooling around, she would have been much more circumspect."

There were several nods of agreement from the stitchers as they settled back to their quilting.

"You said your husband is part of the Guild?" Edie asked.

Theresa nodded. "Yes. Carl Squires. He retired last year, and one of the guys in the Knights of Columbus talked him into joining the Guild this past summer. He was getting bored hanging around the house, and he found he really liked it here. Not only being with the other men, but doing something to help out the parish."

"I wish I could get Gerald involved, but he prefers golf," Clare said.

"This talking and stitching at the same time is really hard. How long will it take for me to be able to do it the way you all do?" Theresa took a few careful stitches, pulled them through, then frowned at the result. "My stitches aren't nearly as nice as yours."

The others encouraged her to keep at it.

"It takes practice," Victoria told her. "And everyone knows these quilts are quilted by a group, so they don't expect every stitch to be just alike. There are bound to be differences from one quilter's work to another."

With little more to be said for the time being, they quilted in silence. Victoria turned on the radio they kept in the room, a small CD player/radio combination that Maggie had contributed a few months previously. It was on an oldies station, and "California Dreaming" played.

Soon, Anna began speaking to Theresa

about moving on to the nine-patch quilt, either by the end of the day's session or the next morning. She explained the quilting pattern they would be stitching on the open squares, and how she, Theresa, could continue to practice by working on the pieced nine-patch blocks, where a simple series of cross-hatching lines would be worked. The others contributed comments from time to time. Everyone but Victoria.

"You're very quiet, Victoria," Maggie finally said.

"I was thinking about Gladys's string quilt," she said, with one of her gentle smiles.

"It's really something," Louise said. "The work that she must have put into it!"

"I can't even imagine sewing all those little pieces together," Theresa said. "I like nice big pieces, maybe four inches square."

"It's a beautiful quilt," Victoria agreed. "And it must have been a great deal of work. But that wasn't what got me thinking. Contemplating, perhaps would be a better word."

She took her time finishing off a thread and cutting another length from the spool. As she carefully lined up the tip with the eye of the needle, she continued.

"I was thinking of how many hundreds of

pieces are in it, and hundreds of different fabrics as well. And yet they all come together to make one beautiful quilt."

She finished knotting the thread and found the spot where she'd left off. It only took a moment for her practiced movement to sink the knot between the layers of fabric and batt.

"There's a quote from Jesse Jackson," Victoria continued. "I don't recall the exact wording, but it's something to the effect that America is not like a blanket, made up of one piece of cloth, but is like a quilt, with many pieces, all held together by a common thread."

There were several nods of agreement as the other Bee members showed their appreciation for the sentiment.

"That's how we are here, in this neighborhood," Victoria said. "Many different people, different races, different religions, different backgrounds. And yet together, we've created a community that's a good place to live."

"Why that's beautiful, Victoria," Anna said.

"Yes, it is," Theresa agreed. Now that she was no longer talking, she could concentrate on forming even and concise stitches, and her confidence grew along with the line of stitches.

"It's kind of like solving mysteries, too," Clare said. "Taking lots of tiny bits and pieces and putting them together until they make a whole picture."

Anna smiled at Clare. Maggie, however, resisted an urge to frown. Leave it to Clare to come up with that one.

"True," Maggie said. "That's what the police do, after all."

"But so do we," Clare insisted, proud of their contributions to the solving of past crimes.

Theresa looked up. "I've heard about how the Quilting Bee helped solve some mysteries."

"I think that was a lot of luck," Maggie said. "Because we knew the people involved, which gave us insight the police didn't have."

"But that's the same situation with Kenny," Clare said, a triumphant tone in her voice. "We know him; we knew his family. And we know people they knew, the people Kate worked with. The people Theresa here worked with for so many years." Her hands came off the quilt to gesture toward the newcomer. "That's why we have to help. The police are too busy and too biased to get to the bottom of it. There's a common thread, all right, and it has to do with Kate and her working while Kenny was away. I don't think the police have done much with that. They decided right away that Kenny was guilty and that's been it."

Maggie hated to slight the police force that way. She did believe in the American system of justice, believed that it worked. For the most part.

But in Kenny's case, she was afraid that Clare might be correct. And while she'd like to believe that the FBI was helping to solve the puzzle, she had heard too much about their burden of work with homeland security to think that they would be a lot of help regarding such a small, local case.

"I'm not sure all crimes are suitable for solving by amateur sleuths," Maggie said. "Despite their success in so many of our favorite mystery novels," she added, with a smile for Clare.

"Maybe not," Clare conceded. "But this one case is perfect for amateurs. Like Victoria said, there are hundreds of pieces to this story. Lots of lives intersecting. Bits and pieces of lives, lives that influenced Kate, leading to her death. When you're making a quilt, not all of the pieces can work in the final top. You know that. Sometimes you have to take out a piece of fabric because it just doesn't fit in. We have to find the pieces here that don't fit."

Maggie thought that might be taking the metaphor too far.

Anna seemed to think so, too. "But you're right, you know. There must be hundreds of people who were involved, even though Kate lived such a quiet life. How can we ever find them all, much less fit them all together?"

"We know the people in this neighborhood. We can talk to them like the friends we are. They're likely to tell us more than they would tell the police. It's a perfect case for us to help with. And we've already done a lot," Clare insisted. "Think of all the people we talked to and all the information we got. We can't prove that she had an affair . . ."

"In fact, it is highly unlikely," Edie inserted.

"So that's one theory disproved," Clare said. Although she'd been reluctant to abandon Kenny's favorite theory, she'd finally had to let it go. "Every bit helps. It's like Victoria said, we have to find the common thread. That's what will bring it all together."

Victoria quoted Sherlock Holmes. "When you have eliminated the impossible, whatever remains, however improbable, must be the truth."

"Oh, that's good," Clare said, giving Victoria a smile of approval.

"Sherlock Holmes," Theresa said with a smile.

Victoria and Clare both returned her smile.

"So you read mysteries, too?" Clare asked.

"Oh, yes. Not as much as I'd like to, but I hope to have more time to read now that I've retired."

As they began a discussion of favorite authors, Maggie concentrated on her stitches, her head bowed over the quilt. "A common thread," she murmured several times, running the words slowly over her tongue as though still working out some fragile new idea.

Slowly, too, the others began to notice. Soon quiet descended as they gave Maggie time to formulate whatever thought she was working on, knowing that she would let them in on it as soon as it took definite shape in her mind.

"Perhaps we've been going about this all wrong," she finally said.

"What do you mean?" Victoria asked.

"We've been following through on Kenny's theory," Clare said, as though defending their actions so far. She'd begun to take this personally. "He's in the best position to know what might have happened."

"But that's the problem. Kenny's theory might not be the correct one. We've pretty much discounted it. Even you've finally admitted that. No one who knew Kate — except Kenny himself, which is a bit strange — can believe that Kate would have an affair. It's just too far-fetched for anyone who knew her. Even a male stalker seems unlikely. So we have to try something else."

Victoria's quiet voice cut in before Clare had a chance to be offended.

"Kenny may be too emotionally invested in this to think logically."

"And he has the post traumatic stress problem which is also messing with his mind," Louise reminded them.

"But what else can we do?"

Clare's eyes had a waif-like look that pained her friends. It was obvious that Kenny wasn't the only one with deep emotional ties to the situation.

"That's the thing. We have to find the common thread." Maggie abandoned her stitching to look around the frame. She met each person's eyes briefly as she spoke her next sentence. "What connected Kate to all these various people?"

Clare looked puzzled. "Her job," she said. "She worked for them, doing bookkeeping work."

"That's right," Maggie said. "Everyone we've talked to has said that she was a marvel at bookkeeping. That it's how she was able to stay at home for so long — because she was so good with managing budgets and making a dollar stretch."

"But how does that help?" Clare asked, still puzzled.

"I don't know — yet," Maggie said. Happy with her new direction, Maggie picked up her needle again. "But that's the angle we should take. For instance, if K.C.'s business was having financial problems, why didn't we find anything about it when we did our online research?"

"Probably trying to keep that information private," Edie said. "Bad for business."

Instinctively, they all looked over to Theresa. Who frowned.

"News to me. I'd heard some rumors, but there are always rumors in business. Every year or two we'd hear that K.C. was going to sell and the new owner would want to downsize, or move the facility, or something. The land value has increased so much over the years that the original lot in Scottsdale is worth a fortune. In fact, it would probably be good business sense to sell the land to a developer and move the car lot to an outlying area."

Edie nodded. "That does make a lot of sense. With all the new development in downtown Scottsdale, the land is increasing in value all the time. This might be the right time to make that kind of a move."

"But would it be worth killing someone to keep that information a secret?" Anna asked. It was definite from her tight-lipped expression that she did not believe this to be true.

"Doesn't seem likely," Edie said. "It's bound to come out. After all, Kenny found out about it, didn't he? I'll bet we will, too, if we ask around."

Maggie nodded. "Hal said he'd heard the same thing, that K.C. was losing money after expanding, with the economy slowing down."

"These things happen, though," Theresa said. "Things will turn around soon enough."

"What about the other places where Kate worked?" Edie asked. "Has Hal heard anything about Nature's Best?"

"He didn't say anything about it, and we did talk about Nature's Best at brunch yesterday. But remember, that's not a local business based here in Scottsdale, like Gilligan's. Nature's Best started in Tucson and has more stores there."

"That leaves the preschool," Clare said.

"I'm not sure preschools are supposed to be money-making endeavors," Victoria said. "Especially when they're associated with churches."

"Well, they have to make enough to cover expenses," Edie said.

"There was some financial information on those grocery stores online," Louise said. "But I seem to recall that the articles said they were doing *better* than expected."

Maggie nodded. "Still, it's something to take into account. Any anomaly."

Clare was smiling broadly now. "I see what you're getting at, Maggie. Like something I've seen in books. Someone could be embezzling money, for instance. Or laundering money." Clare's eyes sparkled with excitement. "Oh, my, this is very exciting. You know what they always say — follow the money."

"Embezzling might explain why Gilligan's is in financial trouble," Edie said. "Everyone seems surprised to hear he has money problems. And he's supposed to be a great businessman. He's received awards from the

Better Business Bureau and some other organizations."

"That's true," Theresa said. "He seems to have a natural talent for seeing where to go next. Though if what you're saying is true, he may be losing his touch."

"Not necessarily." Anna seemed reluctant to let her friend believe the worse of her former boss. They could all see how much she admired him. "It's just that the economy is so bad at the moment. Things will improve. They always do."

"But who could be embezzling from K.C.?" Clare asked.

"No way for us to know," Maggie said. "And there are perfectly legitimate reasons for financial ills, too. Hal mentioned expanding too quickly for instance — something that has caused problems for bigger companies than Gilligan's."

She was about to turn to Theresa, to ask her opinion on who was in a position to tamper with funds at the auto dealership when several loud tones sounded from the radio. It was an attention-getting feature leading in to the station's special news bulletins.

"Just in," the reporter announced, his tones deep and somber. "A hiker in Papago Park has found a body, tentatively identified as that of Kenny Upland, a fugitive since the death of his wife and daughters six months ago."

37

"Oh, no." Clare, her eyes heavy with tears, made the sign of the cross.

Maggie reached for the volume dial and turned the radio up.

Louise sighed heavily. "Sad."

Victoria nodded. "But at least the poor man is at peace now. He's probably having a reunion with his family right now."

"That's a nice thought," Anna said.

"Most recently," the radio announcer continued, "he was named as a person of interest in a gas explosion rigged to destroy the home of car mogul K.C. Gilligan."

As the station returned to their music broadcast, Clare grabbed the radio and tuned in a news/talk station. As expected, they were covering this breaking story, and much more extensively. They had a short interview with the hiker who had come upon the body, after which they launched into the highlights of the Upland case, followed by the more recent Gilligan house explosion. The commentators spoke of the coincidence of the two explosions, talked of the relationship between the two men, then invited callers to join in.

Tears streamed down Clare's cheeks. "That poor man. Who could have killed him?"

"He's at peace now, Clare," Victoria said. She put her arm around Clare's shoulders.

Anna agreed. "He's with Kate and their girls." Although sad, her voice reflected the appropriateness of this.

"I know that some of you haven't been sure that Kenny is innocent," Clare said. "That you've been humoring me. But now we all know."

"Why would you say that?" Maggie looked genuinely puzzled.

"Because the person who did it killed him so that he can't uncover the truth! He must have been getting close."

Louise reminded Clare of something they'd heard. "Several people mentioned suicide in connection with Kenny, remember? Could it be that he killed himself, in a public place?"

"Oh, no . . ." Clare began. But then, perhaps realizing she didn't have enough information to question this last, she turned to Maggie. "You can ask Michael, Maggie. The police will know if it was suicide."

Maggie looked uncertain. "It wasn't in Scottsdale. Papago Park is in Phoenix. I don't know if Michael will know."

But Clare was not to be deterred. "He could find out. You know he could."

The women stitched in silence for the next hour as they listened to callers who recounted their experiences with the Uplands, or who lived close enough to experience the explosion that May day. Even Clare managed to settle down to some serious sewing, setting her stitches carefully, and calming down as she did so. She mumbled quietly the entire time, and Maggie thought she was praying for the soul of Kenny Upland.

Theresa, conscious of being the newcomer in a long established group, remained mostly silent. Until Clare suddenly looked up and suggested that perhaps K.C. had killed him.

"We know that Kenny thought he was the one responsible for killing his wife and children," she reasoned. "And K.C. probably thinks Kenny is responsible for destroying his house."

"Oh, no," Theresa said. "K.C. might leer at the young women at work. He may even have copped a feel in his early days at the dealership. But he just isn't capable of that kind of violence. You'll never make me believe he could become a killer, even if he thought the person had destroyed his home. I've known K.C. for twenty years, and he's a kind man. He loves children and animals. He could never kill someone, and he definitely could not kill children. I believe you can tell a lot about a person from the way that person treats animals."

Clare murmured her agreement, and Maggie and Victoria nodded.

"K.C. is a real soft touch when it comes to animals," Theresa continued. "Like he is with kids. He insisted on caring for the feral cats that came around the dealership when everyone told him to trap them and send them off to the city shelter. At first there were one or two cats that hung around the car lot, and people would share leftover sandwiches with them. When K.C. found out, he brought in a large bag of cat food and some bowls. Then he got some humane traps and caught them — not to turn over to the city shelter, but to have them spayed and neutered at his own expense. Then he'd bring them back and let them roam around the car lot. It became quite a project over the years and quite a large group of cats."

"What a lovely story," Anna said with a sigh.

"K.C. doesn't sound like a murderer," Victoria said. "It's unlikely that someone who loves animals that much could kill a human being in cold blood."

Reluctantly, Clare agreed. She was too much of an animal lover herself to look unfavorably on the person represented in Theresa's story.

"You explained why K.C. and Rosemary never adopted," Edie said. "Did they have animals? Lots of childless couples make dogs or cats into their children."

"No, Rosemary was allergic to dogs and cats both. She had asthma as a child. After she died K.C. told me he thought about getting a dog, but he's not home much and he didn't think it was fair to the animal."

"Hmm." Clare thought this over. "Seems like he could have gotten a companion-type dog and just taken him along to work. He's the boss. Lots of people take their dogs everywhere these days."

"Many people are afraid of dogs, and a lot are allergic," Louise said. "He wouldn't have wanted to lose customers because his dog scared them away, or made them sick."

"I hadn't thought of that." Being such a devoted dog owner herself, Clare always found it hard to believe other people didn't like them. Allergies made more sense.

Just as Louise spoke up about going for some tea, the talk show host broke in with another breaking news announcement.

"This just in. Kenny Upland was found in the desert this morning, in a remote area of Papago Park. Previous reports of his death have proven false. He is seriously injured and has been transported to a local hospital. Let me repeat. Kenny Upland has been found, seriously injured, in Papago Park, and is in critical condition at a local hospital."

Clare jumped up. "He's alive. I have to go light a candle." She rushed from the room.

Anna arose more slowly.

"I think I will, too," she announced, following Clare. "Light a candle for Kenny," she added, in case there was any doubt as to her meaning.

Theresa got to her feet, ready to join her new friend.

Louise too stood. "Why not?" she said.

Without further words, Maggie and Edie followed suit.

Victoria was the last to stand. "We Lutherans don't light candles," she said, "but I can certainly go with you all and say a prayer for his recovery."

■ ■ ■ ■

Fifteen minutes later, they left the church with Edie complaining about those new fangled candles.

"They just are not as satisfying," she said. "Striking a match and setting it to the wick has always been part of the process, and it just isn't the same."

The year before, St. Rose had updated the candles in the church, removing the old-fashioned and dangerous wax ones and installing electronic ones. You deposited your donation in the box, then pressed on the "wick" to light the candle. From a distance they looked real, but as many of the older parishioners agreed, they were just not the same.

"It's like watching Vanna touch the letters instead of turning them," Edie groused.

"Still, these are much safer," Anna said. "And progress can never be stopped."

"Do you think they'll let us visit him?" Clare asked, her mind still on Kenny rather than the church's new candles.

"If he's in bad shape, they might only allow family," Louise said.

"They'll have to let his lawyer see him," Edie said.

"I asked him last time, remember? He didn't have a lawyer."

"Maybe you could get one for him," Anna suggested.

"That's a bit presumptuous, don't you think?" Edie asked.

"He's probably not in any condition to hire someone himself." Clare bit her lip. "But I don't know if he can afford someone."

"The court will appoint a lawyer for him," Maggie said.

"But how long will that take?" Clare sounded worried. "He needs someone to protect his interests. And are the court appointed people any good? Do you think they're all young people just out of school?"

"I'm sure they must be competent," Victoria said, trying to be reassuring.

"I'm not sure anything can be done at the moment," Maggie said. "From what little they said, I think it's likely he's unconscious."

"That's a good point," Louise said. "If the first reports were of a body, whoever found him must have thought he was dead."

"It might have just been an error in the report the news media got," Anna suggested.

"The news people have ways to find things

out," Edie said. "I agree with Louise and Maggie. But you can check around — for instance, you can see if there's a lawyer in the Senior Guild who would take him on or recommend someone who will."

With effusive thanks to Edie for this suggestion, Clare grabbed her purse and hurried out of the room.

38

Maggie waited until Michael walked in to put the steaks under the broiler. One reason Maggie so enjoyed having him over every week was that she put more effort into cooking on those days. She couldn't remember the last time she bothered with a steak and baked potato just for herself. A quick stop at Nature's Best on the way home had provided the ingredients, including the makings for a fresh salad of mixed greens and a selection of fruit she had sliced and arranged on a platter.

"We stayed late at the church, listening to the radio reports about Kenny," she said, after their greeting. "I don't suppose you have any news?" Hope lit her eyes as she watched her son.

"I knew you would ask. But there's nothing new. He's still unconscious with a serious head injury. Someone left him for dead, and he would have been, if that hiker hadn't come along just then. Even though the daytime temperatures are comfortable, it can get hot on the desert floor. He would have been seriously dehydrated in no time."

Michael watched her take the steaks from the broiler and set them on the table. He sniffed appreciatively. "Smells great . . ."

"Since I was running late, I thought something simple would be best," Maggie said. She took a last look around the table to be sure everything was out and sat down. "I stopped at Nature's Best on the way home and got everything I needed. It's such a nice shop, I can't believe I've only now discovered it. And I really think I've had more energy since I started taking the vitamin combination Tony recommended. Clare said the same thing."

Michael frowned. "Tony?"

"He's the pharmacist. I told you about him. A very nice man, very charming. And he belongs to St. Rose," she added.

Michael continued to frown. Maggie wasn't sure what his problem was. She thought Michael would approve of her new vitamin regimen.

"He's very helpful," she continued. "The first time Victoria and I went in, I was just looking around in the pharmacy area and mentioned that I'd been considering a calcium supplement. He was so accommodating, telling me about the various combinations and which might be best. Victoria and I have been stopping there on our way home, and we've noticed that there are a lot of young people who go in and get his advice about supplements."

Michael's face became impassive. Maggie thought of it as his "cop face," but couldn't imagine why he'd be putting it on during their dinner.

"I'm surprised that you've given up your regular stores, Ma. I thought you hated to shop, and liked to keep to the same place so that you knew where everything was and could breeze through."

"I do hate to shop. But staying with the same store doesn't help much. They keep changing things around. Nature's Best is convenient, right there near the church, and it's a small place, so it's easy to get around. And the people who work there are friendly and helpful."

"Like Tony."

"Yes."

Maggie looked over the table, at the empty salad bowl and the fruit platter with only two slices of kiwi left on it. Michael never had cared for the bright green fruit.

"I don't see why you should be concerned

over my shopping habits. You said yourself how good both the salad and the fruit were. And they were so delicious because I got them at Nature's Best. I've noticed a real difference in the organic produce there compared to the usual fare from the big chain stores. It's certainly worth the slightly higher prices."

"You say you've been getting some vitamins there?"

Michael's face sported a formidable frown, making Maggie wonder what was wrong with him this evening. He must have had a hard day on the job. Taken aback by his seeming disapproval, Maggie attempted to laugh it off.

"What? You don't want me to take vitamins? Hoping to get your inheritance early?"

But Michael wouldn't be distracted by her attempt at humor.

"I'm concerned about you. I don't want you to buy pills from just anyone. You can't be sure what kind of additives might be in them. You should keep to known brands, ones that you can trust."

"I'm sure Tony uses the best ingredients, Michael. He has a special blend for post-menopausal women. I'm sure I've had more energy since I've been taking them," she added.

"I understand a lot of young athletes buy their supplements there." His face remained impassive.

Maggie nodded. "I've heard the same. See? Isn't that a good recommendation for his products? Those of us in the Bee who shop there have all noticed a lot of athletic-looking young people buying things in the pharmacy. Older men, too, most of them in their workout clothes. I'm sure it's because Tony is so helpful with his suggestions. And he makes the special combinations of vitamins for different ages and different needs."

"I wouldn't be surprised," Michael mumbled. "Look, Ma, I've been seeing a woman from the white-collar crime division."

Surprised at this sudden change of subject, but delighted by his news, Maggie smiled at her son. "That's wonderful, Michael. Is this something serious?"

But he dismissed any hope she might have in seeing him settled.

"It's too early to tell, Ma. She's a nice woman, and we're enjoying each other's company. But taking it slowly," he added, when Maggie's broad smile reappeared. "I'm just mentioning it to you now because of something she's working on."

Maggie could tell Michael had important

information to disclose, which was confirmed when he began with a warning.

"And don't tell any of your Bee friends about this. It's strictly hush-hush right now, but I don't want you caught up in it if there's a raid there. Or something else."

Now Maggie was fascinated. What was he going to say? Was it about Nature's Best?

"There's an interdepartmental investigation going on right now — into Nature's Best and Tony Sandoval. Scottsdale is working with the DEA and some other federal agencies. I don't have all the details, but I know it's a big project. That's why I'm concerned about you going over there so often."

Maggie was shocked. This was not something she could have anticipated. She'd thought Michael's warnings had to do with his oft voiced comments about the high prices at Nature's Best. She knew he didn't want anyone to take advantage of her — or of anyone else, for that matter.

She was also capable of reading between the lines.

"Do you think it's safe to take the vitamins I got there?"

"You said you've felt good since starting them. It's probably okay. I doubt there would be any illegal substances in the general stuff he has on the shelf."

Maggie nodded. That made sense. She supposed the kind of thing the police and the DEA were interested in would be hidden behind the counter.

"And that's all I'm going to say on the subject," Michael finished.

Maggie nodded again.

"And remember what I said . . . you can't tell anyone. Not even Victoria."

"Michael, I'm not a fool. I also wouldn't do anything that might endanger your career."

Maggie got up to fix dessert. She'd made biscuits for strawberry shortcake, and had sliced the strawberries and covered them with sugar to make the syrup. Now she gathered together the ingredients and brought them to the table.

"This ongoing investigation is very interesting, Michael, because it ties into a decision I came to this morning. I mentioned it to the others and we all agree."

Maggie placed the biscuits on the plates, cutting them in two so that she could scoop strawberries and ice cream into the center.

"Clare is still determined to help Kenny. And Edie thinks he should have a lawyer."

Michael agreed. "Couldn't hurt."

"But I think we've been looking at this all

wrong." Maggie stopped in the middle of inserting the CO_2 canister into the whipped cream maker. "If you discount the domestic problems angle, you're left with Kate as victim. It's too far out to suppose someone targeted the children, unless there was abuse or molestation there, and I can't believe that wouldn't have leaked out."

She squirted the desserts with the fresh whipped cream and placed the dishes on the table. Michael dug right in while she continued her explanation.

"So that leaves Kate as victim. Why would anyone want to kill shy little Kate Upland? Everyone we talked to liked her. Everyone was shocked that Kenny thought she might have had an affair."

"Heck of a thing to say about his wife," Michael said, his mouth full of strawberries and whipped cream. "Great dessert, Ma."

Maggie nodded her acknowledgment of the compliment.

"But everyone also agreed that Kate was a whiz of a bookkeeper. So it brings up the question: did she discover something odd at one of the places where she worked? And was it something big enough to get her killed?"

Maggie finally took a bite of her own dessert, savoring the rich flavor of the sweet strawberries. Michael remained silent as he demolished his shortcake.

"Kate did the bookkeeping — for all of the places she worked. Perhaps there was something going on there. Maybe she was killed because she found someone embezzling, for instance."

Michael's skepticism showed on his face even before he voiced his opinion. "And for that this person not only killed her but her two small children and rigged her house to explode?"

Maggie had to admit it sounded far-fetched when put into those words.

"What about money laundering? From what I read online, that usually involves drug money, and the drug people are supposed to be brutal. Earlier today, I thought that idea far-fetched, but after what you just told me . . . I don't know. It is still hard to believe Kate and Kenny could be involved in drugs. They were such an all-American couple."

Michael shrugged. "They may have looked that way, but we can't know what goes on in someone's home. A lot of vets get hooked while they're in a war zone. They use to try to escape the madness or to help them forget or cope . . . or something . . . Then they come home and they start selling so that can keep themselves supplied. And I'm sorry to say this, Ma, but Kenny's problem with the PTSD makes him a prime candidate for substance abuse. All the more reason for you to stay away from Nature's Best and the whole Upland case."

Maggie didn't want to argue the point, so she didn't say any more on the subject, instead offering Michael seconds on dessert, which he quickly accepted. Michael's earlier information and cautioning made her think drugs were an area of particular interest in the Upland case. She knew he wouldn't say more about Nature's Best and whatever the ongoing investigation might be. But she was suddenly suspicious of the suave Tony Sandoval. And ready to return to Safeway or Fry's for her shopping needs.

39

While Maggie fed Michael, Clare made a call to Bullhead City. When Penny didn't answer the phone, Clare wondered if she would be able to reach her at all. She had to leave a message on the B&B answering machine. She supposed a lot of reporters were bothering them, as Penny had said happened back in May. With Kenny found, media outlets were probably wanting some comment from the family of his victims. Clare felt sorry for Penny and Earl and determined to pray for their peace of mind.

Less than an hour after she left her message, Clare's phone rang. Since she didn't get many calls on her cell phone — she used it mainly for making calls — she hoped it would be Penny. Unfortunately, there would not be any more calls from Kenny.

"Oh, thank you so much for returning my call," Clare began.

"I almost didn't," Penny admitted. Her

voice was dour. "It's happening all over again, just like six months ago. We've stopped watching the television news because chances are we'll have to watch the house . . ." Her voice broke, and Clare heard her take a deep breath. "What was it you were calling about? Is your group coming up this way again?"

"Not right away," Clare said, realizing that this was a good way to begin her conversation without upsetting Penny. "But maybe after the new year. We really enjoyed our stay. Maybe I can bring my husband next time."

They spoke for a moment about the popularity of the B&B early in the year and how soon Clare would need to get in her reservation. Once that was settled, Clare felt she could bring up her real area of interest.

"Penny, I told you that Kenny saved my life after I ran off the road earlier this month. So I promised him I would look into his case. I want to help him more than ever now since he might not recover. If he's innocent, people should know," she declared.

There was a noncommittal sound from the opposite end of the line. But Clare was encouraged since Penny didn't disconnect.

"I know you and Earl were upset when I

told you Kenny's theory of someone stalking Kate. We know now that was highly unlikely. But Maggie has had a very good idea. She thinks we should look at possibilities connected with Kate's work. You know, if someone wanted her killed for some reason involved with her bookkeeping duties. Do you know if there was anything she might have found at one of the places where she worked — something that might have bothered her? We have had several people say she changed a few weeks before she died, and someone said she was thinking of leaving one of her jobs."

"Yes, she did tell me that she was going to give up one of the jobs. And she did sound worried about something the last few times I spoke to her. But I thought it was just the problems in her marriage — you know, with Kenny having those bad episodes and not sleeping well and all. That kind of thing can cause a lot of stress on both partners in a marriage."

"True," Clare said. "I don't suppose she told you if she found any evidence of someone embezzling money? Maybe from the car dealership?"

"Nooo . . ." Penny's voice trailed off, and there was a momentary pause. "Though I wonder . . ."

Clare waited through another moment of silence.

"There *is* something," Penny finally said. "We were given a few things that survived the fire. Not a lot. But Kate had a lovely cherry wood box that she used for her jewelry, and I did get that. She didn't have any expensive jewelry, but since Earl and I gave her most of it, there's a lot of sentimental value attached to the box and its contents."

Clare murmured something about the value of memories, though she didn't think Penny was listening. She was totally wrapped up in her tale.

"Inside the box, mixed in with her bits of jewelry, was a key. I showed it to Earl because I didn't know what it might be for. Or why it would be in her jewelry box."

Clare was literally bouncing in her seat, she was so excited by the direction the conversation had taken. She *knew* that key was going to prove important. Oh, if only they'd known about this when they were there. She could have had the key in her possession.

"Did you figure out what the key opened?" Clare asked.

"No."

Clare tried to hide her disappointment.

The key *had* to be important. Though a little imp on her shoulder warned her that the key might have opened a door or cupboard in Kate's home, and that was long gone.

Penny had resumed her tale.

"It looked like a padlock key, but that didn't make a lot of sense."

"For the pool fence?" Clare suggested. "She might have hid it so the girls couldn't find it."

"I guess," Penny said. "But she never did that while I was visiting. I suggested to Earl that it reminded me of the key to our safe deposit box, but he said it wasn't exactly like it. Which is true. And we had no way to know if she had a bank box or even what bank it would be in."

"Oh, dear, and with Kenny unconscious there's no way to ask him if he knows about one." Clare was thinking fast, but nothing more came to mind. "This could be really important," she said. "Do you mind if I share this information with Maggie and her son? He's a police officer."

"No. Go ahead." Penny's voice didn't show any enthusiasm, but Clare thanked her effusively before hanging up. If she called Maggie right away, she might catch Michael at her house.

40

The mood in the quilt room on Tuesday morning was an odd mixture of excitement and somberness. The Bee members usually enjoyed taking a quilt off the frame and putting another one in, but on this morning, thoughts of Kenny Upland unconscious in a local hospital clouded the atmosphere in the small room. Guilty or innocent, this should not have happened to him.

As expected, they'd finished stitching the maple leaf quilt on Monday and had taken it from the frame to store in the closet. So this morning, they began by putting a new quilt into place. There had been a short discussion on whether or not to start on Edie's blue nine-patch or to pull out a thirties-style tulip quilt top that Maggie had contributed earlier. The tulip would be a straight cross-hatch, while the nine-patch had the beautiful feathered hearts. It wasn't a long debate. They decided on the nine-patch, which would be more interesting to stitch on, Anna said. And as Victoria had said the day before, the blue and white had a welcome soothing quality.

That decided, they turned the radio to the news/talk station, in case there were any updates on Kenny's condition. As they worked, they explained to Theresa how the quilt was pinned into place on the frames and how they rolled the sides in as they completed the stitching.

"I always thought you had to start quilting in the center of the quilt," Theresa said. "I was wondering about that with the maple leaf one."

"It's usually recommended that you start quilting in the center," Louise said, pulling the fabric on her side taut while Maggie pinned the opposite side. "But this kind of frame is an exception. It's much easier to work with a group on frames like this. It's what the pioneer women used for their quilting bees. They lived far apart back then, and they didn't have the chance to get together all the time, so they had to do it all in one day — during a wedding or while the men raised the roof on a house or a barn."

With so many hands, the work went quickly. In no time at all the quilt was in the frame and they were gathering their sewing supplies, ready to sit and begin stitching.

Saving any important information for later, the women had talked about Victoria's experience with the bunco group while they set the quilt top in the frame and Maggie recounted what she'd served Michael for dinner. Now Clare and Maggie updated them on what they had learned the night before. They were farther apart now, with the entire quilt exposed on the frame, but that did not impede conversation. Clare began with a progress report on Kenny, though there was little to tell. The hospital wouldn't give her any information.

"It's the right to privacy laws," Louise told her.

"I know," Clare said. "But it's still frustrating."

Still, she had additional news. "I found him a lawyer, though, right here at the Senior Guild. His name is Walter Jackson, and he knew Kenny and liked him. He's retired, of course, but he said he still takes a case now and then to keep his hand in. And, he's doing it pro bono."

"Good," Edie said. "He needs to have a lawyer, whether he's guilty or innocent."

Clare looked ready to protest this lack of

confidence in Kenny's innocence, then appeared to change her mind. Instead, she plunged into an account of her phone call to Penny.

"After I talked to Penny, I called Maggie and managed to catch Michael before he left. He said he can have someone check on that key she has. They'll be able to tell if it belongs to a safe deposit box."

"I went straight home yesterday and booted up the computer," Edie said. "I liked your idea about looking at this from a different perspective, Maggie. I looked up embezzlement and money laundering, and read up on them to try to understand the possibilities. I must say I think it's the direction to go. Kate would have been in an ideal position to realize one or the other was going on and report it. They are both crimes, but there are a lot of degrees to each. It can be very serious, so it could well be worth killing over. That could be what's in that safe deposit box — proof of whatever she found."

Clare liked that suggestion. "Though it seems to me that K.C.'s place is the most obvious for embezzling. Even though I like K.C., I like Kenny, too. Someone has to be lying."

"But even if an embezzler wanted to kill

Kate, would he or she kill her small children? Just because she might be able to tell someone that money was missing?" Anna was perplexed by this problem and upset that the deaths of two beautiful children might be nothing more than "collateral damage."

"It seems like it would have to be more than that," Maggie murmured.

"I just read something that might throw some suspicion on Nature's Best," Louise said.

They all looked at Louise, surprise on every countenance.

"Someone might be embezzling from Nature's Best?" Anna asked. She seemed puzzled by this assumption. "However did you figure that out?"

But Louise shook her head. "I don't mean I know about embezzling there. It's something else I read recently in a nursing journal. I like to keep up, even though I just do volunteer work these days," she told Theresa.

There were some nods from the others, who knew about Louise's volunteer work. Their fingers continued to move, creating the feathers in the quilting pattern or moving along in straight lines through the nine-patch squares.

"Remember how I told you I knew all about Nature's Best because it's a compounding pharmacy? The article I just read was about a compounding pharmacy in California where the pharmacist and several others were indicted for bringing human growth hormone into the country illegally and then selling it to their customers."

"Growth hormone? Like what they accuse the baseball players of taking?" Edie asked.

"Yes. It's only supposed to be used for very specific medical conditions, but athletes want it now, and men who think it fights aging. So there's definitely a market. With so many baby boomers approaching their sixties, anti-aging products are big business."

Clare tugged at her thread, smoothing down a line of stitching, before looking up at Louise. "So you're saying we should look at Nature's Best, too, since this is something that a woman working with their records might notice."

"Of course that's what she means." Edie sounded exasperated. "That kind of business would require money laundering, not to mention a contact who could provide the drugs. I would think money laundering could leave a noticeable trail if one knows what to look for."

"Drugs," Maggie said, a thoughtful expression on her face. "Drug people are ruthless, you hear that all the time. And drug people are involved in money laundering. I'm thinking money laundering would be more lucrative than embezzling, and it might be worth killing over."

"Where did the pharmacy in your article get the hormone?" Victoria asked. "Mexico?"

"No, they got the drugs from China. But this is just one case, and it doesn't mean anything as regards Nature's Best in particular. But it does create a possibility that the books at that establishment might not be entirely kosher."

"Especially since there are always so many athletic-looking men there." Maggie bit her lip as she thought about that. She recalled seeing that older parishioner who looked so remarkably younger.

"What about steroids?" Victoria asked. "They're illegal, too, aren't they? Could those be brought in from another country and sold under the counter?"

"I'm sure they could be. Wasn't there a case here in Phoenix some years ago about some Russian gang members who were dealing in steroids? I've forgotten the details."

"That's right, they stole a shipment of steroids going to a drugstore," Edie said. "They were Russian, but they weren't part of the so-called Russian mafia."

Maggie almost smiled. Leave it to Edie to remember.

"This is getting very complicated," Clare said.

"You're all amazing," Theresa suddenly said. She left her needle in place in one of the nine-patch squares as she looked at the other women sitting around the frame. "I can't believe that you have so many ideas and possibilities about something that happened six months ago and has stymied the police." She shook her head in wonder before picking up her needle again.

"There's nothing like trying to solve a mystery," Clare said. "That's why we like reading mystery novels so much. I always try to solve the case in the book before the detective does." She sighed with pleasure, just thinking about outsmarting a fictional sleuth.

Theresa took a few more stitches before abandoning her needle once again. "Will you go to the police now — with this new theory? It sounds so good."

"Michael was going to pass along the information about the key," Maggie said.

"I'll let him know about this article Louise read."

She wished she could tell them what Michael had confided to her the night before. It threw a lot of weight behind this new possibility. "I'm sure the police thought of this during the initial investigation months ago," she finally said.

"I don't know," Clare said. "I still think they did as little investigating as possible and just decided that Kenny did it because he was missing. Why go to all that work if you can come up with such an easy solution?"

But Maggie wasn't ready to malign their police department — and, indirectly, her own son — in such a blatant manner. Neither, apparently, was Victoria.

"Now, Clare, we have a fine police department in Scottsdale and I'm sure they checked every possibility before settling on Kenny as their chief suspect."

"It seems to me checking out where the victim works would be pretty basic," Edie said. "They're sure to have done it."

"It wouldn't hurt to talk to K.C. again," Maggie said. "Now that we have a real possibility over at Nature's Best, it would be nice if we could eliminate Gilligan's. Do you think you could come with us, Theresa,

360

if we did? K.C. might be willing to talk to you about whether or not he suspects an embezzler."

Theresa was happy to help, even pulled out her cell phone and called to see if he could accommodate them.

"He can see us right after lunch," she said, as she closed her phone and slipped it back into her purse.

"Excellent," Maggie said. "I'd love to hear what he has to say about the possibility that Kate uncovered something suspicious in his accounts."

"It will be interesting," Theresa agreed. "K.C. prides himself on knowing what's going on in all aspects of his business. So if there is any question about the accounts, I'm sure he'll know."

"But would he tell you?" Edie asked. "It seems presumptuous for you to go there and ask for such personal information."

Maggie frowned. She didn't mind appearing nosy to people, if what she learned was helpful to a larger issue. And the deaths of three innocent people certainly was a larger issue. "It will be up to him. He needn't answer, of course. But we'll explain what we're doing. I'm sure he'll want to help out. I don't know him well, but everyone here at the parish has always said what a good person he is, always ready to help."

Theresa nodded. "He is a good man. I'm sure he'll be willing to hear you out, at least."

"That's all we can ask," Maggie said.

41

In the end, only Theresa, Maggie and Victoria went to see K.C. They didn't want to arrive in a large group and promised to call everyone afterward to "report in." Clare was disappointed at being left behind, even if they called from the car right outside the showroom.

"You're just too close to this whole thing with Kenny," Victoria explained. "You get very emotional, Clare. It would be better if you let those of us with more emotional distance take care of this."

Reluctantly, she agreed that they were correct.

"And I should get back to have lunch with Gerald anyway. He worries about me since the accident." She smiled in a way that let them know this was not necessarily a bad thing.

Maggie was shocked at K.C.'s appearance.

He'd aged in the past ten days. When she'd test driven the hybrid car, K.C. had looked younger than the fifty-six years she knew he carried. Today, however, bags drooped beneath his eyes, and his skin had an unhealthy cast. If she told a newcomer he was sixty-six, she felt sure he would believe her.

Still, his spirit appeared unaltered.

"Come in, come in." He greeted them heartily, wrapping Theresa in a bear hug. "Couldn't stay away, could you?" He chuckled as he released her. "Good to see you again," he added, shaking Maggie's hand.

"We were so sorry to hear about the gas explosion at your house," Theresa told him. Maggie and Victoria agreed.

His eyes clouded over momentarily. "A terrible tragedy. But, with God's help, I'll get through it."

Then he was back to his usual bluff self, turning to Theresa with another welcoming smile. "How are Carl and the kids? I miss seeing you around here, you know." The warmth in his eyes, as well as in his voice, let them know he said this in all sincerity. "But I hope you're enjoying retirement."

"It's great, K.C. You should think about it yourself," she added with a smile.

He offered a bluff reply about giving it some consideration, but they could see it was mere lip service. K.C. was so intrinsically a part of this beehive of a place, it was difficult to picture him anywhere else.

"I hear you've gotten involved over at St. Rose," he said to Theresa.

"Yes. Carl started going to the Senior Guild, you know. He was lonely at home on his own, and he always liked working with wood. And having the other guys to talk to is a big plus."

K.C. shook his head. "That's why I haven't retired. I'd miss all the hustle and bustle." He gestured out into the showroom. "And of course, I'm too young," he added with a chuckle.

Maggie had to agree there was a lot going on outside K.C.'s office. People were everywhere, looking at the cars, checking out brochures, just walking around, intent on errands. Facing days at home — and at a home without a wife, with no children, not even an animal — would definitely be a big change. And things were already changing for K.C.

"We'd welcome you into the Senior Guild in a minute, and you know it," Maggie told him with a grin.

"Oh, I know." He nodded, but his expression was sad.

Then the practiced smile returned. "And

how are you, Maggie? Have you made a decision about that hybrid yet? It's a great little car."

Maggie had to smile at the wheedling tone. She was also happy to see the sparkle in his eye as he tried to make the sale. "I'm afraid I'm still thinking it over. Though with gas prices rising all the time, it's looking more and more attractive."

K.C. turned to Victoria. "And how about you? Thinking of getting a car this year?"

"I admit, I am interested in hybrids." She offered an apologetic smile. "But not at this time."

K.C. sighed, an exaggerated sound that they all knew was pure theater. "Ah, it's a tough life, being a car salesman," he said, making them all laugh.

At his signal, a young man came in from the showroom, offering cold or hot drinks. The women refused, with thanks, explaining that they had just finished lunch. As the young man returned to the main room, K.C. glanced at the three women. Maggie felt an unseemly urge to giggle, looking at him behind his desk, his hands nicely folded before him, just like Sister used to have them do in the first grade.

"Now, what can I do for you lovely ladies?" he asked.

366

The urge to laugh fled, even as relief flooded Maggie that Edie wasn't there. Edie would have taken exception to *that* term, and she would have let him know it, too. She didn't allow anyone to call her lovely lady, little lady, or, heaven forbid, girl.

"You know how Kenny Upland rescued our friend Clare a couple of weeks ago during that big storm?" Maggie began.

"Yes, of course."

Maggie thought that he no longer looked cheery. He'd lost the salesman persona that seemed to come so easily to him. Was he convinced that Kenny was responsible for the destruction of his home?

"Clare is a dear friend of ours, and she's determined to prove that Kenny did not kill his family. We're trying to keep her out of trouble by helping her think things through."

"It's amazing," Theresa said. "You should hear them debating over the quilt frame. I still don't know how they all manage to quilt and talk at the same time." She shook her head in awe.

"So what is it you think I can help with?"

"The media seem sure Kenny caused that explosion at your house, which has brought the whole Upland case to the forefront again."

K.C. frowned. "I wasn't at home that night. I don't know what happened. I just know that I didn't do it myself, which I may have to prove to the insurance company."

"Oh, no." Theresa was instantly sympathetic. "We know you weren't there. And we're sure you wouldn't have destroyed your own home," Theresa assured him, exchanging a quick glance with her companions. The relationship between them was still new enough for her to fear overstepping by answering for them all. But there was no objection from either Maggie or Victoria.

"So the insurance company is sure it wasn't an accident," Victoria said.

K.C. nodded.

"We're not trying to figure out what happened at your house that night, K.C.," Maggie said. "And, by the way, Kenny called Clare's cell phone that night, to let her know he was not responsible."

K.C.'s brows rose, but he did not comment.

"What we're interested in is the original crime. We're trying to determine why someone might have wanted to kill Kate Upland. If it wasn't her husband, I mean. And the best idea we've come up with is the possibility of her uncovering some type of suspicious activity at one of the places where she worked. That was what we wanted to ask you. If you don't mind our butting in, of course." Maggie gave him her best helpless little old lady look. She could appear innocent and guileless, just like an actress playing Miss Marple. And it seemed to work, as K.C. shrugged.

"What exactly did you want to know?"

Maggie suppressed the smile that wanted to appear. This was a sobering business, after all. "Did Kate ever say anything to you about discrepancies in the accounts she worked with? Either here or elsewhere? We know you were friends and helped her out when Kenny was overseas."

K.C. frowned once more. "You think someone might be embezzling from me?"

Maggie was surprised at the quiet voice. She'd expected a theatrical man like K.C. to shout it out for everyone to hear. Perhaps Edie was correct and he would not want to part with such personal information. Maybe letting it get out would be bad for business. Maggie didn't presume to know the answer to that. It seemed to her that it might be helpful to have it known the financial shortfall could be due to criminal activity rather than bad business practices. But then investors might think it showed K.C. was unable to control his staff. It was definitely a Catch-22 business.

"I've heard rumors about financial difficulties at Gilligan's." Maggie put up a hand to stop his interrupting — he looked ready to do so, and she wanted to finish her sentence. "Just rumors, you understand. But I know what a good businessman you are and what a successful business you've always run. So if there are problems, an employee embezzling funds could play into it. At least by my reckoning."

"I see."

K.C. gazed at the three women. Maggie knew that her flattery wasn't going to get him to share information. He was too shrewd for that. But he might feel they could be mutually helpful. That was what she counted on.

"We aren't interested in your personal business situation," Victoria said. Her gentle voice was welcome, as far as Maggie was concerned. She sent her a silent thank you for the help. "We just want to know if there was anything there that could have gotten Kate killed. It seems an extreme kind of murder for a white-collar criminal, but you never know what someone might do if they think they may be going to jail."

"Yes, I can see what you're after," K.C.

said, his voice thoughtful. "The thing is, Kate did mention some odd entries. At the time, I didn't think anything of it, just told her to keep her eye on it and let me know. Then she died. I didn't say anything to the police then. Didn't even think of it, actually. But then Kate's successor told me she'd seen something odd."

He heaved a heavy sigh. "This has nothing to do with the financial situation of the company at the moment. The current fiscal problems have to do with normal business practices, the economy and a too rapid expansion." He frowned again. "I hadn't realized word had gotten out beyond a few people in the local business community."

"You know how it is in Scottsdale," Maggie told him. "In many ways it still is a small town. I heard about it from someone in the local business community, as you put it."

K.C. looked at them for a moment. He picked up a pen from his desk, running it over and under his fingers by turn. His way of relieving tension, Maggie suspected.

"You probably know that I gave my stepson a job." The women nodded. "He searched for his birth mother when he became of age, and Rosemary was delighted to meet him. She wanted to get to know him, and I was happy to indulge her. I'd always wanted a child, so I was glad to offer him a job here."

K.C. paused. His eyes gazed, unfocused, at a spot somewhere out beyond them in the sunny showroom while his fingers continued to twine around the ballpoint pen. After a moment, he returned his attention to the women in his office.

"With two bookkeepers suggesting something might not be right, I called in an auditor. And it now seems that bringing Tyler into the business may not have been the best of ideas after all." He sighed. "I tried to do the right thing by him, treat him like the son I never had. But I guess he wanted to make up for whatever he felt he might have missed growing up."

"You mean . . ." Theresa gulped. "Tyler is embezzling from the company?"

"We can't be certain, but it seems likely." K.C. shook his head, unable to understand his stepson. He dropped the pen on his desk and leaned forward. "And now he's disappeared. I've told the police all this, of course, especially after what happened at the house . . ."

"You don't think he did that, too! Oh, dear," Theresa said.

"He disappeared before or after the explosion at the house?" Maggie asked.

"I'm not sure."

The jovial salesman was gone, replaced by a man betrayed by someone he loved. Or at least, trusted. Maggie could see the disappointment in his eyes, maybe even the edge of despair. No wonder he'd aged.

"He hasn't appeared at work since the explosion, but he wasn't scheduled the day before either, so he may have already been gone. And he's not at his condo."

"It sounds like Tyler is a good suspect then," Victoria said. "Why are the media so sure Kenny did it?"

K.C. shrugged. "Better for ratings, I suppose. Everyone is interested in that story. And the man who got away."

"Not to mention how much more photogenic the Upland house explosion was." Theresa's wry remark surprised Maggie but not K.C., who gave a wan smile.

Maggie nodded, agreeing with both of them. The flames shooting out of the roof of the Upland house — or shooting out from where the roof had been — did make for a riveting picture. And then there was the shock value. The beautiful woman and her equally beautiful children, dead, and left in the house. She hated to even think about it.

"Do you think Tyler could have done it?"

Somehow the question didn't seem as intrusive, coming as it did from Victoria. She had such a soothing voice and a gentle way of saying things.

"I can't believe Tyler could kill someone. Especially a woman and two children. But set up an explosion at my house?" K.C.'s eyes were infinitely sad. "Yes, I think he might have done something like that. I don't think he meant to harm me."

Perhaps he saw the skeptical look in Maggie's eyes. And Theresa's because he decided to elaborate.

"I was at a dinner in Tucson that had been on my calendar for months."

There was a moment of silence while they considered this.

"After speaking to the auditor, I did some very serious thinking. And a bit of investigating of my own," he added, eyes twinkling now as he looked at Maggie and Victoria. "You ladies aren't the only ones who can solve a mystery, you know. I knew Tyler had recently purchased a condo, but I didn't know it was one of those high-rise condos on the waterfront in Scottsdale. And while I've considered him an up and coming young executive here, I don't pay him enough for that kind of mortgage, though I would have helped him with it if he'd asked me," he concluded.

How sad, Maggie thought. Tyler stole, endangering the company, in order to provide himself with the kind of lifestyle he felt he deserved. And he could have had it for the mere asking. She could see from the sorrow in his eyes that K.C. loved the young man like a son.

"Maybe a taste of the good life made him think he needed it now, that he didn't want to wait to inherit," Maggie suggested.

As they stood to leave, Theresa urged K.C. to join her family for Thanksgiving dinner. He gave her an indefinite maybe for an answer, but Maggie hoped he would accept. He needed some relaxation, and she thought Theresa and her family could probably provide it.

42

After all their probing questions and creative speculation, things ended in a rather dull way and seemed, at first, to have nothing to do with the Quilting Bee.

As in most of the country, people in the valley invaded the malls for the Black Friday ritual of shopping for bargains. In downtown Scottsdale, however, things were somewhat different.

Although there was no reason for the Senior Guild to meet on the Friday after Thanksgiving, the Quilting Bee decided to gather. They always liked to quilt together and were in the midst of their "investigation" concerning the Upland case, so they wanted time to talk. None of them cared to join the throngs of shoppers out on that day, and no one in the Bee had out of town company. It was also a sad truth that many older, retired people had nowhere else to go on most days and would just as soon arrive at the church for a long visit with friends. Working on whatever projects they had going was almost incidental, so the Bee women were not the only Senior Guild members at the church that morning.

Even their newest member came, bubbling over with news about her pregnant daughter and filled with excitement about her first grandchild.

"She made the announcement at the dinner table," Theresa told them. "Right after we said grace. I'm telling you, it made a wonderful thing to be thankful about."

Maggie reported the latest development of her newest granddaughter, who could blow bubbles and was close to rolling over. Victoria described the meal she'd had at the Phoenician, courtesy of her niece and her family. Louise had tried a new recipe for stuffing that included apples and corn bread; Anna told them about the success of her pumpkin/pecan pie. Edie complained that the neighbor who'd invited her to dinner left the television on during the meal.

Work was progressing nicely on the blue nine-patch quilt when they finally got around to Kenny, K.C., Tyler, and Kate. They'd spent most of Wednesday morning talking about their visit with K.C. and his suspicions about Tyler, so they naturally returned to that subject.

"Did K.C. join you for Thanksgiving dinner?" Victoria asked, remembering that Theresa had invited him to join her family.

Theresa gave a wide smile in answer. "He sure did. I was happy to have him, and I think he enjoyed himself. He's just as happy about the new baby as we are. In fact, he insisted on giving her a check — to start the baby's college fund, he said. I think he feels like an uncle to my kids."

"Did he say anything about Tyler?" Clare asked.

"No, he didn't. And I didn't like to ask. It was a holiday, and I thought he needed some time away from all that."

Maggie nodded, agreeing with Theresa.

Even Edie agreed. "That would hardly be Thanksgiving dinner conversation," she said.

"Anyway, we know he's working with the police," Maggie reminded them.

"I've been watching the paper to see if they find him." Clare clipped her thread and reached for the spool. As she threaded her needle and made the knot, she looked over to Maggie. "Have you heard anything from Michael about the safe deposit box key?"

Maggie had not. "He worked yesterday and only popped in to eat. But he did tell me he hadn't heard anything from the police in Bullhead City who were supposed to pick it up. And then they have to pass it to the Scottsdale PD, so I don't know how long that will take."

"And we don't even know if it is a safe deposit box key," Anna reminded them.

"Oh, it has to be." Clare's facial expression reflected her confident tone. "It would be the perfect place for Kate to hide proof of whatever she found."

"I wonder if we'll ever know," Anna wondered.

"Sure we will." Edie's voice was firmly positive. "We found out who Deep Throat was, didn't we? Didn't think I'd live to see that day. So why wouldn't we learn who killed Kate Upland?"

Maggie had to admit that, put that way, it seemed destined to happen. "Let's just hope it doesn't take thirty years."

43

The beginning of the end had echoes of that day two weeks ago when Clare started it all with a phone call to Maggie.

Clare left early that Friday, saying she had to stop at Nature's Best to pick up something for Gerald's lunch. "He won't be happy if he has to have leftover turkey," she said. "He likes it well enough, but not two days in a row. He's already unhappy about missing his usual Friday golf game, but the courses are all really expensive Thanksgiving weekend because of the out of towners. I hope they'll have some nice roast beef at the Nature's Best deli."

Barely five minutes later, Maggie's phone rang. Anna and Theresa had already left the church, but Maggie, Victoria and Edie were storing the sewing things in the closet while Louise arranged a sheet over the quilt frame to keep their work clean.

"Maggie?"

She wasn't whispering this time, so Maggie instantly recognized Clare's voice. And, as before, she was excited about something.

"Clare." Maggie smiled at the others. "Did you call to tell us the roast beef was irresistible?"

But Clare had no time for chit chat.

"Maggie, I'm at Nature's Best. You have to come over here. They're raiding it!"

"Raiding it?" Maggie's eyebrows lifted as she puzzled over this. Perhaps she'd heard incorrectly. "Who's raiding it?"

Victoria, Louise and Edie stopped what they were doing to listen. Edie sidled closer to see if she could hear Clare's side of the conversation.

"The police, Maggie. And I saw someone in a shirt that said DEA."

Clare's voice, while still excited, dropped a bit. *She probably doesn't want everyone around her listening in,* Maggie thought. And she knew there were people around her; she could hear the murmur of a crowd through the open line.

"I can't explain over the phone," Clare said. "Come over. Park in the lot next door."

There was the distinctive click of a phone disconnecting.

"What's happening?" Victoria asked.

"Clare said that the police are raiding

Nature's Best. The DEA, too. Come on, let's go," Maggie said, grabbing her purse. "She said to park in the lot next door."

She headed for the door, closely followed by Victoria, Louise and Edie.

Within minutes, they were looking for Clare in the small crowd outside Nature's Best. They recognized several faces as Senior Guild members, a few others as people who lived in the vicinity. Police cars and vans that Maggie thought might have to do with evidence collecting were grouped outside the store. Yellow police tape encircled a wide area around the store, effectively keeping people back. Far enough back to make it difficult to know what was really happening.

In the parking lot outside the store, and taking up whatever space the police were not using, were remote broadcast vans from all of the area's television stations. Several helicopters circled overhead. Maggie was sure the noon news broadcasts were all carrying this "breaking news" story. She briefly regretted not being home to watch it. There would probably be more information available through the media than standing out there in the parking lot outside the store. Still, the air of excitement wouldn't be evident in her living room.

They found Clare standing with a young woman wearing a Nature's Best polo shirt, whom Clare quickly introduced to them. Young and blonde, her red eyes were an indication of her feelings about the current situation.

Clare greeted them eagerly, excitement spilling over. *If she was a child, she'd be bouncing on her toes,* Maggie thought.

"You'll never believe it," she told them. "They've arrested Tony."

Maggie, Victoria, Louise and Edie all exclaimed in surprise. Though Maggie, remembering Michael's warning, was perhaps less surprised than the others. Louise saw the DEA shirts and nodded thoughtfully.

"I got here just in time for the perp walk." Clare's voice rose at being able to relate such exciting news to her friends.

"The what?" Victoria's eyebrows rose.

"You know, the perp walk," Clare insisted.

But Edie preempted the explanation. "It's when they put handcuffs on the person and walk them out past all the media."

The short, succinct answer almost made Maggie smile. She felt sure Clare would have taken several sentences to explain it, probably bringing in examples from television or the movies.

"I do feel bad for his family." Victoria shook her head sadly. "Tony seemed like such a nice person."

"He is," Heather said. "His family, too." She twisted her hands anxiously in front of her. "He has two young sons, you know. Wouldn't it be awful to turn on the television and see your dad being arrested?" Her voice filled with horrified dread.

The older women all nodded solemnly. It was indeed a sad thing for the children.

But Edie had a more practical outlook. "Well, then, he should have kept to law-abiding practices."

Heather just stared at her for a moment, then took a crumpled tissue from her pocket and wiped her nose. It was obvious to all of them that she had been crying.

"I was just coming in to work when I saw the police cars drive up," Heather told them. "I'm on for noon today." She glanced down at her watch, frowning at the dial. "I guess I won't be working today after all, huh?"

Maggie put her arm around the young woman's shoulders. "I'm sure the store will be closed for the rest of the day."

"It might be closed for a few days," Louise added.

"Everyone is saying Mr. Sandoval was selling illegal drugs," Heather said. Unlike Clare, Heather spoke in a low voice, as though she was ashamed to recount such damaging information. "I was afraid to go inside, in case they arrest me, too. And I don't know anything about the pharmacy or any illegal drugs." A lone tear trailed from her frightened eyes. "I have a daughter," she added, as though that explained her fright. And of course, it did.

"It looks like they're taking all the files and computers," Edie announced.

The women watched, along with all the other neighbors and shoppers, fascinated by such activity right there in their neighborhood. They saw more than one person capturing the scene with cell phone cameras. Teens stood behind the newscasters when they could, mugging for the cameras, more interested in appearing on television than with the scandal of local drug sales.

They stayed for almost an hour, though there was little else to see. They spoke to others they knew in the crowd, and everyone related their experience and what they had seen. Maggie was relieved when Victoria suggested they had seen enough. "I guess I'll have to find another vitamin provider after all," she said. Her voice was so dull, Victoria didn't even tease her about it.

When she finally got home, Maggie was surprised to find a message from Michael, asking her to call him as soon as she returned.

Worried, as any mother would be by such a cryptic message, Maggie quickly dialed her son's cell phone.

"Michael, what is it?"

Her concern turned to relief as soon as Michael began.

"I have news about the Upland case," he said.

Not sure if he was about to tell her that Kenny was innocent after all or that they had definitive proof he'd killed his family, Maggie waited. She had to remind herself to keep breathing.

"Kenny is clear in the explosion at K.C. Gilligan's house. There's been an arrest."

"That's good," Maggie said, still not sure how this could be called "the Upland case." It seemed to her that this was a completely separate issue. It was mainly the media that claimed Kenny was responsible for that disaster. "Was it Tyler Gilligan?"

She heard Michael's exasperated sigh.

"I'm not even going to ask how you know

that," he said.

"So he really did set that bomb, or whatever it was, in K.C.'s house."

"He did. And he planned it particularly so that Kenny would be blamed. Luckily for K.C., Tyler didn't know how to arrange for a big fire like the one at the Upland house. He managed a gas explosion, but the explosion itself took out most of the oxygen, so it put out the fire. I understand from the arson people that using natural gas to start a fire is very tricky and a method for experts."

"So Tyler didn't have anything to do with the original crime at the Uplands'."

Maggie was disappointed. She'd hoped finding the embezzler would pinpoint Kate's killer. But now it looked like two of the businesses where Kate worked had illegal activity going on. What were the odds! She would have scoffed at that in a mystery novel, unless the bookkeeper herself was involved. Too much coincidence. But then real life was full of surprises, and true crime was often more complicated than fiction.

"I also learned that Kenny was never a real suspect in the Gilligan explosion," Michael continued. "The media liked him for that because it made a good story. And that was fine with the investigators. They hoped it would make the real suspect feel comfortable that he'd gotten away with it. That's when they make mistakes, which Tyler did. He was ready to flee to California and went back to his condo for some things."

"Amazing," Maggie said.

"Just wanted to let you know what's happening," Michael said. "I've got to go."

"Wait." Her anxious tone kept her son from disconnecting. "Michael, I've just come from Nature's Best."

"So you saw what's happening there."

"Clare said she got there just in time to see the 'perp walk.' Terrible term," she added.

"How did you happen to be there?"

Maggie could "see" Michael's frown even though they were miles apart.

"Clare left early so she could pick up some lunch meat. She called us and told us about the raid, and we joined her there. It was just as we were leaving anyway. A lot of Senior Guild people stopped to see what was happening. There would have been a lot more people if it had been on a regular weekday."

"I think that's why they planned on today. I only found out this morning, though. They wanted to catch Sandoval by surprise, and that made today good as well. They'll be building their case for a while, but from what I hear, Sandoval is already talking."

"So he really was dealing in drugs." Maggie sighed, disappointed in learning this about a man she'd previously admired.

"He was selling illegal steroids and HGH. That's growth hormone, you know."

"Yes, I do know, Michael. I'm old, not stupid. It's what a lot of older men think will keep them young," she added, shaking her head at the folly and vanity of so many aging men.

Maggie could hear voices on Michael's side and realized he must be working. "Thanks for calling," she told him. "I'll let Clare know about Tyler. She'll be interested."

"Let's hope this will be the end of it."

But Maggie knew it couldn't be the end. They still didn't know who killed Kate Upland. Unless Michael thought Kenny had done it.

Maggie sighed. Would they ever find the truth about what happened to Kate?

44

Maggie was glad that, before leaving Nature's Best the previous day, the Quilting Bee had agreed to meet on Saturday. They took seats around the quilt frame with varying levels of excitement, anxious to discuss the previous day's happenings.

"I can't believe I missed all the excitement at Nature's Best yesterday," Theresa said, picking up her needle and thread. After a week of stitching with the Bee, she was much more confident about her ability. She tucked the needle in without hesitation, pulling her knot between the layers with one quick jerk of her wrist.

"It was exciting, all right," Clare said. "Gerald didn't even mind a late lunch of leftover turkey because I had so much to tell him."

"I looked up that article I'd seen about the compounding pharmacy," Louise said. "I wanted to compare what was said in that to what the local media reported about Nature's Best."

"Were there similarities?" Edie asked.

"Generally, I guess. There were a lot of different agencies involved there, too."

They had seen men and women at Nature's Best the day before wearing shirts sporting a veritable vegetable soup of initials. FBI, DEA, ICE. According to the news reports, the FDA and the IRS were also involved.

"Not too many specifics were the same, though," Louise went on. "The pharmacist who was arrested in the report I read was getting human growth hormone from China and making his own version to sell. Anabolic steroids, too. He sold most of the drugs over the internet, so he was arrested for mail fraud, too. A lot of charges were mentioned. Conspiracy, smuggling, mail fraud, distribution of growth hormone, even asset forfeiture."

Edie nodded, a smug expression on her sharp features. "He'll have to pay the price for bringing in those drugs and selling them in this country."

"If Tony is facing similar charges, it will go hard on his family." Anna shook her head sadly. "The family will have to pay for his bad judgment. Didn't you say he had young sons?"

"Yes," Maggie said. "He had a photo up at the pharmacy of two young boys in soccer uniforms. Maybe eight and ten. It is a shame."

"They haven't mentioned the charges against Tony yet," Louise said, pulling a length of thread from the spool. "But I assume they will involve many of the same charges. The paper this morning said he was getting his supplies from Mexico."

"Did you see the paper?" Clare asked. "They mentioned simultaneous raids in Tucson and Nogales that were related to the investigation at Nature's Best. It's really a big deal."

"We should put the radio on the news/talk station so that we can catch their news on the hour," Edie said, rising from her chair to change from the oldies station currently tuned in.

"Maggie has other news," Clare announced. While Maggie had called her after talking to Michael, they had not spoken to everyone in the Bee, so they didn't know who had heard about the arrest of Tyler Gilligan.

"Michael called yesterday. They've arrested Tyler Gilligan for the explosion at

K.C.'s house."

"I saw that in the paper," Theresa said. "It was such a small item I almost missed it. But I'd talked to someone from the car dealership who told me about it, so I was looking for it."

"I noticed it, too," Edie said. "Terrible thing, after all K.C. did for him." She clicked her tongue and shook her head. "These young people have no appreciation for all the older generation does."

No one commented on what was a common complaint from Edie.

"I'm sure Tyler's arrest would have warranted more coverage if it hadn't come at the same time as the Nature's Best raid. That's a much bigger story," Louise said.

"Michael said the fire investigators never seriously considered Kenny as a suspect in that explosion. It wasn't set up the same as the one at Kenny's house. Michael said they figure he was trying to implicate Kenny by using what he knew from news reports. Tyler thought it would be enough to turn on the gas jets and turn off the pilot on the stove, but apparently you need to do more than that if you want a fire. He said something about the blast taking all the oxygen out of the air and killing whatever fire was there from the initial spark. I don't understand all of it."

"I did some online reading on that after the Upland house explosion and fire," Edie said. "It's not easy to burn down a house using natural gas. You have to use something else to create the fire — gasoline or something along that line. I read that only a real pro uses gas in an arson case."

"That's what Michael told me," Maggie said.

"I guess Tyler became the number-one suspect when he turned up missing right after the explosion," Theresa said. "Isn't it interesting? I can't help wondering if he would have been clear, or at least not such a prime suspect, if he'd just continued going in to work as usual."

"Why did he run off that way?" Anna asked. "Does anyone know?"

"My friend at the dealership said the people who know him figure he panicked. She also says a lot of people there think he *was* trying to kill K.C. — even though K.C. won't admit it. K.C. doesn't want to believe Tyler could do that, but the people who worked with him disagree."

"It's an impersonal way of killing someone," Edie said. She elaborated when she received several quizzical looks. Theresa even said "What?"

"Think about it. To shoot or stab or strangle someone, you have to get up close and personal. In most cases you would be face to face with the victim. But setting up an explosion and fire means you don't have to be there when the person dies. You don't have to see them die."

Maggie nodded. It was an excellent observation. "I guess he could even tell himself that K.C. wouldn't suffer, as the smoke inhalation would have killed him. I understand people just get sleepy from lack of oxygen and drop off."

"I feel so bad for K.C.," Theresa said. "He had grown to love Tyler. He really saw him as the son he never had."

Before things became too maudlin, Maggie turned to Clare.

"Have you been able to contact Kenny?"

"No." Clare's voice reflected her frustration. "They won't tell me anything when I call the hospital."

"It's the new privacy rules, and they're careful to enforce them," Louise reminded her.

"I know, but it's still frustrating not to know how he's doing. But Walter . . . you know, the lawyer here at the Senior Guild who offered to represent Kenny? He has been able to find out that Kenny is still in a coma. But he also said they expect him to wake from it soon. Something about brain waves, I think."

Victoria snipped her thread and reached for the spool. "I wonder if they'll ever learn who attacked him."

"Probably some young hoodlum." It was one of Edie's pet theories that young hoodlums and gang members were responsible for most of the crimes committed in the valley.

They were all distracted by the ringing of a cell phone, something that rarely happened at Quilting Bee sessions.

Clare fumbled with her purse to retrieve her phone, spoke for a moment and returned it to its special pocket. Everyone could see that she was excited; she was grinning and her eyes sparkled.

"Oh, my gosh," she began. "That was Walter. Kenny woke up. Walter has seen him and is on his way over to see us." Clare was so excited, she stumbled over the words.

Within fifteen minutes of the call, Walter was standing in the door of the Quilting Bee room.

"Things are really moving now," he told them. "This is quite an interesting case, and I thank you for getting me involved, Clare. The police were there questioning Kenny, and from the questions they asked, I think they may now have some doubt about his guilt."

"Really?" Clare smiled a broad, happy grin. "That's wonderful. Do they know who really did it?"

"If they do, they aren't telling me. It's an impression I got, from years of experience with interrogations," he said.

"Did Kenny say who hit him?"

Walter shook his head. "He doesn't know. He doesn't remember anything about the attack. The doctor says that isn't unusual and he may or may not recall something later.

"However," Walter continued, "I learned something very interesting from one of the cops I know. You know that Kenny was found in the desert near a homeless camp where he had been staying. Well, guess where Tyler Gilligan was hiding out?"

"Not in the homeless camp?" Clare almost bounced in her chair as she awaited his answer.

"Got it in one," he replied. "It's quite a coincidence, isn't it?"

Clare could hardly contain her excitement. "Do you think there's a connection?"

"Wouldn't that be incredible?" Theresa said.

"Not that incredible, if you think about it," Louise said. "Kenny was there because a lot of homeless men are veterans, so he could hide out among them and not feel like an outsider. And he knew he was safe there, that they wouldn't turn him in because of the special bond they shared. Tyler, though, was not in his element out on the streets. If he tried to kill his stepfather, then ran in a panic when he didn't succeed, he didn't have time to plan out what he wanted to do, or where to go. We know he tried to blame Kenny for the explosion, so he had to be familiar with the Upland case. If he ended up in that camp and saw Kenny there, he'd probably recognize him. Then he could have just grabbed something handy and bashed his head in. He wasn't reasoning very well. He might have thought they would dismiss both cases — the Upland and the Gilligan arsons — if Kenny was found dead in the desert."

"Maybe." Theresa seemed unconvinced.

Maggie could see how Louise had reasoned it out, and it made sense to her, too.

Even Walter nodded. "That's some excellent logic, Louise. I tend to agree. I think they're going to be looking at Tyler for the attack on Kenny. And my cop friend already told me they have forensic evidence connected to that. They retrieved epithelials from the rock used to bash Kenny, and they found clothing fibers on some nearby cholla. If Tyler did it, they'll have him."

"Epithelials," Clare repeated, seeming to savor the word as it rolled over her tongue. "And fibers. It's just like *CSI*." She grinned happily as she pulled her thread through the quilt. "But it would never work in a novel. Too contrived," she said with a shake of her head. "Personally, though," she added, grinning widely, "I like it."

45

Six weeks later

A cool January morning had evolved into a warm, sunny afternoon. At the Browne ranch, in the shadow of the McDowell mountains, Hal and his family turned their traditional Sunday brunch into a party to welcome in the new year — even though it was already several days into that year. All of the Brownes were present, and many of their friends, including all of the Quilting Bee members and their spouses. Walter Jackson and his wife were there, and Michael's friend from white-collar crimes, Lauren Whitehorse, whom he was still dating but declined to call a girlfriend. So it was inevitable that talk would get to the Upland case, which was still far from over. Walter claimed the complicated cases swirling around Kate Upland would drag on for years.

"At least Kenny is a free man now, and he

can get treatment for his PTSD." Clare still felt a special bond with Kenny, whom she insisted saved her life that day in the storm. She kept in touch and had even invited him to the party. She was disappointed when he declined, but Maggie was not surprised. Kenny was unused to crowds and would have been stressed, which was not good for his PTSD.

"What's become of Tony Sandoval?" Louise asked.

"He and his family are in the Witness Protection Program," Lauren said, "so they have new identities and are probably in another state. I'm sure they got him a job that has nothing to do with pharmacology."

There was some laughter at that.

"Still, it's a shame," Maggie said. "All that specialized education wasted. And I liked Tony. Besides his knowledge of supplements, he had a kind of old-world charm that was very appealing."

"Kind of like Cary Grant in those old movies," Clare added.

Maggie saw the mischievous twinkle in her son Bobby's eye and spoke before he could.

"Anyone who says 'Cary who?' can leave right now."

Bobby laughed good-naturedly with the others.

Before Clare could bring up examples of Cary Grant's debonair style, Victoria took them back to Maggie's comment about Tony. "We all liked Tony," she said. "He knows how to charm people, like a good salesman."

"I think he provided a real service with his special blends of vitamins," Maggie insisted.

This proved too much for her sons.

"Yeah, he did. For the rich old men who were trying to defeat Father Time," Frank said, still chuckling.

"Don't forget the rich jocks," Bobby said, to more laughter.

Poor Tony, Maggie thought. He felt so passionately about keeping up one's health with the proper vitamins and diet. And he'd been reduced to nothing more than a joke at an afternoon party.

Still, Maggie was used to the teasing of her boys. "Go ahead and laugh," she said. "I got some name-brand vitamins that are supposed to be specially formulated for women my age, but they don't give me the same energy I'd noticed with Tony's."

"They might have had a bit of something extra in them," Bobby teased. "Give you a little boost, you know."

Maggie laughed along with the others, but she did feel bad about the whole situation at Nature's Best.

"I tried to warn Ma to stay away from Nature's Best, but she's not real good at listening," Michael said.

This brought hooting and laughter from his brothers, and a few chuckles from the Bee women.

"I thought you were concerned that I was spending too much money on groceries," Maggie said, "and I'm perfectly capable of budgeting myself. You have to admit the entire situation there was not something any of us would have expected to find in downtown Scottsdale."

"Oh, I don't know about that." Bobby raised an expressive eyebrow. "The club scene is down there, so it's a good spot for selling designer drugs. In fact, I'm surprised he wasn't into that. He could have made a fortune."

"Tony's contacts were getting after him to start selling ecstasy and some other club drugs," Michael said. "As you say, he was in a good location. But he was still resisting when he was arrested."

"I wonder why," Edie said. "Like Bobby said, he could have made a lot of money."

"Because Tony is basically a good man," Victoria suggested. "And a family man."

Michael nodded. "He felt he was providing a service. He didn't view it as allowing rich old men to beat aging, he felt he was helping them face up to it. He sold them vitamins and other health items, too, and made suggestions about diet. He felt he was adjusting their mental attitudes toward aging and a healthy lifestyle. When he started selling products to the athletes, he did the same with them. Most of the body builders really appreciated his suggestions, too. They're big into health drinks and smoothies and all that stuff."

Lauren nodded. "His clients are loyal. None of them want to testify against him."

"Besides," Hal said, "if they do, they'll be admitting to buying illegal substances. They'd have to get immunity first, or take the fifth."

"Leave it to a lawyer to change them from loyal supporters to selfish slobs," Frank said.

Appreciative laughter rang out. Lawyer bashing at parties was usually acceptable, even if your brother was one.

"How did he ever get involved with those dreadful men who killed Kate?" Victoria asked. "I've been following the story in the paper, but I still don't understand that part

404

of it. As you said, he was a nice man who felt he was helping people. I'm sure he thought his substances were safer than those available on the black market."

"He started out selling the HGH to a few older friends at his fitness club. Then he was asked about steroids by some of the weight lifters. It was all word of mouth. As his client list burgeoned, he needed larger quantities of supplies to manufacture the drugs. That's how he managed to get mixed up with some very nasty drug types from Mexico."

"And was he making so much money, he had to launder it?" Edie asked. "You'd think he could have listed it as income from the drug store. Prescription drugs are so expensive."

"It wasn't his money that was being laundered," Lauren said. "The contact who was selling him supplies was blackmailing him into laundering drug money for his organization. Once Kate started working there, it didn't take her long to see that Tony was finagling his books. That's when he began having second thoughts."

"It was a sad day when that parent heard him say he needed help with his books and relayed the news to Kate," Victoria said.

"I don't understand why he didn't keep

doing them himself," Anna said. "He must have known an outside accountant would find a problem."

"Maybe that was the point," Louise suggested. "Maybe he *wanted* to be caught."

"Who knows what he was thinking," Michael said. "But that's the point when he figured it was all going to come out and contacted someone at the DEA. He said he would testify for immunity and a new life for himself and his family. But his contact must have gotten wind of it. Or just realized Kate was a threat. When Kate was killed, it scared the hell out of Tony and he changed his mind about testifying. He was afraid his family would be next, and he was probably right. But the feds knew what was going on, so they figured they would just continue the investigation on their own."

"But if that's the case," Maggie asked, "why didn't they know this drug contact killed Kate and the girls?"

Michael shrugged. "Probably just one of those things that happens when more than one organization is working a case. Not enough sharing of information between departments. Who knows? The local detectives were working the Upland case, and Kenny looked good for it. He was missing, and continued to be missing. They wouldn't really know about a federal drug investigation or that it could tie in with a murder in their jurisdiction."

"My Lord," Sara said, "it's like something straight out of Hollywood."

"Oh, it is," Clare said, excitement in her voice. "Kenny's been contacted by several people from Hollywood. They want to make a movie of his story."

"Is he going to do it?" Maggie wondered if such a thing would be good or bad for his mental health.

"He's still trying to decide."

"I suggested he get an agent to handle it for him," Walter said. "Negotiating with Hollywood is a special field. He needs someone who knows what they're doing so he doesn't get taken advantage of. Or have the story twisted in such a way that he comes out looking bad."

Clare nodded solemnly. *As if she's had lots of experience with Hollywood,* Maggie thought with an inward grin.

"So our theory that Kate was killed because of her work was correct." Clare smiled proudly at this acknowledgement of their deductive powers.

"Oh, you were a big help," Lauren said. "That key you learned about, from Kate's mother? As you suspected, it was for a safe deposit box. There was a flash drive in it, with copies of all the spreadsheets she was working with from both Gilligan's and Nature's Best."

"But hadn't you already raided Nature's Best by the time you got that?" Maggie asked.

"Yes, but it's still good evidence," Lauren said. "It will be especially helpful in the Upland case, if anyone is ever charged. We're also checking the spreadsheets against what was taken from Nature's Best, in case any changes were made to try to cover up what Kate found."

"It's a shame that no one may ever be charged with killing Kate and the girls. It was such a terrible thing." Maggie sighed.

"But Kenny can get on with his life now. He's really trying to," Clare said. "The VA has offered him a job working with other returning veterans who suffer from PTSD and urging them to get help. He's in a unique position to explain how not getting treatment contributed to ruining his life."

"It was Clare's persistence that finally cleared Kenny," Gerald said, raising his glass toward his wife in a silent toast. Pride shone in his face as he beamed at her.

Clare blushed bright red, but her eyes sparkled. "It's another success for the Quilting Bee," she said, "though I guess it all would have come out eventually, after the raid on Nature's Best."

"Maybe," Gerald agreed, "but you were the one who really got things going when you saw Kenny that day. And you wouldn't let anyone tell you that he was guilty."

"I feel bad admitting it now," Maggie said, "but there were times when I doubted Kenny's innocence."

"We all did," Victoria assured her.

"Not me," Clare said. "I always believed in him."

Edie rolled her eyes at Clare's smug tone.

"If he had made a few more phone calls to your cell, we might have caught up with him sooner," Michael said. "Maybe before Tyler managed to find and almost kill him."

Soon after that Quilting Bee meeting where Louise had reasoned that Tyler was a good candidate for Kenny's attacker, the papers had proved her correct. Within days of his arrest, Tyler was charged with assault and attempted murder for that incident. Just as Louise had theorized, Tyler had been at the homeless camp when he recognized Kenny. Thinking he might make everything go away if Kenny's body was found, he lured him away from the others and hit him with a convenient rock, leaving him for dead.

"What?" Clare looked over at Michael, clearly puzzled. "Calling me? How would that have helped?"

Edie snorted. "They must have tapped your phone, Clare."

Michael nodded. "Ma told me Kenny called you, and I passed that information along. Unfortunately, Tyler found him before we did."

Clare appeared stunned. Maggie, for one, wasn't surprised at her reaction. She knew she was upset because she hadn't known. She would have found it very exciting, having her phone tapped. And while she might be indignant now, she would soon enough be telling all her friends in the Senior Guild, explaining how it had played a part in the investigation.

"How is K.C. managing?" Maggie asked Theresa.

"He's sticking by Tyler," she replied. "And I'm not surprised. People find it hard to believe, but he just tells them that Tyler's his stepson and you don't abandon your son."

"It takes a special person to be so forgiving," Anna said.

"I'll say." Edie shook her head. "That boy

410

caused tens of thousands of dollars worth of damage at K.C.'s house and tried to kill him, too. I'm sure I wouldn't forgive so readily."

"He still doesn't believe that Tyler tried to kill him," Theresa said. "He keeps saying that dinner was on his calendar for months, so Tyler knew he would be gone. That high-priced lawyer he hired to defend Tyler is trying to get that particular charge dropped."

"He probably will, too," Walter said. "He's a good lawyer, and well worth his high fees."

"There's still plenty that will keep him in jail for a long time," Michael said. "There's the arson, which he confessed to before he lawyered up."

"He'll say his client was coerced," Walter said. "Or badgered into confessing."

"Then there's the attempted murder charge in the attack on Kenny," Michael said. "A good lawyer may get that down to assault, but he won't get off easily. There's a lot of forensic evidence, the kind of thing juries like these days."

"After evading capture for so long by living on the street, why did he go back to his condo?" Victoria asked.

"Tyler didn't know much about life on the street," Michael said, "but he quickly

411

learned that the library is a popular spot with the homeless population. He traded his nice jacket for an old and dirty one, then just shuffled into the main library, the way he saw others do. Once there, he checked the newspapers and some online news sources. That's when he saw media accounts pointing to Kenny as the main suspect in the Gilligan arson. They made such a big deal out of the similarities to the Upland case, talking about how Kenny was still out there and how his wife had worked for Gilligan's . . ." Michael shook his head in disgust. "He didn't realize that Kenny was not an official suspect. He thought he had gotten away with it after all. He decided to hightail it to California, then come back here pretending he'd been gone the whole time on some kind of emergency back in his hometown. He stopped at the condo to clean up and pick up a few things before leaving."

"He's not real good at planning things out, is he?" Frank laughed at such simplistic reasoning.

"Hey, if crooks were smart, we'd never catch any of them," Michael said, bringing on more laughter.

"Do you think he'll try to get off on an insanity plea?" Edie asked. One of her rants on the justice system had to do with the way lawyers were able to manipulate that particular plea.

"The arson at K.C.'s house took planning," Victoria said. "After all, he was trying to frame Kenny for it. Could he say he was out of his mind when he did all that planning?" She looked toward Walter for an opinion.

Walter shrugged. "Felons try all kinds of things. It depends on his lawyer."

"He might be able to get away with temporary insanity when it comes to his attack on Kenny," Maggie said. "That had to be a spur of the moment thing. He might be able to say it drove him mad to see Kenny, who was accused of terrible crimes, after all."

There was a quiet moment while they thought this over.

"He may have been out of his mind with fear when he saw Kenny and acted without thinking," Michael conceded. "He panicked when he realized he might go to prison." He shook his head. "He doesn't have the mind of a real criminal."

"Tyler is greedy, but he isn't a killer," Theresa said. "He would never have attempted to kill K.C. if he couldn't do it long distance."

"That's what Edie said," Clare replied.

413

"About arson being an impersonal way to kill someone."

"Of course it is," Edie said. "You don't have to look the victim in the face, don't have to see him at all."

Michael nodded. "It's a good observation. As Frank mentioned, Tyler isn't much at planning. His attempt to burn down K.C.'s place was a dismal failure. He wanted to implicate Kenny, of course, but he didn't do enough research to know that just turning on the gas jet would not be enough to cause a fire."

Edie shook her head. "I still don't understand why he didn't drive off that first night, then abandon the car in California." There were several nods of agreement. "Staying here in town, and in a homeless camp of all places. That just doesn't make any sense."

"He obviously wasn't thinking straight," Louise said.

"He's not very smart," Theresa said. "Not like K.C. None of us at Gilligan's could believe it when K.C. decided he would take the place over one day. He'll drive it right into the ground — no pun intended," she added with an apologetic smile. She received a few wry grins.

Michael provided more insight into Tyler's thought processes. "He was still in town, getting ready to leave, when the explosion at the house happened. He expected it to take hours, that it wouldn't go up until the wee hours of the morning. But the UPS guy stopped at K.C.'s with a package and he rang the doorbell. It was the spark from the doorbell ringing that caused the gas to explode. And since there was no accelerant, there was no fire. But when Tyler heard the report on the news, he panicked, pure and simple. He figured we'd be looking for his car. That was why he didn't drive off. If the explosion had happened overnight or first thing in the morning the way he thought it would, he would have been in California."

"It's interesting to hear the news reporters now talking about how different the two explosions were." Maggie smiled. "We had discussed that at the Quilting Bee, about the lack of a fire, but no one else seemed to notice it. Until Tyler was arrested, that is."

"Anyone who thinks the media is always right is crazy," Edie said, then was surprised at the laughter generated by her comment.

"This time, Ma, and her friends," Sara said, nodding toward the other Bee members, "managed to solve the mystery without getting themselves in any danger."

"Solving murders is still not a proper hobby for a retired woman," Michael said, narrowing his eyes at his mother.

"Of course not." Maggie smiled. At least he hadn't blurted out her age in front of everyone. Not that she was vain about it, but she did enjoy the fact that people rarely guessed her correct age. "But quilting is." Maggie turned to her youngest son. "As I've often told you, we just like to discuss the local news while we quilt."

General laughter drowned out any reply Michael might have made. Maggie and her Quilting Bee friends smiled complacently at one another. They enjoyed both their hobbies — quilting and solving murders. There were no plans to quit either one any time soon.

ABOUT THE AUTHOR

Annette Mahon is an avid reader who always wanted to write novels of her own. A retired librarian, she is also a quilter and enjoys including quilts and quilters in her novels. A native of Hilo, Hawaii, she now resides in Arizona with her husband and a spoiled Australian Shepherd. Visit her at www.annettemahon.com. E-mail her at annette@annettemahon.com.

The employees of Thorndike Press hope you have enjoyed this Large Print book. All our Thorndike, Wheeler, and Kennebec Large Print titles are designed for easy reading, and all our books are made to last. Other Thorndike Press Large Print books are available at your library, through selected bookstores, or directly from us.

For information about titles, please call:
   (800) 223-1244

or visit our Web site at:
   http://gale.cengage.com/thorndike

To share your comments, please write:
   Publisher
   Thorndike Press
   295 Kennedy Memorial Drive
   Waterville, ME 04901